S0-AUA-045

Other Books by Joseph Machlis

The Enjoyment of Music
Introduction to Contemporary Music
Lisa's Boy
The Career of Magda V.
Stefan in Love

Under the Name of George Selcamm

The Night Is for Music
Fifty-seventh Street

Allegro

Allegro

A NOVEL

JOSEPH MACHLIS

W· W· NORTON & COMPANY
New York · London

Printed in the United States of America
First Edition

The text of this book was composed in 11/13 Janson
Composition and Manufacturing by the Haddon Craftsmen, Inc.

Library of Congress Cataloging-in-Publication Data

Machlis, Joseph, 1906–
Allegro : a novel / Joseph Machlis.
p. cm
ISBN 0-393-04075-5
I. Title.
PS3563.A31157A79 1997
813'.54—dc21 96-53542
CIP

W. W. Norton & Company, Inc., 500 Fifth Avenue, New York, N.Y. 10110
http://www.wwnorton.com

W. W. Norton & Company Ltd., 10 Coptic Street, London WC1A 1PU

1 2 3 4 5 6 7 8 9 0

For

Florence Rome

I

1

I REMEMBER WHEN the idea first came to me that I might one day be a concert violinist. Isaac Stern was playing that night in Carnegie Hall. I sat next to Julia in the top row of the family circle. (When I spoke to her, she was Mom, but in my mind I called her Julia, same as my father did. If he could, why couldn't I? It brought her closer.)

Julia put her arm around me and drew me to her. "Maybe you'll be standing down there someday," she whispered in my ear. "And all these people will come to hear you."

"Not a chance, Mom," I whispered back. "They'll all be dead."

Julia gave me that look which told me I had just said something clever. I loved to see it in her eyes. I thought about her prophecy and liked it.

Stern had begun his last encore, Kreisler's *Schön Rosmarin.* The sound floated up from the stage, wonderfully clear and beautiful. Julia swayed from side to side in time with the waltz rhythm. Not that she had a good word to say for the Viennese. They had been terrible to the Jews under Hitler and, according to her, were just as anti-Semitic now. She admired Stern for refusing to play in Vienna. It showed he was a real person.

The concert ended. Julia let out a sigh. "Such an artist," she said. "I could listen to him all night."

We started down the long staircase from the family circle. Julia was afraid of heights and clung to me; I liked that. When we reached the lobby, she glanced at her wristwatch. "Your father won't be home until eleven. How about a cup of coffee?" She always said "your father" instead of "Dad" and made it sound vaguely like a reproach.

"Sure." I was all for adventure.

Once we reached the Automat, Julia had trouble making up her mind. She complained about being overweight and insisted that she put on pounds simply by looking at sweets. She ended with a wedge of cherry pie on which floated a ball of pistachio ice cream. I chose the same.

"Did you notice how he held his bow?" I asked as she dug into the pie. "A little higher up than most. That's what makes his tone so rich. I'd know his vibrato anywhere." I admired several violinists, but Stern was definitely at the top of the list. "I enjoyed his encores," I said, "because I'm studying them. He made them sound easy."

"For him they are." She smiled and finished her ice cream with a deep sigh. Then she looked at her watch. "Time to go," she announced. "Your father won't sleep until we're safely home."

Home was a four-room apartment on West 102nd Street off Broadway. Julia complained that the neighborhood was not as good as it used to be; the Jews were moving out while Hispanics and blacks were moving in. However, the apartment was pleasant and, more important, rent-controlled. Dad was waiting for us in the kitchen, hunched over a cup of coffee and tomorrow's *Times*. He was in his undershirt, which showed the little black curls on his arms and chest. He was a perfect contrast with Julia: thin, wiry, and dark, a quiet, unassuming man who put up with her outbursts, whether of anger or laughter, with unfailing patience. "So how was it?" he asked, without looking up.

Julia's exuberant contralto boomed through the kitchen. "Wonderful! He lifts you into another world."

Knowing her tendency to exaggerate, Dad turned to me. "Did you enjoy it too?"

"I sure did. He's great."

"Our Danny should only end up playing like that," Julia said, "and I'll be quite satisfied."

Dad turned to her. "Are you comparing Danny to Isaac Stern?"

"Who's comparing? I'm only giving him something to try for. What I want him to learn is that if Stern could make it, so can he. He's got to work hard, and it'll come, God willing."

"God has nothing to do with it," Dad replied. His atheism balanced my mother's religious feeling. He had flirted with communism in his youth and never forgot Marx's dictum that religion is the opium of the people. "Hard work is not enough. You need talent, lots of it. And luck."

"There you go, putting doubts in his mind." Julia was on familiar ground and made the most of it. "How can he develop confidence if you keep telling him how hard it is to succeed?" Sooner or later, in their arguments about me—their favorite topic—they reached a point where they discussed me as if I weren't there. Julia did not mince words. "It's not enough that you stopped yourself. Now you want to stop him."

"I didn't stop myself," Dad answered defensively. "It was the wrong time. The Depression was no time to start a career. Then came the war. And when that was over, it was too late."

Dad had begun as a promising violinist, but nothing had come of it. He ended up in the pit in Broadway musicals, when he was lucky enough to find work, and gave lessons on the side. He considered this a perfectly respectable way to make a living, even if it fell short of what he had expected. He was certainly not alone in this; the story was true of many musicians of his generation. But he hated to see Julia fill my mind with the same hoopla that he had once swallowed whole. He knew only too well where it led.

"Excuses, excuses," Julia cried, her voice adding an exclamation mark to each word. "This wasn't right, that wasn't right. Nonsense! You have to want a career with all your heart, and you've got to keep fighting until you get it. The minute you settle for something less, you've lost it. Danny has the talent, he has the guts, he's got me—and you—" she remembered to add, "to help him. I know he'll make it, and with God's help he will."

"I've no objection," Dad said affably. "Try and get it, I always say."

"And I always say, 'If you don't even try, you don't stand a chance.' " With that she kissed me good night and swept into the bedroom.

I opened the sofa in the living room, which served as my bed, and fell asleep almost immediately. I awoke a little later and became aware of Julia bending over me, lightly brushing my hair back from my forehead. I pretended to be asleep. Why? Because I usually tried to do what was clearly expected of me. When I finally opened my eyes, she said, "I came to make sure you were sleeping."

"I was."

"I have trouble falling asleep these days. I've too much on my mind." She sat down on the side of the bed. "When the noise is around me all day, I keep going, but when it grows quiet at night, I remember sad things." She was referring, I knew, to the death of my brother, Robbie, who succumbed to polio when he was nine, just before the Salk vaccine was perfected. I was too young at the time to remember him. "You can recover from an illness," she continued, "or a love affair. But you never recover from the death of your child." Her voice was low and tight. "I ask myself how could God do such a thing to me. Then I remember I've no right to ask. He has a plan and a purpose, whether we understand it or not."

I loved it when she spoke to me as if I were a close friend. She bent over me, and her voice dropped to an intense whisper. "Now I watch over you as I watched over Robbie. I want you to get everything you deserve. And I won't let anything stand in your way. I want to be proud of you like Isaac Stern's mother must be of him." She stroked my cheek. "More than anything, I want you to be happy."

She planted a kiss on my forehead and vanished into the darkness. I lay very still, allowing the meaning of her words to sink in. I wanted all the wonderful things she promised me. I wanted them for my sake, but even more for hers.

2

THE AUDITION WITH my new teacher, Dmitri Stamos, was set for the first Tuesday in September. "I'm going with Danny," Julia announced to my father. "And don't tell me I can't."

"Who said anything?"

In a gentler tone she added, "You yourself said it was time for a change."

Dad shrugged. "I've taught him long enough. I guess I could still show him a thing or two, but he'll be better off in a school, if they take him. He'll be in a musical atmosphere and meet other students instead of working by himself."

Julia bristled. "What do you mean, if they take him? They're lucky to get him."

"That's what you and I think, but will they?"

Once again they had forgotten I was there. "I must say, Phil, you don't have much faith in the boy. I sometimes think you're not even concerned about his future. He's your son as well as mine."

Dad had heard all this before, but for once he answered back. "Maybe I'm concerned in a different way from you."

"What's that supposed to mean?"

"I never wanted him to be a wunderkind. You know what they say: The *wunder* goes and the *kind* remains. All those old geezers in the violin section of the Philharmonic, each one of them began as a prodigy. The only kid on the block who played the violin and his aunt Rosie kept saying, 'Mark my words, he'll end up in Carnegie Hall.' Well, he did end up in Carnegie Hall, but not the way Rosie meant. Now he sits there with his buddies sawing away while Milstein or Stern is up front, and he keeps thinking, What does that one have that I don't? The answer is: talent!" He pronounced the word as if it were in capital letters. "You keep telling Danny he's gonna be a great violinist. I think you're making a mistake. D'you realize how many things have to mesh before a star is born? Being at the right place at the right time, knowing the right people, getting the right breaks. And plenty of luck. Do you remember Woody Allen's film about sex, all those sperm rushing forward to meet the egg and only one making it? The others just got lost. Well, it's the same in art." Dad grinned.

"So why can't our boy be the one? Answer me that, smarty."

"I never said he couldn't."

She was not mollified. "I believe in him, and I want him to believe in himself. Is that so wrong?"

"No."

"Good. For once we agree."

Julia generated a lot of excitement as we prepared to leave. As a matter of fact she was considerably more nervous than I was. She saw to it that I wore my navy blue suit—what I called my bar mitzvah suit—with a clean white shirt and tie. I balked at the tie but gave in. She brushed down my hair, which immediately stood up again, and made me shine my shoes. Finally she inspected me and pronounced me fit to go.

It was one of those late-summer mornings when the city is floating in sunlight. We made our way up Broadway to the music school on Claremont Avenue. The audition was scheduled in Stamos's studio, a pleasant room with two enormous windows overlooking a little park, beyond which was visible the dome of Grant's Tomb, flanked by the Hudson. Stamos, one of the foremost violin teachers in town, was a commanding figure in his late fifties, with a shock of iron-gray hair, the swarthy complexion and fiery eyes of his Greek heritage, and a pair of bushy black eyebrows that looked as if they were about to fly off his face. I imagined him as a Mediterranean pirate of old with a long earring dangling from one ear. Everything about him was larger than life: his laughter; his gestures; his dramatic pauses. "So what you play for me?" he boomed.

I was overcome with shyness in the great man's presence. "Chaconne by Bach."

"Is good." He nodded vigorously for me to begin.

I tuned up, adjusted the violin under my chin and sounded the opening chords of the theme, digging my bow into the strings to produce a full sound. I was extremely nervous at first but calmed down as I reached the complex passages that followed. Soon I was too preoccupied with my fingers to think of my nerves.

Stamos listened to the end. "Not bad," he said, "not bad at all." At the time I did not know that this from him was high praise indeed. "What else you play?" he asked. "Something slow. I want hear your legato."

I had prepared Paganini's Caprice No. 1, but in response to his request I switched to an arrangement of Chopin's Nocturne in E-flat and played the melody as expressively as I could.

Stamos nodded his approval when the piece was finished. "You are very musical, my boy. But you must"—his pronunciation was closer to *mahst*—"not play that piece. It belongs on the piano. Why Wilhelmj arranges it for violin?" As he walked to the bench by the window where my mother was sitting, he answered his question. "To make money, of course." He made this sound like a most reprehensible goal.

He sat down beside Julia. "Mrs. Sachs, your son is very talented. I will take him. I recommend him for scholarship. But there is problem. His violin is garbage. He must have new one."

"It was my husband's old fiddle," Julia said.

"Good enough for beginner, but not anymore. Now Danny needs real violin. Can you buy him one?"

"How much would it cost?"

"I cannot say. Twelve hundred. Maybe a little more."

Julia winced but immediately regained her composure. "If we have to, we will."

Stamos shook his head approvingly. "Is good. Then he can begin."

His friendliness loosened Julia's tongue. "My husband bought him a toy violin when he was three. He made like he was playing it for hours on end. His father is concertmaster of the orchestra in *Follies*. It's a big hit on Broadway. He began to teach Danny when he was five. Phil couldn't get over how fast the boy learned. 'When I show him something,' Phil told me, 'he already knows it.' Everybody who heard him said he was a genius."

Stamos smiled. "Genius is big word, Mrs. Sachs. Mozart was genius, and Beethoven. Let's say that your son is big talent." He rose as a sign that the interview was over. "Come Tuesday at three," he said to me. "Your first lesson. It is new chapter in your life. I think it will be good one."

"I know it will," Julia said fervently.

Stamos shook hands with us. We left.

"Did you like him?" Julia asked as we walked toward Broadway.

"Why wouldn't I? He liked my playing, didn't he?"

A coffee shop came into view on the corner opposite. "Let's celebrate," Julia announced, and led the way.

The celebration consisted of blueberry pie and butter pecan ice cream. "From what your father gives me," Julia said, "I saved a thousand for a fur coat. It'll go for your violin instead."

"Gee, Mom!" I stopped, too overcome to go on. In my view of the world Dad and I were earth people who had our feet on the ground, but Julia was from another planet. When she put her mind to it, anything was possible. "I don't want you to go without your fur coat." The words rushed out before I could stop them. What if she believed me?

"Why not? A violin is more important. I'll get an imitation fur, and from far it'll look like the real thing, believe me." She swallowed the ice cream slowly and added coquettishly, "Maybe someday you'll buy me the real thing. Know what? I'll enjoy it just as much then."

I gazed at her round face. It seemed to me that she was the best mother in the world, and I loved her very much. I only hoped I would deserve what she was doing for me. I would have liked to tell her this, but I felt awkward. As a matter of fact, whenever I felt anything deeply, my first concern was not to let anyone see it. So I took her hand instead and murmured, "Thanks, Mom, thanks for everything."

Julia washed down the ice cream with a sip of coffee and wiped her lips. She gave me a loving look and stroked my cheek. "We did a fine job this morning, you and me. As Mr. Stamos said, a new chapter is opening in your life. God willing, it'll be a happy one."

3

THE VIOLIN SHOP on Forty-fourth Street was a dark, musty place, with dust dancing in the gray light from a narrow window. The smell of violin varnish hung in the air. The wall was covered with a profusion of instruments—half and three-quarter sizes for young players and full-size instruments for older ones. Mr. Yankelovich, the dealer, was a friendly man with a gaunt face and bad teeth. He had sold Dad an instrument years before and greeted us warmly. When Dad told him that I was going to study with Dmitri Stamos, he said, "A terrific teacher. Your boy is lucky to be with him."

"He's just beginning," Julia explained.

"If you had half a million dollars," the dealer said, "I'd advise you to buy a Strad. In ten years it'll be worth five times that much."

"If I had half a million dollars," Julia asked, "would I be here?"

"Of course you would, buying that Strad. But I have just the right thing for you. A German instrument from around 1850. In perfect condition."

He lifted the violin from the wall and handed it to Dad. As with most German instruments, its gleaming varnish was a shade lighter than that of the Italian ones. "It has a sweet tone. Just right for Bach," Mr. Yankelovich said.

Dad ran some scales and arpeggios across the strings, followed by vigorous double stops. "I like it," he said. "Danny, try it."

I played the opening passage of the Chaconne. The instrument sang to me; I loved its brave, happy tone. "Terrific, no?" Mr. Yankelovich inquired.

I nodded agreement.

Mr. Yankelovich turned to Dad. "It's a twelve-hundred-dollar instrument, but since you're an old customer, I'm letting you have it for a thousand even. A real bargain!"

Dad shook his head. "I wasn't intending to go over seven-fifty. The union has a fund for its members to buy their instruments. The trouble is, when you borrow money, you have to pay it back. No, we'll stick to the seven-fifty limit. When Danny needs a better violin a few years from now, we can always come back."

I looked at Julia. Why wasn't she offering her nest egg? She seemed to have forgotten all about her promise, and I had too much pride to remind her.

We left with a modern French violin that didn't speak to me at all. I was heartbroken but took care not to show my disappointment. After we had walked a block, Julia suddenly stopped. "We're going back," she said.

"Why?" Dad asked.

"Danny liked the other violin, and we're going to get it for him."

"How d'you expect to do that?" Dad inquired.

She explained about the fur coat that she could do without. "How do you know what he feels about it?" Dad asked. "He never said a word."

"He didn't have to," Julia said as we turned back. I breathed more easily.

My parents haggled with Mr. Yankelovich over the exact terms and reached agreement at eight hundred. He wrapped my violin in a purple silk scarf and carefully fitted it into its case. "I'm throwing in the bow as a present," he said. "A French bow by a pupil of Tortelier. It'll bring you luck, Danny." He shut the case.

Dad turned to me with a smile and said, "Take it." I did, hugging the case with both arms as if I were bearing a treasure. Mr. Yankelovich escorted us to the door, shook hands with my parents, and showered us with good wishes.

"When I was little," Julia said, "I used to read stories about King Arthur. He named his sword Excalibur and set out to conquer the world with it. This is your Excalibur, Danny."

"How do you remember such things?" Dad asked. No matter how many years they had been together, Julia continued to amaze him.

When we got home, I shut myself in my parents' room to be alone with my violin; I needed to get to know it. I flipped the bow through the air over and over again, enjoying the sharp retort it made. I unwrapped the instrument, positioned it under my chin, and sounded each of the strings in turn. They were like the voices of four friends, and I even attached faces to them. The G had a rich resonance; its face was fat and friendly. The D was warm and mellow; it wore glasses. The A was like a song: a handsome face, like a movie star's. And the E was bright and tense: a thin face with hollow cheeks. Then I launched into my favorite Paganini Caprice, the one with the wide leaps.

Dad opened the door and shut it carefully behind him. He sat down and listened until the end of the piece. "Sounds great," he said.

I could not tell whether he was praising me or the violin. Unlike Julia, he rarely praised my playing; neither did he light into me as she did when she was displeased with me. Yet curiously enough, it was Julia's approval I kept trying to win, rather than his, which I knew I had. Julia was the one I had to convince.

My lessons with Dad had brought us close together. I had enjoyed them and was not altogether happy that they had come to an end. But I knew that he approved the change to Mr. Stamos. "You'll be better off in a school," he told me. "Means you'll be studying subjects besides the violin. Like harmony and ear training. They're very important." I nodded energetically, to show that I intended to try hard.

He put his hand on my shoulder and said, "You'll go far, my boy. Much farther than I did."

Coming from Dad, this was quite a statement. I was not prepared for it and felt flustered. "Thanks," I blurted out without knowing exactly what I was thanking him for. The violin? The lessons? Or his being uniformly kind and supportive?

By the time I went to sleep that night I had already forgotten the name of King Arthur's sword. But I liked Julia's comparison. The violin was my weapon. I would go forth and do battle with it. And win.

I counted the days until my lesson with Stamos. When the day finally arrived, there was a fierce argument between my parents. In the morning Julia said, "I don't want us to be late."

Dad caught her up on this. "What do you mean 'us'? You're not going with him, are you?"

"Why not? I'd like to hear what Stamos teaches him. Why shouldn't I be there?"

"Because a lesson is private business between teacher and pupil. No outsider is supposed to listen in."

"I'm not exactly an outsider. Besides, Stamos knows I teach the piano. I'm a musician too." She had taught beginners early in their marriage. Her pupils had dropped off in recent years, but she still spoke as if she were professionally active. "I'll know what he's talking about, and if Danny practices wrong, I'll be able to correct him. So what's so terrible if I go along?"

It didn't occur to either of them to ask how I felt about the matter. In any case, Dad lost the battle. When it was time for me to leave, Julia came with me.

Dad's misgivings turned out to be unjustified. Stamos was too much the ham not to enjoy an audience. He welcomed Julia, who settled into the bench by the window, and proceeded as if she were not there.

I never forgot that first lesson. I was enveloped by Stamos's presence, spellbound by his dramatic voice and gestures. He spoke to me as no one ever had. "What is music? It is two separate things, like body and soul. One side is physical. Trills, scales, arpeggios, double stops, harmonics—what is known as technique." He pronounced the word with a guttural sound deep in the throat, as if it were spelled *tekhneek*. "You must practice over and over until the technique is perfect, so that you will be master of the notes, not their slave. Then you are free to think of the other side, the important side, what the music says. The notes are like words; they are speaking to you, they are saying thoughts and feelings. This is what the true artist tells to you. It is like Mahler says, 'The best things in music are not in the notes.' To bring out the soul of music, you must have soul yourself. You must feel; then you will make your audience feel. You must never be one of those who play notes fast and loud without feeling. Music is the language of the soul. Always remember that."

All this was accompanied by extravagant sweeps of the arms,

up-and-down racing of the bushy eyebrows, and a wide variety of facial expressions. I listened as I never had before. Fortunately Stamos's generalities were a prelude to the lesson itself, which dealt with such concrete matters as the positioning of hand and fingers, the role of wrist and elbow, the secret of playing in pitch, the motion of the bow, and—most important of all—the resulting quality of tone. By the end of the hour I was exhausted from the sheer intensity of my concentration.

I was silent as we came down from Stamos's studio. Then I said, "Wow! I feel as if a truck ran over me."

"He's a great teacher," Julia replied. "We're lucky we found him."

She gave my father a detailed report of the lesson. It was ingrained in her thinking to view the events in her life in cosmic terms, for she ended her account with "There's a God in heaven, and He has a plan. All we have to do is follow it."

Dad, ever the skeptic, asked, "And how do you know what His plan is?" Julia put him in his place with a withering look.

4

THE STUDENT LOUNGE, its sofas and armchairs covered in bright colors, was a large, open area where you could relax. I didn't. I sat in an armchair in the corner, wishing that someone would speak to me. The students all seemed to know one another, so that I felt very much the outsider. I found it difficult to talk to strangers; besides, I had the feeling that if I tried to join a group, I would not be welcome.

On a sofa nearby sat a blond boy and two girls. He was obviously telling jokes, for the girls kept bursting into laughter. I would have liked to join them but didn't know how. I finally mustered up the courage to go over to them, but instead of asking if I could sit with them, I heard myself blurt out, "Is the cafeteria around here?" It was my second visit to the school, and I did not yet know my way around.

The boy, without hesitation, pointed to a corridor. "Follow that hallway," he said, and smiled at the girls in a peculiar way.

I wondered what was so peculiar and soon found out: The corridor led to the street. In short, I had been given the exact treatment I expected. I retraced my steps to the lounge, hurled the word *asshole* at him, and continued until I found the cafeteria.

I was munching a sandwich when the boy appeared and stopped at my table. "Sorry you were pissed off. Can't you take a joke?'

I gave him a sour look. "Some joke. I'm still laughing."

He sat down. "There was something about you that made me do it, the way you came over."

"Now you're saying it's my fault you made a fool of me."

"You were asking for it."

"Sure, I'll take a course by mail. Next time I come over, I'll be right on. That is, if there is a next time."

"Aw, come off it. I'm trying to be friendly. My name's Steve Hammer." He held out his hand.

I took it. "Danny Sachs."

"Who do you study with?"

"Mr. Stamos."

"He's my teacher too. In fact I'm going up for my lesson."

"I guess I come after you."

Steve rose. "See ya upstairs."

"Where's your violin?" I asked.

"In my locker. Get one, and you won't have to drag your fiddle around with you."

I nodded, and Steve left.

When I went into Stamos's studio an hour later, Steve was playing the final section of the Bruch Concerto. I thought he had a fine tone and played with great technical ease but without any real involvement. When he finished the movement,

Stamos turned to me and said, “You two know each other?”

“We met downstairs.”

“Danny, play something for Steve. That Paganini Caprice you played for me.”

I took my instrument out of its case and tossed off the piece. It was Steve’s turn to be amazed. “You sure play a mean violin,” he said.

Stamos smiled happily. “You two are going to be my prize pupils.”

Steve packed up and made for the door. As he passed me, “I’ll wait for you downstairs,” he said.

Stamos did not believe in assigning technical exercises to his students. The exercises instead were derived from whatever music was being studied. In this way technique became not an end in itself but something related to the composition. This meant that technical control and musical understanding went hand in hand, each feeding the other. He had asked me to prepare the *Kreutzer Sonata* and showed me ingenious ways of transforming the piece into a series of exercises in various rhythms dealing with specific technical problems. That done, he addressed himself to the music itself. “Notice,” he said, pointing to the first page of the rondo, “how Beethoven repeats the measure, each time a tone higher. What means that? He wants more intensity. You must therefore give a bigger tone. The third time still higher. So you build structure like architect builds a building. Each time the phrase returns, it has greater strength, greater meaning.”

Again I listened with an intensity of which I had never thought myself capable; I tried to store in my mind everything Stamos said, so that when I was home, I would remember every word and act on it. When I left the room, my head was spinning.

Steve was waiting for me in the lounge. “How was it?” he asked.

“Whew! He wears me out. I never met anyone like him.”

“There isn’t anyone like him.”

"Is he always like this?"

"Yeah. He just goes on and on. Like a hurricane. I wait for him to stop, but he can't. He has too much to give."

We walked down Riverside Drive toward the subway. A September haze wreathed the Jersey shore; the Hudson, calm and majestic, flowed slowly toward the bay. The leaves fluttered lazily in the late-summer breeze, and the trees held out their branches as if begging a favor. I let Steve do most of the talking; I didn't want to show him how much I enjoyed being with him. He had an active mind and jumped from one subject to the next. If he asked a question, he never bothered to wait for an answer. He kept jabbing his long, thin fingers through his blond hair. When he had thoroughly messed it up, he took a small comb out of his breast pocket and drew it back from his forehead until everything was in order again. He was extremely good-looking, and knew it.

"You like to read?" he asked.

"Uh-huh, but with school and practicing, I don't get much in."

"Funny thing, when I read, especially if it's a story, I keep changing it in my head, so that I'm actually following two stories, the one on the page and the one I'm making up. That ever happen to you?"

Without waiting for me to answer, he said, "Did you ever stop to think what fun it would be if we could unscrew our arms and legs and send them out on their own? They could then come back and report to us what had happened to them."

"How could they come back if they had no brain to tell them where to go?"

"You're being realistic. I'm dealing with sci fi. Suppose you had a magic formula to make you invisible. You could watch people, and they wouldn't know you were there. You'd find out what they're really like."

"Why would you wanna know?"

"If you did, you could control them."

"I guess so," I conceded without enthusiasm. The prospect

did not particularly attract me, but I was being polite.

We parted at the subway station. I wanted to ask Steve when I could see him again but didn't. He was easily the most interesting fellow I had ever met, and a damn good violinist besides. As I went down the stairs to the subway, the excitement of the past week swept over me. All at once I had found a teacher, a school, and a friend.

5

ON SUNDAY MORNING the telephone rang. It was Steve. "How about coming over later?" he said.

"Where do you live?" I maintained a casual air. It would never do to show how delighted I was by his invitation.

Steve lived in one of those old houses on Riverside Drive. By my standards, the building was elegant; it had an elevator. The apartment was spacious, with old-fashioned high ceilings and a view of the Hudson. When I commented on the size of the living room, Steve responded, "They don't make 'em like this anymore."

We spent the afternoon playing for each other. I admired Steve's natural way of handling the violin. His was the kind of facility that couldn't be learned; you either had it or you didn't. We were very different. He had the ideal build, at least a head taller than I was, with broad shoulders that tapered down to a narrow waist, whereas I thought of myself as chunky. His blond hair lay smoothly on his head, while my dark brown mop looked constantly in need of brushing. He was extremely careful of his appearance. His clothes looked as if they had been made specially for him; mine looked as if I had tumbled into them. When he played, he stood up straight and quiet, in the posture made famous by Heifetz, while I was carried away by my feelings and swayed from side to side. He wanted his playing to be cool and aristocratic; I wanted the listener to feel everything I felt. He could charm the pants off anybody; I was always saying things I shouldn't. He was talkative and boisterous, while I tended to be quiet and reserved. We did have one thing in common: He obviously enjoyed my company, and I certainly enjoyed his.

I also enjoyed playing with him. We practiced Bach's Concerto for Two Violins and managed to stay together even in the tricky passages where the tempo changed. "We make a good team," Steve said. "We'll find a cellist and violist and start playing quartets." I eagerly assented.

I was immensely flattered when, in the next weeks, Steve began referring to me as his best friend. "What about me?" he asked with a grin. "Am I yours?"

"You're not only my best friend," I replied, "but my only one."

"How come?" He sounded surprised.

"I've always been a loner."

"Don't tell me you prefer your own company. I hate to be alone."

"I don't make friends easily. Besides, when you make a friend, you're taking a chance."

"Whaddya mean?"

"He can take away his friendship whenever he likes."

Steve laughed. "Why would I do that?"

"You can't trust people," I explained. "And you can't depend on their feelings."

"Where did you learn that?

"I didn't learn it. I just know it."

"Well, if you ever need me, Danny, I'll be there for you. You'll see."

I hoped he was right.

Having Steve for a friend meant having someone to share things with. We were soon inseparable. On days when we didn't see each other, we talked on the phone two or three times. When we met, we would slap our palms together; this became our special handshake long before high fives became popular. Steve was a movie buff. As a result, films became a much more important part of my life than they had ever been. He introduced me to the works of the great Italian directors—Rossellini, de Sica, Fellini—whom he worshiped. "They're for real," he said of them reverently; "they don't fuck around."

Steve organized a string quartet; we met at his house every Tuesday evening. He played first violin, I second; then we switched. We rehearsed two works at each session: a Haydn quartet followed by a Mozart or early Beethoven. I was by temperament a soloist, but I found it exciting to explore the chamber music literature. "This is different from playing by yourself," I told Steve. "Here you're part of a group and everything depends on teamwork. I like it."

"As much as playing solo?"

"In a different way."

I was particularly pleased that Julia took a liking to Steve. "I used to worry that you were too much alone," she confessed. "It's much better for you to have a friend." She assumed a knowing expression as she added, "A wise man said, 'To make a friend, you must shut one eye. To keep him—both.' "

I had occasion to shut both eyes sooner than I expected. A competition was announced for the post of concertmaster in the student orchestra. I decided to try out for it even though Stamos didn't encourage his prize pupils to join the orchestra; their true goal, he felt, should be a solo career. At the same time he knew that they could not help benefiting from the experience. Steve and I both joined and thoroughly enjoyed the rehearsals. Steve announced that he would not enter the competition, which greatly improved my chance of winning. I carefully prepared the works I had to play before the jury and looked forward to an easy victory.

At the last minute Steve changed his mind without telling me. I was totally unprepared for the announcement on the bulletin board that Steven Hammer had won. To my disappointment at losing was added the bitter knowledge that my best friend had pulled a fast one on me. In a fury I telephoned him. "Why didn't you tell me?" I demanded.

"Why would I tell you we were competing against each other? I knew it would upset you."

"Then why didn't you stay out?"

"Because it seemed foolish not to try. Look, Danny, I didn't win because I'm a better violinist than you, only a better sight reader. What's the big deal?"

"Nothing, except that I trusted you and you lied to me."

Steve tried to answer, but I hung up. What was the use? I couldn't make him see that his behavior constituted a betrayal of our friendship.

Over the next days I could not put Steve's treachery out of my mind. Friendship, it turned out, was an even riskier business than I had supposed. Had not all my fears come true? Why hadn't I seen through him from the start? He's a no-good son of a bitch, I told myself, and was sorry I had ever come to know him. The wonderful hours we had spent together no longer seemed so wonderful. From here on I would go it alone. That way I couldn't be hurt again.

I confided my unhappiness to my mother. To my surprise Julia defended Steve. "You're being too hard on him," she said. "He didn't tell you because he didn't want to hurt you. You shouldn't break off with him; you two were such good friends. You expect too much from people. Remember what I told you about shutting both eyes."

Stamos too made light of my defeat. "Your future is not in the orchestra. It is on the concert stage."

"If I'm so great, how come I lost?"

"Because in the orchestra sight-reading is very important, and your strong point it is not. You must understand about good sight readers. The first or second time they play a piece, that is as good as it will ever be. But for the artist, he may not read the music so good the first time, but every time he repeats it he understands it more, his interpretation grows." Stamos summed up with a wave of his hand. "You win one, lose one, it is all a lottery. And the first lesson you must learn is how to lose. More important even than how to win. Next competition is for concerto with orchestra." He smiled confidently and shook his leonine mane. "That one you win."

That week I discovered how much Steve meant to me. I kept thinking about him; I missed our walks and our conversations. Suddenly there was no one to do things with, no one to telephone. A great emptiness was closing in on me; each day I felt more bereft. I wanted to phone, but my pride would not allow it. I struggled with the temptation but was determined not to give in. On the sixth day my will suddenly crumpled. I dialed Steve's number. At the sound of his voice I came to my senses and hung up.

When I arrived for my lesson on Saturday, Steve came out of Stamos's room. "Hi, stranger," he said, and grinned as if nothing were amiss. I didn't reply.

After the lesson I went down to the lounge. Steve was waiting for me. "You still mad at me?" he asked.

I said nothing.

He put his arm around my shoulder. "Look, Danny, you're being silly. You'd have a right to be sore if I'd done something against you. I just didn't want us to be running neck to neck for the same prize. Besides, in case I lost, I didn't want you to know."

It had never occurred to me that Steve entertained such a fear of losing. I remained sullen. "It's the principle," I growled.

"Principle, my ass. If it was going to make things easier between us, I had a right to do it. Anyway, you're a damn good fiddler, but you're not cut out to be a concertmaster. So what are you all steamed up about?"

He gave me one of his surefire smiles; his face crinkled up, and tiny lines were etched around the corners of his eyes. Beneath the warmth of that smile the remnants of my anger evaporated. I had my best friend back. What more did I need?

6

THE VAGUELY FRIGHTENING world of girls. Where they were concerned, I envied Steve his cool. Flirting, for him, was as enjoyable a game as tennis or handball. A master of light banter, he held forth in the student lounge with an inexhaustible stream of jokes. This was a game at which I was singularly inept. My throat went dry, my palms sweated, and for the life of me I couldn't think of anything amusing to say. "You have to relax," Steve instructed me. "It's like playing double stops. The minute you tense up, you go flat. Just remember, they're as scared of you as you are of them."

I found this precept helpful and in time overcame my shyness sufficiently to carry on some semblance of conversation. Since I was dealing with fellow students, a safe opening gambit was to ask the girl I was talking to how her lesson had gone. If she was a violinist, we at once had something in common. At about this time Steve began to pay attention to a pianist named Louise Schonfeld. I focused on her friend Ruth Lasker. The four of us saw each other every Saturday morning and gravitated to the same table in the cafeteria.

Steve was an excellent mimic. When he described his lesson, he imitated Stamos's accent and gestures. "You mahst make like this, the bow very loose and martellato." Steve extended his left arm to support an imaginary violin, while the right flailed the air. "Baht if you not careful, you will play sharp. You mahst compensate by pressing a leetle lower on the string." Steve grinned. "I did and played flat. Ya can't win."

I kept my eyes on Ruth. Her softness appealed to me, and I liked the way her hair trailed off into soft down on her cheek. Her voice was gentle, as were the curves of her body. "Good thing you can't play sharp on the piano," she said. "All you have to do is hit the right key." She smiled. "Not that that's so easy."

Steve proposed a double date for the following Saturday night. The girls accepted. Since Ruth lived in the Bronx and Louise in Brooklyn, we decided to meet at Steve's house. His parents would be away, and he could have a Chinese dinner sent in.

On our walk down Riverside Drive he held forth on the possibilities of the evening. "You still a virgin?" he inquired, even though he guessed the answer.

With considerable embarrassment I admitted that I was. Thereupon Steve dispensed advice like a true man of the world. "Saturday night you're going to find out what it's all about." He considered this as important an event as being born. "You're going to lose your cherry." When I looked puzzled, he explained, "That's what they used to call it before our time."

"Where did you hear it?"

"From my uncle."

Because I was speaking to my best friend, I considered it pointless to hide my apprehension. "I'm not even sure I know how to go about it."

"If the bees and butterflies know, why wouldn't you?"

It was a good point. I felt considerably relieved.

"First thing you do"—Steve continued his instruction—"is buy a condom. Mustn't be without one. Better, get several in case the first one breaks. They sometimes do." As an afterthought: "Or in case you feel like doing it again."

"I'll be satisfied to get through it once."

"My first time I didn't do so well," Steve confessed. "But it got better each time. Now I think it's the greatest."

"Better than practicing?" I asked with a laugh.

"Much. Why do you suppose everybody loves doing it?"

That night, as I tried to fall asleep, I couldn't get Ruth out of my mind. We were walking through a subterranean garden filled with flowering bushes more luxuriant than any I had ever seen. I held Ruth's hand in mine and led her to the shade of a huge tree. We lay down where the grass was cool and soft. I undressed her and removed my clothes; her eagerness matched mine. She kissed me, slipping her tongue between my lips as in the movies. I fondled her breasts and strayed lower; now I lay on top of her. One push and I reached the climax; the stuff came pouring out of me before I could hold it back.

Breathing heavily, I buried my head in the pillow, then reached for a towel and wiped the stain off my pajamas; I didn't want my mother to see it. People said that you'd go out of your mind if you did it too often, but how much was too often? I shook my head from side to side to make sure my brains were still there, and fell asleep.

Saturday dragged. Thoughts of the evening ahead kept popping into my head, making it difficult for me to concentrate on practicing. It occurred to me that I ought to try on the condom for size. I fetched the packet from my coat pocket and unfurled the white rubber sheath on my penis; it was a perfect fit. The sight aroused me, and even though it was much too soon, I played with myself again. When I finished, it occurred to me that the rehearsal had gone very well; what would the performance be like?

The girls arrived at Steve's punctually at seven. He looked extremely handsome in a blue blazer and pair of gray slacks. No matter what I wore, I could never compete with him either in clothes or looks. With the Chinese dinner Steve served his father's best white wine; he had chilled it in advance. He was an expansive host who knew how to keep his guests amused. "A Frenchman, an Englishman, and a Chinaman were marooned on a desert island . . ." The girls giggled at the punch line, which spurred Steve on to his next joke. Here too I was easily overshadowed, but didn't mind; I was having too good a time.

After dinner Steve brought out his violin. Accompanied by Louise, he played the first movement of Mozart's Sonata in A. When they finished, Ruth and I applauded. I wished Steve would ask Ruth and me to play the next movement, but he didn't, and I was too diffident to suggest it. It was Ruth who did. I enjoyed playing on Steve's violin, which was considerably better than mine. This time Louise and he applauded.

Steve kept the evening moving. The concert over, he rolled back the rug, put on a recording of Mick Jagger, and asked Louise to dance. Head bobbing, fingers snapping, he looked great. "I can't get no satisfaction," the million-dollar voice wailed as Steve and Louise executed the latest dance steps. I remained on the sidelines. Despite my fine sense of rhythm, I had never learned to dance. Ruth tried to teach me, but after a few halfhearted attempts I begged off, embarrassed by my clumsiness. "You have to have it in you," I explained to her. "Remember the kids in school who were not supposed to sing because they were listeners. Well, I'm a watcher."

When the dance ended, Steve turned on the television, which gave him an excuse to dim the lights. Then he and Louise paired off on a settee to watch an old film. After a while I saw them tiptoe out, undoubtedly on their way to Steve's room. I was alone with Ruth.

We were sitting on the sofa. I put my arm around her shoulder and drew her closer; she didn't object. This gave me the courage to place my other hand on her breast, which I fondled while pressing my lips against hers. When there was still no objection, I lowered my hand. It was a scenario I had reviewed in my mind again and again, each step leading inevitably to the next. She responded to my kiss. After a few minutes I was ready to move on. My heart beat faster as I let my hand drop to her knee and, drawing a deep breath, I slipped it underneath her skirt.

She suddenly sat bolt upright, grasped me firmly by the wrist, and removed my hand. "What do you think you're doing?" she asked as she stood up, turned on the light, and faced me.

The sudden bright light made me squint. I felt as if I had been caught in some shameful act. "I'm trying to make love to you," I said defensively.

"You call that love?" She seemed annoyed yet at the same time faintly amused.

"Who cares what you call it?" Sullenly: "That's what it is."

"No, it isn't."

I was ready to go over to the offensive. "So why'd you lead me on?"

"Lead you on? I was just being nice to you. Why not? I like you fine. But that doesn't mean I'm ready to go the whole way with you."

"Plenty of girls would," I said, trying to sound as if I believed it.

"And plenty of girls wouldn't. I'm one of those."

"Then you're missing a lot of fun." I could not help feeling that my man-of-the-world stance was not convincing.

She suddenly returned to the couch, sat down beside me, and turned her face to me. "It would be fun if I meant something to you. I'm not just someone for you to push that thing of yours into. I'm a person. If you want to make love to me, you have to get to know me as a person and make me feel I'm someone in your life. Then"—she cocked her head coquettishly—"it would be different."

"That takes a long time." I realized I sounded peevish.

"Sure it does. But it's worth waiting for."

"How would you know?"

"I don't. I've only imagined it. But I trust my feelings. The other way it's just push push push and finished. That's not what I want."

I suddenly stopped trying to deceive her. "You make me feel like a fool."

"You aren't a fool. You're a very talented guy, probably the most talented in the school. With luck you'll end up being a famous artist, maybe even a great one. But you know very little about people, what they're like and how they feel. I don't either, but I do try to figure them out."

My disappointment, though intense at first, had dissipated.

So had my embarrassment. In spite of her refusal, I was beginning to like her. "You're so much smarter than I am," I told her with true admiration.

"No, I'm not. Only a little more mature. That's because girls mature faster than boys."

Suddenly, without warning, she bent forward and pressed her lips against mine. Then she opened her mouth, sucked in my lips, and daintily passed the tip of her tongue over mine. My feeling of rejection left me; I responded with a delight as great as my surprise. When she released me, I stared at her. "Wow!" I exclaimed.

She smiled. "Let's be friends. That may not be as exciting as having sex, but it'll mean more." She ran her fingers through my hair. "Who knows? I might even fall in love with you."

I looked at her nonplussed. "You're something!" I finally said.

"Not something," she corrected me. "Just someone."

I put my hand in my pocket. As my finger touched the packet of condoms, something of my disappointment returned. "If Steve had asked you," I said, "you'd have said yes."

She became coolly analytical. "First of all, he wouldn't have asked me because I'm not his type. Second of all, if he had I'd have said no the same as I said to you. I won't sleep with anyone unless I feel something for him. And I can't feel anything for him unless I get to know him. So there you are, smarty." She became coquettish again. "But *no* can become *yes*—if everything else is right."

That night, as I emptied my pockets before going to bed, I let the packet of condoms rest in the palm of my hand and smiled. It was not the first time that a rehearsal had gone better than the performance.

7

My sense of failure about the evening returned when Steve called the next day. "Why'dja leave?" he wanted to know.

"What was I supposed to do, hang around?"

"What bugged you?"

"She wouldn't give. She went so far and no further."

"Maybe you didn't handle her right."

"Tell me about it."

"Don't be a sore loser."

"I'm supposed to dance with joy because you had a good time?"

"I set it up for you, didn't I?"

"She has a thing about giving out only if she loves the guy."

"Where'd she get that idea?"

"Maybe she read about it."

"No use crying about it. Better luck next time."

"There won't be no next time."

"How about my fixing up another double date?"

I considered that and decided against it. "Not now. I've more important things on my mind."

"Like what?"

"The concerto competition is coming up. I'm gonna enter it."

"This time you'll win."

"Think so?"

"You're the best fiddler in the school. No one comes near you."

"You do."

"I won last time. Now it's your turn."

"So I've got to practice like the devil for the next two months. Girls only get in the way."

"You need some fun too."

"I don't mind putting it off." I enjoyed saying this; it showed I was ready for more serious things.

More and more I looked forward to my lessons with Dmitri Stamos. The man emitted a psychic force that held me in his spell from the moment I entered his studio. "Well, Danilo," he would say, "what you bring me today?" From there the lesson proceeded with solid instruction in the basics of violin playing, interspersed with philosophic musings on life and art, anecdotes about great composers and performers, and descriptions of various personages he had encountered in the course of his career. Stamos obviously considered these detours as important as the main discourse. So did I.

What I especially enjoyed were his nostalgic memories of his homeland—the clear blue of the Athenian sky or the beauty of the Parthenon as it caught the rays of the morning sun—and his intensely personal view of the spiritual power of music. Stamos was a mystic. He was convinced that we had inhabited the earth in a previous existence and would return to it again. His conception of God combined the frailties of the Greek gods with the compassionate humanity of Christ. He had prepared for the priesthood in his youth and still scrupulously observed the rites of the Greek Orthodox Church. His life was marked by a monastic simplicity. He rose at five in the morning and spent almost two hours in prayer and meditation. "Music," he told me, "expresses feelings no human tongue can say. It is the prayer of the universe; it gives thanks to God for creating the world." He riveted me with his intense gaze, bushy eyebrows traveling up and down his forehead, eyes blazing. "We see only the outside things. The truth is hidden deep underneath, where only the soul can see." He held up my violin. "You think this instrument could make such sounds if it did not have a soul?" His voice fell to a reverent whisper. "That is why it must tell only the truth." I wasn't sure I knew what all this meant, but it sounded wonderful.

His exalted vision did not prevent Stamos from recognizing the practical problems of a musician's life. "You love music?

Good, you can walk in forest and play to heart's content. No one will stop you. But what you really want is to stand onstage in Carnegie Hall and play to audience. In other words, you want career. This is completely other problem. The world is not waiting for you; she will try to stop you as much as she can. You must want success with all your heart; you must fight for it and never give up." Holding up his hand, he spread the long, bony fingers wide apart, then tightened them into a fist. "For this you must be strong."

Stamos pointed to the window. "Believe me, it is not easy out there. It is not like here at school where everyone knows you and likes you. Out there is struggle. You must play concert if you feel good or bad. Your audience paid to hear you and is waiting to sit in judgment, a monster with many heads eager to eat you up. And the critics wait to write review and wipe you out. You think artist's life is easy? I tell you, my boy, it is not. But if this is what you are meant to be, it is your destiny."

I mustered the courage to ask, "You think I was meant to?"

Stamos thought hard. "Is possible," he said at length. "You have the talent and good head on your shoulders. You also need luck, much luck, but that no one can tell before."

I practiced hard in the weeks before the concerto competition and felt I was ready for it. "I don't like competitions," I confided to Stamos. "Makes me feel like a racehorse speeding down the track for the final lap."

"Is not good feeling?" he asked.

"No."

He smiled. "Is good feeling if you win."

As the night of the performance approached, Julia entered into the spirit of it. The competition seemed to mobilize all her fighting instincts. She was full of advice. "When you come out onstage," she exhorted me, "look at the judges before you begin to play. Eye contact is half the battle."

Dad objected to the fuss she was making. "It's only a school event. Why build it up into something more?"

"Because it's a rehearsal for what he'll face later."

As usual, they discussed me as though I weren't there. "You only make him nervous," Dad said, "with that kind of talk."

"It's important," Julia asserted, "he should start thinking of himself as a winner."

"It's important," Dad countered, "he should start thinking of himself as a musician."

"Fat lot of good that'll do him unless he convinces people that he is." She shared Stamos's view of the world as a jungle. "It's tough out there, and he'll have to fight for his place. That's what it's all about, and the sooner he knows it, the better for him."

Dad sighed. "We sure don't see eye to eye."

"You can say that again!" she shot back.

The contest took place at the end of April. In the unanimous opinion of the judges, I was the winner and was chosen to play the Beethoven Concerto with the orchestra. Steve was among the first to congratulate me. "Didn't I tell you?" he said. He was the runner-up and didn't seem to mind this at all. I couldn't help noticing how much better a loser he was than I. It was a quality I genuinely envied in my friend.

The concerto concert was the culminating event of the school year. As the date approached, I suffered an attack of nerves. What if, in the middle of the performance, I suddenly forgot? Steve reassured me. "Everybody's afraid of forgetting. There'd be no problem if we could play with the notes, as they used to. But it's not done anymore. Practice it once with the music and once without, so it'll sink in. You'll have to play without notes for the rest of your life; you may as well get used to it."

My imagination conjured up one catastrophe after another. What if I broke a string? What if, as I was playing, I fell a measure behind the orchestra? The conductor would glare at me; everyone in the audience could hear what was wrong. What if my hands broke out in a sweat, my fingers went sliding over the strings and played excruciatingly off pitch? A recurrent dream of my childhood returned to plague me. I lay on my back in some kind of box. Two men in black arrived with hammers and began to nail down the top. I tried to cry out, to tell them not to box me in, but my voice stuck in my throat. I lay paralyzed with fear as the top slowly descended on me, and awoke with a start, my heart pounding, my mouth dry.

There was also a ridiculous dream. I stood in the center of the stage facing a crowded auditorium. Without warning a crucial button came loose, my trousers and shorts fell down and left me stark naked in front of the audience, which burst into laughter as I tried to cover myself with my violin.

The night before the concert I had trouble falling asleep. Julia came beside my bed. "I knew you were awake," she said.

"I guess I'm nervous."

"I'll get you a glass of warm milk." Warm milk was her remedy for all ills—physical, mental, or spiritual. "If you're so tense now," she asked, "what'll it be like when you play in Carnegie Hall?"

I pondered the question. "I guess it'll be easier by then, Mom," I finally said.

"Look, dear, you worked hard, you practiced well, so what can go wrong? Now go to sleep, and you'll see, it'll all come out fine."

Her words had a strangely calming effect on me; at length I fell asleep. Although I didn't know it then, this was to be the pattern of all my concerts, a pattern of worry probably deeply embedded in my nature.

I slept fitfully, awoke early, and played through the concerto, concentrating on the cadenzas. Once with the notes, twice without. Everything seemed to be in order. Toward evening I put on my tuxedo, the first I had ever owned, and surveyed myself in the mirror. The dinner jacket made my shoulders seem broader, so that I looked taller. I appraised myself item by item. Height, medium. Eyes, dark brown. Hair, dark brown and curly but brushed down neatly. Build, not bad. Looks, passable. Personality, plenty. Overall, B plus. Steve, I reflected, would have made an A.

At eight I was in the greenroom, struggling with my nerves. Suddenly I could not remember how the concerto began. In a panic I pulled out the music for a last look. My hands were sweating. I wiped them and tested the top button of my trousers. Soon a burst of applause from the hall told me that the *Egmont* Overture was over. *Now!* I grabbed my violin, walked onstage, and bowed to the audience. I was greeted by a splatter of applause and a blur of faces; I turned away to tune my instrument. In front of me sat my parents and Stamos, also Steve. They came especially to hear me, I told myself. They want me to do my best, and I'm not going to disappoint them.

The orchestra opened with a brave fortissimo, and as I listened, my fears dropped from me. I let myself float on Beethoven's lengthy introduction, its powerful harmonies lifting my spirit. I positioned the violin under my chin and played the opening notes with the sweetness they require. The sound gave me courage. I had no time to think of trousers, broken strings, or forgetting. I was engaged by more important matters, such as playing the right notes. Before I knew it, the opening section was over; the orchestra introduced the glorious second theme, and I remembered Stamos's words: *It must sound as if the heavens are opening.* I let the melody sing its way into the hall as it floated stepwise up the scale, each note melting into the next. It *was* as if the heavens were opening.

In the second movement, a serene meditation, I tried for a singing legato. Whom was I playing for? My teacher? My mother? The sea of faces before me? Or simply for the joy of playing? No matter. The sound was pouring out of my violin. By a strange illusion it seemed to be pouring out of me, from the innermost part of me; it flowed from me into the violin and from the violin out into the world. I was part of the music, and the music was part of me. Better still, I *was* the music; the music and I were one. At the same time I stood outside it, watching, listening, judging, to make sure that it was coming out exactly as I wanted it to.

The finale demanded lightness of heart and bow. I tried to capture the outdoor scene that I felt lay at the heart of this movement. My long hours of practice had prepared me well; the staccato notes leaped off my bow with the utmost clarity and ease. The conductor took the final section at a whirlwind clip that brought out its bravura quality. We ended bravely, arousing a storm of bravos that told me what I wanted to hear: I had charmed my public, dazzled them, and, most important of all, moved them. I took a deep breath and acknowledged the applause with a low bow. I had come through my first trial, and victory was sweet.

Friends and fellow students crowded into the greenroom to congratulate me. Steve came up grinning. "You did it!" he exclaimed as we clapped palms together in our secret greeting.

Julia kissed me; she had tears in her eyes. Dad embraced me.

Stamos appeared and enfolded me in an operatic embrace, with a kiss on each cheek. "My dear boy," he intoned in his majestic baritone, "this is the best I ever hear you play. What I always say? Artist needs public and public needs artist." He turned and indicated a thin middle-aged man standing next to him. "I have great pleasure to present you to Mr. Amos Schein."

I realized from Stamos's tone that Mr. Amos Schein was an important person. He shook my hand. "Congratulations. You played very well, very well indeed."

"When Mr. Schein says you played very well," Stamos intoned grandly, underpinning the words with a sweep of his hand, "you must believe him. He does not give praise lightly."

Schein offered me his card. "Call me tomorrow, we'll talk," he said, and made room for the next well-wisher.

There was a party in the students' cafeteria. Platters of cold cuts, potato salad, and coleslaw were flanked by cans of Pepsi and Tab. I was ravenously hungry and devoured two sandwiches. Most of the talk was about my performance. As I told Julia when we finally left, "I could have listened to them all night."

"Why not?" was her answer. "You certainly deserved what they said."

When we came home, a blanket of fatigue suddenly descended upon me. I slumped into an armchair. "Whew, this takes a lot out of you, that's for sure. But I loved it."

Dad sat down beside me. "My boy," he said gently, "you made your mother and me very proud of you tonight."

The thought occurred to me that it was not easy for him to talk to me. I realized for the first time that my father was a very shy man.

Julia sat down on the other side of me and stroked my cheek. "I'm making a wish." She smiled happily. "That we should have many more nights like this."

"We will, Mom," I said, and felt that in some fundamental way the evening was her doing as much as mine.

8

TWO DAYS LATER I found myself on Fifth Avenue outside the apartment house where Amos Schein lived. It was across the street from the Metropolitan Museum of Art, in a neighborhood unfamiliar to me. The lobby was very grand, with enormous chandeliers, a marble staircase that led nowhere, and a huge tapestry on one wall. Mr. Schein lived on the twenty-third floor. A servant answered the doorbell and ushered me into the living room. "Mr. Schein will see you in a moment," he announced, and disappeared.

The room was of the kind I had seen only in the movies. Paintings hung on the wall; little tables were scattered about with lamps on them and a profusion of knickknacks. I walked around looking at the paintings. In one corner, to my astonishment, I faced a suit of armor straight out of the Age of Knighthood. A red plume rose gallantly from its helmet. It was here that Schein found me.

"You like it?" he asked.

"Looks like in a museum."

"You're right, it is a museum piece," he said. "It's supposed to have been worn at the Battle of Agincourt. Know when that was?"

"The one in *Henry V*? I saw the movie."

"Yeah. That's how you kids learn Shakespeare nowadays. From Laurence Olivier. 'We few, we happy few, we band of brothers,' " he suddenly declaimed.

I was vastly impressed by his erudition, not realizing that since the Olivier film the opening line of Henry's speech had become familiar to millions.

"It's over five hundred years old," Schein said, lightly tapping the breastplate. "If you and I could come back five hundred years from now, what a different world we'd see. We can't even begin to imagine it." He sat down on the sofa and motioned me to the chair opposite. "I wanted to talk to you because I was very much impressed with your playing." He spoke slowly, with the authority of one who was accustomed to be listened to at board meetings. "I wanted to find out a little about you. Tell me about yourself."

I was puzzled. "What's there to tell? I study with Mr. Stamos and practice the violin most of the time. That's about it."

"How much do you practice?"

"After school, about three, four hours every day. Maybe a bit more on weekends."

"Good. Mr. Stamos says it's not how long you practice that matters but how well."

"It's not easy to keep my mind on the music the whole time, but I do most of the time."

"What does your father do?"

"He plays the violin in Broadway shows. Right now he's with *Follies*. He taught me before I went to Mr. Stamos."

"Is there any problem at home with your studying? I mean, a financial problem."

"No. When Dad's working, we're fine. In between shows it's not so good."

"When I was your age," Schein said, "I had to work all day and tried to get an education at night. That was not easy. You're lucky you can spend your days studying. I'm glad to see you're taking advantage of the opportunity."

I nodded to show that I agreed with the sentiment.

"I'll tell you why I wanted to see you." Schein continued. "I think you have what it takes to become an important violinist. And I'm going to help you. I've helped a few young musicians in my day. Some turned out very well; one or two didn't. It's all part of the game. In any case, I want nothing to stand in your way. If you have to go to Europe for a competition and your family finds it a problem, you can count on me. Come here." He rose and led the way to the study adjoining the main room. "See these?" He pointed to two violins attached to the wall. "One is a Strad, the other a Guarneri. You'll have your choice when you make your debut in Carnegie Hall."

I looked at the instruments in disbelief, fascinated by the rich patina of the varnish. "Wow! You mean that?" I exclaimed.

"Sure. The violins are dead hanging on the wall. They come to life only when an artist plays them. And I hope you will be such an artist."

I threw a puzzled glance in Schein's direction. "What do I have to do in return?"

Schein smiled. "I see you have a practical mind, my boy. Good. You'll need it. You don't have to do anything for me except be normally friendly. Maybe play at my house once in a while when my wife gives a party. You'll enjoy that. And sometimes come along with me on a trip if I don't feel like going by myself. That's about it, I guess."

"It sounds like very little," I said, trying to be polite. Then: "One thing puzzles me, if you don't mind my asking."

"What is it?"

"Why would you want to help me?"

If Schein was surprised by my question, he did not show it. "I'd have to tell you the story of my life to answer that," he said, "which would take too long. Let's just say that I love music and think it worthwhile to help talented young musicians. Also, in a way I made my money from music—I developed a gadget used in television units—so there's no reason why I shouldn't give some of it back to music." I nodded to show that I understood his reasoning. "Let's drink to it," Schein continued. "Coffee. I don't serve liquor to minors."

The servant brought two cups of coffee and a plate of chocolate cookies. My sweet tooth got the better of me; I ate three. I felt relaxed and happy in the presence of my patron. He closed the interview in an admonitory mood. "A career is a serious thing, my boy. Believe me. Many are called, but few are chosen. I have a hunch you'll be one of the few. Keep working away; you're on the right track. But remember one thing: You would make it anyway whether I helped you or not. Having me behind you may make it a little easier, nothing more. You have what it takes, and that's what's important."

I walked down Fifth Avenue on a cloud. What would my parents say when I told them? It sounded too good to be true, but it *was* true. I hurried home with the news.

9

One morning at the music school Ruth Lasker came up to me. "Why've you been avoiding me?" she asked.

"Who's been avoiding you?" I asked innocently, knowing that I had been.

"Don't pretend you don't know what I'm talking about."

Since she insisted, I decided to tell the truth. "I thought you didn't like me."

Her soft-gray eyes opened wide. "Where'd you get that idea?"

Mysteriously I answered: "I have my reasons."

"Well, you're wrong. I like you very much."

Her tone left no room for doubt. "All right then," I said, suddenly friendly, "let's take a walk."

It was a sunny day in late April, with that holiday look the city assumes on Saturday morning. Children were playing in Riverside Park, and the Hudson was as serene and majestic as ever. "You were wonderful the other night," Ruth said. "I never thought you'd play like that."

"What'dja expect? That I'd be a dog?"

"I don't know what I expected, but you were something else. So"—she stopped, hunting for the right word—"so pure."

I smiled. "That's a funny way of putting it."

"It's true. You have such a mature style."

"You thought I'd be childish?"

"Stop putting words into my mouth. I did think you acted kind of childish that night, and I didn't expect you to be so different onstage."

I waved my hand in a superior way. "That's my public image."

"It's a very nice one. What did Mr. Stamos say?"

"He said that if I were dead, he'd call me a genius. Since I'm still alive, he thought I was very talented."

"You're lucky to have a teacher who builds you up. Mine tears me down."

"Why do you listen to her? She has no pipeline to God."

"She talks as if she did."

"Some of them tear you down because it makes them feel important."

"When she's in a good mood, she's fine. But when she's not, you'd better watch out."

I was enjoying Ruth's company. She was pretty, she was giving, and she took me seriously. "I like talking to you," I said. "You mean what you say, and no bullshit."

"And I like talking to you. You don't kid around like your friend Steve. He drives me up the wall. And you're talented."

"How about smart?"

"Stop fishing."

We turned back toward the school. When we arrived, I asked, "Can I see you sometime?"

"Why not? Call me and you'll come over. Maybe we'll play sonatas. Do you sight-read?"

"Not too well. Mr. Stamos says that's my weak point. But if you tell me what we'll play beforehand, I could look it over."

"How about Sunday afternoon? We could go through Mozart's Sonata in A and Beethoven's in E-flat."

I usually spent Sunday afternoon with Steve but didn't mind a change. It would make me a little more independent of him. "You have the music?"

"I've got lots of chamber music."

"How come?"

"I'm not headed for a concert career. That's not my thing. I'll probably accompany singers, play trios and quartets, or work with a violinist. Maybe even," she added coquettishly, "with one I like."

"It's a deal. What time Sunday?"

"Two o'clock." She gave me the address.

I took the two sonatas out of the library and read them through. My reluctance to play at sight stemmed from my dislike of the unexpected. Once I played through a piece, I knew what to expect and felt comfortable with it. I saw that in both sonatas the slow movement gave me an opportunity for the songful lyricism that was my strong point.

On Sunday I took the subway to the Bronx. Ruth lived in a six-story apartment house on Vyse Avenue. The neighborhood, like my own, was in transition: The Jews were moving out; blacks and Hispanics were moving in. Her parents, like mine, remained because the rent was controlled. The apartment was comfortable. The sofa in the living room was covered with a flowered chintz and brightly colored cushions; a print of van Gogh's *Sunflowers* enlivened the wall. The piano, an upright, was in excellent condition. Ruth's parents listened to the Mozart sonata; then they had to leave. The Beethoven, I thought, had more substance. I had not yet learned to appreciate Mozart's profundity.

Ruth had remarkable facility at the piano. Scales, arpeggios, double notes, trills, octaves—she took them all in stride. Her sense of rhythm was finely attuned to mine, so that I really enjoyed playing with her. "You have my beat," I told her, "and you accompany out of this world."

"That's the wrong word," she corrected me. "The piano part in these sonatas isn't accompaniment. It's as important as the violin part. In fact they're talking to each other like equals. So stop thinking that you're playing a solo with piano accompaniment."

I accepted the correction. "I told you you were smarter," I said as we began the finale.

I was delighted at the way the session went. When we finished, I said, "Mr. Stamos is right when he tells me to play more chamber music. It makes you listen to what the other person is doing. He says soloists listen too much to themselves."

We repeated the Mozart sonata after the Beethoven; it went more smoothly, and I got more out of the music. Then Ruth fixed some supper. "How about a movie?" I asked when we sat down to eat.

"I'd love it."

An embarrassing thought tore through my mind; my face grew red. "There's only one problem," I said, and pulled two dollars out of my pocket. "This is all I have."

Ruth gave me a very feminine smile. "You never heard of women's lib? We'll go dutch, like friends."

We saw Jack Nicholson in *Easy Rider.* In the course of it I managed to rest my elbow against hers on the arm between our seats. I wondered if she would move away and was delighted when she didn't. This was the first of a series of Sunday afternoons in the course of which we explored the piano-violin literature, concentrating on the sonatas of Mozart and Beethoven but ultimately moving on to Grieg, Brahms, and Franck. After several movies I was emboldened to put my arm around her shoulder. I still fantasized about her in my solitary bouts with passion, but the image in my mind was subtly changing from sex object to someone I really liked. At the same time I keenly remembered her reprimand during our first evening and was determined to do nothing to upset our friendship. This time she would have to make the first move. I could wait.

With the passing weeks I took ever greater pleasure in Ruth's company. She listened to me, encouraged me, and understood me. Increasingly I relied on her good sense and her ability to see things as they really were. With her I could let my guard down and was not afraid of revealing my hopes and dreams. "As far back as I can remember," I told her, "I wanted to be somebody. And I knew I could only be somebody by playing the violin. The first time my mom took me to Carnegie Hall I knew I'd stand on that stage someday and people would listen." This was not quite true; it was Julia who put the idea into my head. But the idea stuck.

Ruth was thoughtful. "There are different ways of loving music, I guess. I love to play it, but it doesn't mean I want to be alone on a stage and have a thousand eyes on me. That would make me uncomfortable. Once I share the spotlight with somebody else, I'm fine. What I need is someone to hide behind. That's why I know I'm not a soloist."

I was suddenly impelled to be completely honest about myself. "I guess what I really want is an ego trip. I want people to take notice of me and admire me. When I enter a room, I want them to say, 'Look, there's Danny Sachs.' I may as well admit it. I know it's childish to care so much what people think of me, but I do."

"No, it's not childish. After all, artists work like dogs to get to the top and to stay there once they're there. They may think they're serving the public, but basically they're serving themselves."

As long as I was baring my soul, I decided I might as well go the whole way. "And I want my mom to be proud of me. I want her to feel it was worth doing all she did for me." I wouldn't have confessed this to Steve out of fear that he'd laugh at me but felt comfortable admitting it to Ruth.

She asked me about Steve. "He's my best friend," I told her, "yet I never have the feeling I can really depend on him."

"He's a lot of fun," Ruth said, "but I don't think he knows what friendship is. He's strictly out for himself. You'll find that out sooner or later."

"I already did," I said, remembering how hurt I felt after the competition for concertmaster. "My trouble with Steve is I need him more than he needs me." I paused a moment before adding, "I'm sure glad I found another friend."

Our relationship developed so naturally that when we finally became lovers, it seemed to grow inevitably out of all that had preceded. One evening in June Ruth's parents were attending a wedding. Instead of going to see a film we sat talking in the living room. At one point she put her arms around me and kissed me. Then, without a word, she led me to her room. She took off her clothes and lay down on the bed. I took off mine. I remember the moment when I stood naked before her. I felt a wonderful pride in my body, pride in my nakedness, and an excitement I had never experienced before.

I lay down beside her and surrendered to the flow of tenderness between us. Pressing up against her, I curved my knees between hers and passed my hands over her body. Her skin felt wonderfully soft to my fingertips; there was something miraculous about that softness. Her eager response made me feel like a conqueror. Nothing could stop me; nothing could defeat me. Ruth looked down at my erect penis and curled her fingers around its hard surface. "Looks like a piece of sculpture," she said, "and feels like one."

"Except that it's alive," I answered. She laughed.

The fact that Ruth was a little older than I was made it easier for me. She turned on her back to receive me. Once I was in her, I abandoned all thought for the sheer joy of being, a pure physical joy so intense that seemed to reach back millions of years before I was born. I pushed my way to climax, or was I the one being pushed? At the same time part of me split off to stand a little distance away and watch from the outside, which only added to the excitement of this marvelous moment.

Ruth's orgasm came soon after mine. Her breath came fast; her fingers dug into my back; I loved feeling them against my skin. Then we lay quietly in each other's arms, listening to the beat of our hearts; a delicious sense of peace warmed my being. "Whoever invented this," I said at length, "had a great thing going."

"Who d'you suppose did?" she asked.

"God, I guess. He should've patented it. He'd have made a fortune."

Ruth suddenly raised herself on her elbow and gave me a searching look. "By the way, I've a question to ask."

"When people say, 'By the way,' I know it's important."

"It is."

"Out with it."

"Do you love me?"

"Wow! That's a tall order."

"Well, do you?"

I knitted my brow. "I'll have to think about it." Abruptly I pulled her to me and pressed my lips on hers. Then: "Come to think of it, I do."

10

People liked to be invited to Amos Schein's musical evenings. The food was good, the atmosphere friendly, and the mix of guests—from the arts, business, television, plus the usual contingent of hangers-on—was apt to be interesting.

Amos was a charming host who let his friends do pretty much as they pleased, except for the hour of music when they had to sit quietly and listen.

He cultivated a brusque manner, perhaps thinking that it made him seem more important. His life had followed the pattern of the American dream, from a childhood of poverty during the Depression to success four decades later. Like many a self-made man, he liked to think that others could do just as well if they worked as hard; that was what America was about. At the same time he suspected that they couldn't; this reinforced his sense of his own uniqueness. In any case, he thought our government spent too much money coddling the poor; this was why he voted Republican.

When he was a boy, he had had some lessons on the violin, which stopped because his parents couldn't afford them; he had retained his love of the instrument. He endowed a professorship in violin at the Juilliard School—it bore his name—and several chairs in violin in local orchestras. He also owned the two rare violins he had shown me and did not mind lending them out—heavily insured, of course—to deserving young artists.

Schein had faith in capitalism because it encouraged people to acquire things. He himself was an avid collector. Two Seurats, a Matisse, and a Modigliani graced his walls. The Agincourt suit of armor was one of the high points of his collection. Another was his second wife, Valerie; she was thirty years his junior. He had divorced his first wife, after a long companionable marriage, expressly to acquire Valerie. She was pretty in a platinum blond way; her baby blue eyes had a way of opening wide with wonder. She wore designer clothes with a flair and habitually read the society columns to learn about the parties she hadn't been invited to. She had no particular feeling for music, but when her husband developed an interest in a young violinist, she attended to his wants and saw to it that he had a new suit to wear when he played at Amos's musicales. She also had him to dinner once a month. (The young violinist was usually male.

Mr. Schein believed that girls should stick to the flute or harp.)

It was Stamos who had persuaded Schein to attend my concert at the school. His last protégé had disappointed him, and he was ready to take on someone new. He decided at once that I would do. From that night on he believed in my talent and tried to help me in every way he could. He began by asking me to play at his last musicale of the season, in the middle of May. Mr. Stamos told me that it was a great honor to be asked to play in Amos Schein's house.

I couldn't wait to share the news with Ruth, who was to accompany me. I suggested that we play a sonata by Mozart and one by Beethoven, but she knew better. "Most of those people don't know a thing about music. They're there for the party. The Beethoven will be more than enough for them, followed by a piece that's easy to take, like the Rondo Capriccioso or one of Sarasate's Spanish dances. We'll be lucky if they don't talk and drink while we play."

I wanted my parents to attend the musicale. What did Ruth think? "Why not?" she said. "Ask him. He won't say no."

She was right. "Of course you can invite your parents," Schein said. "I'll be delighted to meet them."

Julia's first impulse was to decline the invitation; she didn't think she had the right dress for the occasion. "It's a high-class affair," she said. "I don't want you to be ashamed of me."

"Come off it, Mom. You wear whatever you have, and it'll be fine. They're coming to hear me play, not to see your dress. And if they do look, they'll see how pretty you are."

This was hardly the kind of speech that Julia could resist. She kissed me and said yes.

She wore her best dress, a blue silk, for the party, and Dad had his hair cut. When they arrived at Mr. Schein's, he welcomed them warmly and introduced them to his guests. He then led them to the Agincourt armor and explained that it was over five hundred years old. Julia said, "We should look so good in five hundred years." After examining the cuirass and breastplate, she added, "But tell me, wasn't it a bit awkward for them to—how shall I say?—go to the bathroom?"

Schein laughed. "I'm sure they found a way."

Dad, from his Communist days, had retained a general disapproval of wealth. He felt there was something vaguely immoral about it because of the things people had to do to acquire it. Nevertheless, he found the atmosphere of Mr. Schein's apartment attractive, especially when he was served white wine in a beautiful goblet. "Y'know what?" he whispered to Julia. "If I had my choice, I might even decide to be a millionaire."

"Don't tell me you're selling out to the enemy."

"I didn't say I was. I only said I could be tempted."

"I have news for you, sweetheart. They're not going to."

I went to Schein's study to warm up. I was tense but nowhere near as nervous as I had been before my concert at school. Ruth, who looked lovely in a black taffeta dress with a wide skirt, kept my spirits up. "Just remember, you're playing for Mr. Schein. The others don't know from nothing."

Her remark cheered me up. I stopped playing and said, "Let's have a kiss." She obliged.

Dmitri Stamos was very much in evidence in the drawing room, his dark eyes blazing, leonine mane waving, arms flailing the air. He loved parties, and he loved an audience; here he had both. He remembered Julia and greeted her warmly. "Madame, you will have great pleasure from your son," he informed her in his grandest manner.

Lucite folding chairs were distributed throughout the room. The host made a little speech to introduce me. "We are about to hear a very talented young man who is not yet known to the public. But he soon will be; you can take my word for it." He forgot to mention the pianist; his wife reminded him to do so. Ruth sat down at the piano, and I took my place in front of it.

As had happened at school, once I was in the music my nervousness dropped from me; the sheer joy of playing was enough to calm me. Besides, I had excellent support at the piano. Ruth's beat never wavered; her tempos were vigorous but unhurried. We played the *Kreutzer Sonata*. At the end of the first movement a well-known wine merchant broke into enthusiastic applause but stopped in embarrassment when he realized that he was not supposed to applaud between movements. I pretended not to notice and attacked the scherzo with a confident staccato. In the slow movement I revealed the singing tone that typified Stamos's teaching. The rondo finale was all vivacity and charm.

We followed this with the *Spanish Dance* by Sarasate and Saint-Saëns's Rondo Capriccioso. When we finished, Mr. Schein's guests crowded around us to tell us how much they had enjoyed our playing. Then the doors of the dining room were thrown open, and a buffet supper was served. Stamos piled a generous helping of lobster salad on his plate, along with a warm croissant. I did the same. Schein approached with a question. "I'm thinking ahead for Danny," he said to Stamos. "Would he be ready for his debut sometime next season?"

Stamos thought. "He could be." With a smile to me: "He's a hard worker. What have you in mind?"

"Carnegie Hall. Where else? We should reserve the date now."

"He's ready for it," Stamos said. "They do not hear anything like that since Heifetz made his debut." As usual, he was exaggerating, but it was good to hear. "You know the famous story of that debut, of course. Mischa Elman is in box with Godowsky. In the intermission Mischa wipes his forehead and says, 'It's a hot night tonight.' 'Not for pianists,' Godowsky answers."

Schein had heard the story at least a dozen times, but he laughed politely. "Danny could start with the Bach Chaconne; he has the right tone for it. Then the *Kreutzer Sonata*. I haven't heard it played that well in a long time. He's a rare combination. Sizzling technique, yet so musical. And he projects like a house on fire."

Stamos's hand made a lordly gesture in the air. "Don't forget his sound. Rich and full like great tenor singing. This is how a sound should be."

"I have the right instrument for him. Come see." Schein led Stamos and me into his study, where the two violins gleamed on the wall.

Stamos removed the one nearest him and carefully examined it. "Which Guarneri is this?"

"Del Gesù."

"Oh." There was reverence in his voice. "And the Stradivarius?"

"Cremona, 1715. His great period. Its price is going up. I could get a quarter million for it."

"More," Stamos asserted confidently.

"Then it's settled," Schein said. "Danny will make his debut as soon as we can get Carnegie Hall." He looked pleased. He liked important matters to be settled smoothly, without fuss.

On our way home Dad reproached Julia. "That was a stupid remark you made about the armor."

"What remark?" Julia asked innocently, although she knew perfectly well which one he meant.

"About the knights having to go to the bathroom."

"They had to go, didn't they? What was so stupid about it?"

"Mr. Schein was embarrassed by it."

"Not at all. He laughed. He's got to go too, so what's so embarrassing? Stop being impressed by his wealth." She turned around to me; I was walking behind them with Ruth. "Tell your father not to be so refined. He can be a pain in the ass when he's that way." She threw back her head and laughed the hearty laugh that made her whole body shake.

I watched her and felt happy. It had been a wonderful evening, and I was glad my parents had been there to share it with me.

11

THE FOURTH OF July weekend was approaching. Schein invited Mr. Stamos and me to his house in East Hampton. Except for an occasional trip to Jones Beach I had rarely been out of the city, and I looked forward to the visit with considerable excitement.

It turned out that at the last moment Schein had to fly to London. There was no reason to change our plans, he told us. "Valerie's busy in town, but the housekeeper is out there, and we have a heated pool. You'll have a fine time."

Stamos kept up a steady stream of talk as the train sped through the Long Island landscape. He enjoyed gossiping about the musical celebrities of the day. In a more serious vein he spoke to me about his youth. "The Nazis do terrible things in Greece. I was in the Resistance. My unit specializes in blowing up trains. I must say, I am very good at it. When a person is young, he has courage. And if he is not afraid to die, you have no power over him."

He had been a friend of the Greek pianist Gina Bachauer. "In small country, artist holds special place, like ambassador to the world. Greece is very proud of Gina. She is big woman"—he curved both arms to indicate her girth—"and onstage she moves like a queen. One day we are on plane to Egypt, where she goes to play for our troops. Pilot orders us to attach parachutes in case we must leave plane. Gina points to little door at her feet and says, 'You expect me to go through that?' And she laughs. Not only great artist but great human being. The two not always are together."

He thought for a moment and added something I never forgot: "People think artist is superior human being. They are wrong. He is only superior talent."

He discussed the great violinists of the past. "Heifetz plays like god. Such taste and elegance. Kreisler has the Viennese charm. You cannot resist him. Mischa Elman has beautiful sound, like singer, but no taste at all. Also two women, Lea Luboshutz and Erica Morini." He shrugged his shoulders to indicate that he did not regard them highly. "I do not like when orchestra takes women into violin section. It is a man's instrument. Jacques Thibaud fine violinist, but the French school is superficial. Not like Russian or German. During the war he collaborates with the Nazis. He wants to be on winning side. He makes big mistake." Stamos smiled. The idea that Thibaud had guessed wrong seemed to please him enormously.

Schein's house stood a considerable distance from the road. The grounds had a manicured look; the pool was set back from the house. We decided to take a swim. I had forgotten to bring swimming trunks, but the housekeeper produced a pair. Stamos was an excellent swimmer. I was so-so but enjoyed being in the water. By the time dinner was served I was ravenous. The meal consisted of a seafood salad garnished with huge Long Island tomatoes and the sweetest corn on the cob I had ever tasted.

We watched television awhile. What with the trip and the swimming, we were ready to turn in at ten. "It's so quiet here," I said, "you can almost hear it." The song of the crickets only accentuated the stillness.

The guest suite consisted of two bedrooms joined by a bathroom. I fell into a deep sleep almost at once. It was very dark when I suddenly came awake. The door to my room was ajar, and in the doorway, silhouetted against the night-light in the bathroom, I made out Stamos's tall figure. His shadow reached all the way to my bed. I watched in silence, too astonished to make a move, as the shadow edged slowly forward. Stamos advanced noiselessly and lay down beside me. His eyes shone in the half-light. He carefully lifted the coverlet and let one arm rest lightly across my chest. "You sweet boy," he murmured, "you lovely boy."

I had the strange sense that all this was happening not to me but to someone else, that it was taking place in a dream. What to do? I was too much in awe of my teacher to cry out, too dumbfounded to try to stop him. I caught the wild, imploring look in his eyes, a look of entreaty such as I had never seen there before. His lips passed lightly across my chest, then began to descend. He eased himself down, an inch at a time, until his face was on my thighs, then still lower, until he opened my pajamas and gently inserted my penis in his mouth.

I lay quite still, paralyzed by the conflicting emotions that coursed through me. The sensation in my crotch vaguely reminded me of the moment when the lips of Ruth's vagina parted to receive me. I shut my eyes and pictured her, holding on to the image until I had an erection. Stamos's lips continued to move slowly, caressingly up and down, until almost against my will I exploded into his mouth. Then, as stealthily as he had arrived, he eased himself off the bed and vanished behind the half-open door. Not a word had passed between us.

I turned around and buried my head in the pillow. Too agitated to think, I abandoned myself to the wild wave of anger and guilt that poured over me. And behind these, I experienced a terrible sense of having been used, of having been betrayed. I was keenly aware of how much I owed Stamos for all he had given me, but I did not owe him sex. Caught unawares, I had let myself be overwhelmed; I hadn't even tried to defend myself. A deep sense of shame engulfed me. Why hadn't I cried out, pushed his head away, jumped off the bed, locked myself in the bathroom? Why had I allowed him to have his way? I felt that in some strange manner I was to blame for the assault. It was almost as if I had invited it. But I hadn't done a thing; I was innocent! How could I have known what was in his mind? What should I have done? Punched him in the mouth? How could I? I looked about desperately as the night began to lift. Could I possibly face him after what had happened? I gotta get out of here, I told myself. Right now!

I took off my pajamas, threw on my clothes, packed my

overnight bag, and tiptoed down the carpeted staircase leading to the lower floor. A simple lock held the door. I opened it and walked out of the house.

Dawn was coming up over the sea. I walked along the empty street, not knowing where I was going. Everything was in place as though nothing were amiss. How could this be after what had happened? A car passed. I hailed it, and asked the driver how far it was to the station. "It's on my way," he said. "Hop in."

The station was deserted. I sat down on a bench, slipped my hand into my pocket, and fingered its contents. I had my return ticket and six dollars, more than enough to get me home. Shutting my eyes, I rested my head against the wall behind me.

The guilty feeling returned, but this time I argued with it. Stamos was my teacher; I respected and admired him more than anyone I knew. The question that troubled me was why he had picked on me. Was there something about me that had encouraged him? It bothered me even more that instead of being horrified, I had responded to the experience. But if someone was sucking your cock and you kept thinking of your girl while he did it, how could you not respond? You might even enjoy it. The main thing was that I must never let such a thing happen again. It had happened because we were alone in the house, with only the bathroom between our rooms, and Stamos had taken advantage of the opportunity. If Mr. or Mrs. Schein had been there, he would never have dared. The thought came to me that once I had talked the matter over with Steve, I would see it all much more clearly. I wondered if Stamos had ever made a pass at him. If so, how had Steve reacted? In any case, I would call my best friend as soon as I hit the city.

The train to New York was still an hour away. I sat quietly. My thoughts were whirling; I couldn't bring them into order. I wanted to talk, but there was no one to talk to. I felt like crying, but there was no one to cry with. Instead I dozed off. When I awoke, the ticket office was open; the station was beginning to stir. Finally the train arrived.

A new thought came to torment me. How would I face Stamos at my next lesson? Would I have to change teachers? The prospect was little short of terrifying, especially with the possibility of my Carnegie Hall debut less than a year away. I could not even consider it. A much more acceptable solution presented itself. I would go into my next lesson as if nothing untoward had happened between us. I would not mention the incident or give any indication that I remembered it. My every instinct told me that Stamos would do the same. We would wipe what had happened clean off the slate. It was the only way.

This brought me to my next decision. I was not going to tell Steve what had happened. He had no right to know about it. This was Stamos's secret, covered over by the jovial manner and the grand gestures. Hidden deep underneath was that look of entreaty in his eyes, the terrible humbling of his pride when he let his guard down. Why would I betray his secret to Steve, who would blab it to everyone he knew even if he swore a thousand times he wouldn't? It came to me that I owed Stamos this small act of loyalty. Steve would never know the truth, Ruth would never know, only I would, and I would keep the knowledge locked deep inside me.

Suddenly I remembered the subterranean garden that had haunted my childhood dreams. The garden of innocence I had lost forever. Wasn't this what the story of Adam and Eve was about? You grew up; you lost your innocence; you faced problems you had never had to face before. You kept wanting to go back to the lost paradise, but there was no returning.

A gentle sorrow filled my heart, mixed with resignation. By the time the train entered the tunnel under the East River, I was myself again.

12

My lesson with Stamos was two days away, and I dreaded the encounter. But the instant I entered the studio on Saturday, I knew that he too had decided to ignore the incident. His greeting was as jovial as ever: "And how is Danilo today?" I breathed more easily.

We discussed the Moscow violin competition, the date of which had just been announced. He was emphatic on the subject. "There should be law against competitions. I think they are terrible. When I am asked to be on jury, I say no. On principle. But I must admit that if you win, it is shortcut to career. Suddenly everybody knows your name, managers fight to get you, it takes ten years off your struggle. Not for every winner. Many you never hear of again. This is because juries stupid. They pick wrong winner."

I asked the basic question: "You think I should apply?"

"Why not? After all, someone must win, and you have as good chance as any. Moscow big village like Cleveland." His booming laughter filled the room. "Not interesting, except for Kremlin. Not beautiful like Leningrad. But go. You will enjoy."

Ruth soon brought an interesting piece of news. She had learned from Steve's girlfriend that he intended to enter the competition but was not going to tell me about it.

"Why not?" I demanded, feeling a little bit hurt even though I knew by now that I could expect anything from my best friend.

"People like to keep it a secret," she explained. "In case you lose, you don't want your friends to know."

"But I'd have to know if he disappeared for a couple of weeks."

"Maybe he doesn't want to put the idea into your head. After all, he has a much better chance if you don't go."

"I hate competitions," I said, "but I think I have to try. It seems like the next step."

I had the usual difficulty in reaching a decision, going around and around in the familiar circle from yes to no and back to yes. In the meantime Ruth gathered the necessary information, and I sent in an application, along with the required tape of my playing. I didn't tell Julia until I was notified that I had been accepted. She was thrilled at the notion that her son was going to win the Moscow competition. How else? Dad was more skeptical. "He'll be up against first-rate players from all over the world. That's a tall order."

"There you go again with your doubts. How can he win if you keep telling him he'll lose?"

For once Dad stood his ground. "I never told him that. But I want him to be realistic."

"Take a chance, I say. What've got to lose?"

"The fare is over a thousand dollars. That's what we've got to lose."

"We'll manage, just as we did with the violin. I'd rather spend on that than a fur coat."

Mention of the hypothetical fur coat persuaded Dad that he had lost the argument. He felt defensive. "Get it straight, I'm not against his going. It'll be a great experience for him. If you must know, I envy him. To be young and going to Moscow. It's like in Chekhov's play. The three sisters keep saying they'll never get there."

Never having seen the play, Julia did not grasp the allusion. But she knew she had won.

The question of the airfare was solved in short order. Stamos appealed to Amos Schein, who said he would pay for the trip. As Stamos put it, "He loves competition." My real problem was Steve. I tried on several occasions to tell him that I was a contestant but lost my nerve. Yet I realized that I could not indefinitely postpone the disclosure. I pictured his astonishment if we met on the plane or ran into each other in Moscow. In either case Steve would accuse me of having willfully withheld the truth. The date of our departure was approaching; I had to do something. Finally, when only a fortnight remained, I confessed that I had been admitted to the competition.

We were walking along Riverside Drive on our way from school. Steve grinned pleasantly. "I knew it all along."

"How come?"

"You'll learn sooner or later, sonny boy, there are no secrets in the music world."

"After all, you didn't tell me either."

"I'm not reproaching you. We both decided not to tell. What's wrong with that?"

"If we're best friends, we're not supposed to keep secrets from each other. That's what's wrong."

"Sure we're friends. But when both of us enter the same competition, we're also enemies. Friendly enemies."

"I'm not your enemy," I responded hotly.

"Be honest about it, Danny. You want me to lose so you'll be sure to win. What's friendly about that?"

"It's not true."

"Stop lying to yourself and you'll see that it is."

I made an honest effort to assess my motives. "I don't mind your getting second prize," I said at length, "as long as I win the first."

"That's decent of you. I'm not so generous. I want you to lose so I come out on top."

"Thanks for telling me."

"The difference between us is," Steve said, still grinning, "that I don't try to kid myself."

To prepare me for the ordeal, Stamos offered to give me some extra lessons. The first of these was to take place at his apartment on West Seventy-second Street. "You come Thursday at five," he said. "Yes?"

That set off another crisis in me. Under no circumstances was I going to his apartment. If in order to win in Moscow I had to be alone with him in his studio, I would rather lose. How could I make it clear to him that the lessons had to take place at the school? I hemmed and hawed but knew there was only one way out: for me to tell him so. I finally roused myself to dial his number and from sheer tension broke into a sweat.

"Ah, Danilo!" The voice was affable, reassuring.

"I called to say—" My wits scattered. Overwhelmed with embarrassment, I fell silent.

"What?"

I rallied sufficiently to be able to postpone the moment of truth. "I wanted to tell you how much I appreciate all you're doing for me."

"Bah! You not need to thank me. It is natural for teacher to want pupil to do well."

I swallowed hard and took the plunge. "About the lesson on Thursday . . . could it be at school?"

There was a silence. I could practically hear the wheels of his mind turning, absorbing my message and appraising it. "Why you say that?"

"I'm used to the room at school and feel more comfortable there. I'll play better there," I added, to bolster my case.

There was another silence. Then he said with finality, "It is more convenient for me to give extra lessons at home."

He was reminding me of his generous offer. It left me no alternative but to explain that I could not accept it. "I don't want to be a burden to you, Maestro. I'll simply have to do without the extra lessons." To make my ultimatum more palatable, I decided to change the subject. "The girl who accompanied me at Mr. Schein's . . . did you like her playing?"

"She is fine accompanist. Very talented."

"Well, I'm in love with her. We hope to get married." That said it all.

"When?" he asked.

"Oh, not yet. Someday in the future. When I can afford it."

The news must have made Stamos realize that I was not

going to yield, for he suddenly did. "I tell you what, Danilo. I give you lesson at school. Come Thursday a little later. Five-thirty."

"Thank you, Maestro, thank you very much." I hung up, jubilant.

Steve and I spent much time discussing the details of our trip. As the momentous day of our departure approached, he remained as calm as ever, but I steadily grew more tense. I had difficulty falling asleep at night. My mind spun around and around, envisaging the opportunities that would open up for me if I won: instant fame, concerts all over Europe and America, and, of prime importance to a beginning artist, a manager, who would stand behind me, fight for me, and guide me through the jungle. How could I sleep if all these choices were opening up before me? Only one thing was necessary for me to be able to grasp them: I had to win.

Julia shared my excitement. She refused even to consider the possibility that I might not come out first. That only increased my apprehension. So many things could go wrong. I might break a string or have a memory lapse or miss a cue. I knew the competition pieces backward and forward. As a matter of fact I was afraid to overpractice them because that might make them lose their freshness. At the same time I couldn't hold back from practicing. Between all these conflicting impulses and my insomnia, I was not in very good shape on the sunny June morning when my parents took me to the airport.

This being my first trip out of the country, Julia kept up a steady stream of advice. "Be careful of what you eat. I hear the food there is terrible. And for heaven's sake, don't talk to strangers. Their secret police watch foreigners all the time; you might get into trouble.

"Mom, I don't speak a word of Russian, so there's no chance of that."

"Oh, yes, there is. Their agents speak very good English. Be careful."

"Trouble is"—Dad turned to Julia—"you watch too many spy

movies." Although he had given up his faith in communism, he was still considerably to the left of my mother; that allowed room for interminable arguments in which neither of them ever convinced the other.

Ruth, Steve, and his parents were waiting for us at the airport, which seemed to be in a state of bedlam. It was time to say good-bye. Julia embraced me and invoked her favorite protector. "May God be with you," she said, her eyes filling with tears.

Dad was less emotional. He pressed me close to him and whispered in my ear, "Knock 'em dead!" I suddenly realized how much I loved him.

I kissed Ruth and felt very close to her.

The Swissair plane lifted off on schedule. Steve sat in the row behind me since both of us had requested window seats. For the first time I saw the New York skyline from the air and was overwhelmed by its beauty. All those slender towers of steel and glass thrusting up to the sun. What a city was mine! I sat back in my seat, took a deep breath, and surrendered to the excitement of starting out on an adventure.

13

THE SOUND OF Russian teased my ear; gentle vowels alternated with spurts of *shtch*'s and *kh*'s deep in the throat. As Stamos had indicated, outside the Kremlin Moscow was not particularly interesting. In any case I was too busy practicing to have time for sight-seeing. Stolid-looking apartment houses were built around huge courtyards, and there were several large hotels in the wedding-cake style dating from Stalin's time. I walked across the bridge over the Moskva River and stood looking down at the gray-green water below. This was something I would never have taken time to do in New York.

My problems were of an interior kind. My ambition got the better of me; I was consumed by the desire to win. This was strong enough to disrupt my sleep. The instant my head touched the pillow, my brain began to whirl with thoughts of the contest. I could win only if I was the best or if the judges thought so, but no magic formula could guarantee the outcome. This left me no alternative but to worry about it.

Steve, on the other hand, was altogether relaxed. "If I win, I win," he announced, "and if I don't, I'll have a good time anyway. I don't have to make first prize. I'll be satisfied with second or third." I knew him well enough to know that he was not pretending; this was how he thought. I envied him his carefree attitude but could not hope to match it.

The dormitory to which I was assigned was a large room that housed eight contestants. Steve was assigned to another dorm. Unfortunately I was not used to sleeping in a group. As I lay trying to fall asleep, a variety of sounds disturbed me. However, I soon made friends with an English boy named Eric Glenwood, who had brought along an extra pair of ear stopples. Made of wax, they could be molded to the ear and blocked out sounds. I found them very useful.

When I did manage to fall asleep, my old anxiety dreams came back to haunt me: the one about the long wooden box in which they hammered the lid down over my face; the one in which my trousers fell down, leaving me naked in the center of the stage. I woke up from these misadventures more exhausted than when I lay down.

I was fascinated by Eric's British accent, so much more tense and focused than the flabby inflections of New York speech. Eric and Steve became buddies and came to my assistance with sleeping pills that enabled me to get some rest. The only trouble was that I was a little groggy the next day. Eric, ever resourceful, remedied this with some amphetamine pills. They were rightly called uppers; they cleared my head and left me feeling as energetic as if a fragrant wind had blown the cobwebs from my brain. Even more, they lifted the burden of my self-doubt and made the sun shine again. I did not want to make a habit of these drugs, but they did help. Steve supplied the necessary rationale: "Unusual stress calls for unusual remedies." Who could argue with so reasonable a view?

In order to break our daily routine of practicing, the three of us went swimming in the huge outdoor pool in the center of Moscow. When we stood naked in the locker room, I pretended not to look but was curious to see if Steve's penis was bigger than mine. He must have read my mind, for he said, "Sure, mine looks bigger, but the real test is when they stand up. Some gain in size, and some lose."

I laughed to hide my embarrassment. "Which is yours?"

"I'm not telling."

Eric drew the proper conclusion. "It's not the size that counts but how you use it."

To my astonishment, middle-aged women were moving freely through the locker room with pails and mops. On our first visit we went through all the motions of modesty, but by our third swim we had learned to disregard the ladies as completely as they disregarded us. Noteworthy was the shape of the pool. You swam through a special channel straight into the locker room; that made it possible to keep the pool open even in cold weather. This, I insisted to Steve and Eric, was the greatest discovery since the invention of the wheel.

The day of the first round approached. The contestants drew lots to decide in what order they would perform. I was scheduled to play on the first Friday in June. Haunted by my fear of a memory lapse, I practiced furiously. When Friday came, buoyed by Eric's magic pills, I was ready.

The contest took place in the great hall of the Conservatory. The entrance was dominated by the statue of Tchaikovsky, which I touched on my way in for good luck. In these matters I was superstitious. The judges sat in a group in the balcony, taking notes. My accompanist was a middle-aged lady who seemed to know the entire repertory. On the strength of a single rehearsal she followed me with ease. I began with the unaccompanied Partita in D-minor of Bach, the one with the Chaconne; then came the piano-violin Sonata in E-flat of Beethoven, and three Paganini Caprices.

I had already discovered that passages making severe technical demands on me were in a sense easier to play than those requiring thought and feeling, because my fingers were kept so busy that I had no time to be aware of my nerves. My intonation was impeccable, my tone sang, and I thought the Bach came off exceptionally well. I was warmly applauded and knew that I had played my best. I returned to the auditorium to hear the contestants who followed me. Eric impressed me as an excellent violinist but was the only one who did.

I did not practice the next day; I needed the rest. This enabled me to hear Steve. He was thoroughly relaxed onstage; his natural facility stood him in good stead, but I was not impressed by his musical interpretation. Steve was brilliant technically, I decided, but superficial. Still, I could see that he would have much to offer a certain kind of audience.

On Sunday evening the names of those who had been admitted to the second round were posted. I grew tense as I approached the bulletin board; it would be a severe blow to my pride if my name was not there. It was, along with Steve's, but the mortality rate was high. Of the thirty candidates, ten had been eliminated, Eric among them. This made no sense to me, but as Dmitri Stamos maintained, no jury's decision ever made sense.

Steve and I celebrated our victory by getting high on vodka. Eric joined us. He was downcast by his defeat; we consoled him. He was leaving early the next morning; the Soviet authorities were not disposed to keep feeding a contestant once he was out of the running. Eric liked his two new American friends sufficiently to present us with a decent supply of his magic pills.

Soon Steve disappeared. He was pursuing a pretty violinist from Yugoslavia and could not afford to waste an evening. "Why don't you find yourself a girl?" he said to me. "It'll take your mind off this damn competition."

I shook my head. "My mind is somewhere else."

"But you need a bit of fun once in a while. Relax, man!"

"I can't when I'm pushing so hard."

Steve grinned. "I'm pushing too, but somewhere else."

I realized that he and I differed fundamentally in this area. I was perfectly satisfied to have one girl. Now that I had connected with Ruth, I was relieved not to have to look any further. Steve, on the other hand, was continually on the prowl. No sooner had he made one conquest than he began to plan the next. As a result, he never stayed with one girl long enough to get to know her. It struck me that what Steve thought of as a form of pursuing was actually a form of running away; he kept too busy to connect with anyone.

By chance I did find a girl. Her name was Carla, and she was from Rome. She had played the same morning as I, stayed to hear the other contestants, and came over to me to tell me how much she had enjoyed my playing. She had studied at the Royal College of Music in London and spoke excellent English. I felt guilty about not being faithful to Ruth but not enough to stop flirting with Carla. We took to each other at once; I had a strange feeling that I had known her for years. She had a fine mind and was utterly self-possessed; she also had a sense of humor.

We had to move quickly since both of us knew that once the competition was over we might never see each other again. This lent our relationship a certain excitement; we were going to crowd whatever happened between us into days instead of months or years, and we were going to enjoy it that much more. Also, because of Ruth, there was for me something vaguely sinful about the affair.

Carla loved Schubert, as did I, and Szymanowski, whose music I did not know. Also Ravel, although he had left only one major work for the violin. She actually played Ravel's *Tzigane* in the second round. She was an opera enthusiast and managed to get us tickets to the Bolshoi. We heard three operas that were obviously popular in Moscow but had never made it to New York, Rimsky-Korsakov's *The Legend of the Invisible City of Kitezh*, to which the Russians gave a lavish production in the style of a fairy tale; Tchaikovsky's *Mazeppa* (I couldn't tell whether the fat heroine was Mazeppa's wife, mother, daughter, or mistress); and Anton Rubinstein's *Demon*, an old-fashioned account of the struggle between good and evil in the soul of man. During intermissions the audiences rushed to the food counters and devoured meatballs on black bread, followed by huge scoops of *marozhineh* (ice cream).

Carla wanted me to accompany her on a visit to the Pushkin Museum. Her mother was Russian and had recited his poetry to her when she was little. "How cultural!" I protested, and begged off. She was secure enough in her playing to take time off for this pilgrimage. I wasn't.

We dined together after she had paid her gesture of homage. At the end of the evening she let me come home with her. She was staying with a Russian family, friends of her father, a businessman who came to Moscow twice a year. Their son was away at the University of Leningrad, and they let Carla have his room. She was strong on decorum. We arrived after her hosts had gone to bed, so they wouldn't know she had a visitor.

It was wonderful to make love to her; she enjoyed sex, had no inhibitions, and made me feel that she liked me very much. Whatever guilt I felt about my disloyalty to Ruth I assuaged with the reflection that she would never find out about it. At the same time I realized how lucky I was to have her in my life. With Ruth I was enveloped in a glow of tenderness. Carla, on the other hand, was primarily occupied with her own pleasure. Since our friendship had taken shape so quickly, there was no reason why she should be overly concerned with me. I did not make the mistake of expecting more from her than she could give. It was well past midnight when I kissed her good night and tiptoed out of the apartment, feeling altogether satisfied with myself.

I was vastly relieved to survive the second round of the competition. So was Steve. "I didn't think I'd make it," he confided in me. "The best way is not to expect anything. Then whatever you get is so much gravy." We both hunkered down to intense preparation for the last round. The winner was to be chosen from among six finalists. There was a steady buildup of tension as the contest ground to its last stage. Now I really needed Eric's gift—a sleeping pill at night and an upper to rescue me in the morning.

Carla was one of the finalists. This upset me no end. The thought that the girl who lay in my arms might snatch my victory from me was more than I could face. Steve couldn't understand why I was so disgruntled. "Stop carrying on, Danny. What if you hadn't gotten to know her? She'd simply be another contestant."

"But I did get to know her. Why didn't she stay home," I asked morosely, "and marry a rich Italian and have kids?"

"That kind of talk is no longer in style, my boy."

"Have you heard her?"

"No. But I'm told she plays like a house on fire."

"I don't want to hear her. And if she wins, I'll never forgive her." I thought a moment. "To lose to a girl . . . what a drag!"

On the last three nights before the finals Carla and I did not make love; our minds were elsewhere. Although I had said I wouldn't, I went to hear her performance and was thrown into a depression. She was an extraordinary violinist: wonderful bow arm, luscious tone, blazing technique, faultless intonation, and real musicianship. What right had she to be that good? I was convinced that she would take first prize and prayed to God to let me win, even though I didn't believe He existed; it was best, I felt, to be on the safe side. Then I realized that my anger would get me nowhere. The only thing that would bring me through was to play better than Carla. That was a tall order.

I didn't sleep at all the night before I was scheduled to play. In spite of that, I came through without a mishap. As a matter of fact the challenge seemed to give me more energy; I played my best. I never forgot the moment when I ran into Steve outside the Conservatory and he blurted out, "You did it, Danny!"

I couldn't believe him and suddenly remembered my first day at the school when he sent me down the wrong corridor. "You're not joking, Steve?"

"Look, this is nothing to joke about. Come inside and you'll see for yourself."

With beating heart I approached the bulletin board and read that I had won the first prize. The blood rushed to my head, along with a thrilling awareness of the magnitude of my victory: a series of appearances with the major orchestras of Europe and offers from any number of managers. Winning the Tchaikovsky meant having my career handed to me on a silver platter. As I stood in front of the bulletin board, I realized that a new chapter had opened in my life. At the same time the feeling of unreality remained, as though it could not possibly be that this wonderful thing had actually happened to me.

The second prize went to a Russian boy; the third to Carla. Steve took his defeat in stride. "They were not going to have two American winners, that's for sure. I knew all along you'd win."

"How did you know?"

"Because you were far and away the best."

"It doesn't always work that way. You have to remember, a lot of politics goes into these competitions."

"It didn't hurt you to be an American. The Soviets want to improve their relations with the United States, and this is one way of doing it. But you did play a blue streak above everyone else."

"Even Carla?"

Steve thought before he answered. "I'm not sure. She was outstanding. What counted against her, I think, is that she's a woman. Russians are way behind on that score. They've never let a woman win first prize."

"What you're saying is"—I bristled—"that I didn't really deserve to win. Thanks."

"Stop being sensitive. You made it, so be thankful for that."

I decided to change the subject. "Are you disappointed that you didn't?"

"Not too much. After all, I got into the final round, so it wasn't a total loss. Now I'll have the guts to enter other competitions."

Another question flashed through my mind: Are you sorry I won? I did not ask it. I didn't think that Steve begrudged me my good luck. He could be selfish and thoughtless, but he was not mean. What if it had been the other way around? Would I have rejoiced in his triumph if I myself had lost? I had to admit that I wouldn't have.

Carla went through all the motions of congratulating me; she embraced me and said how happy she was for me. But I knew she took my victory as a personal affront, one that she was no more disposed to forgive than I would have been if she had won. We did not discuss the matter. I sensed that she explained her defeat on political grounds: first, that I was an American and second, that she was a woman. An unattractive element of rivalry had entered our friendship, and I was not sorry that it was drawing to a close. Carla, I decided, would make a fine companion for some man—as long as he was not a violinist.

The awarding of the prize took place in the great hall of the Conservatory. There was a huge public, much applause, and much festivity. Afterward Steve and I, along with several other contestants, sat drinking vodka till three in the morning. That night I did not need any of Eric's pills.

Our last day in the Soviet Union was enlivened by a visit to Lenin's Tomb in the Kremlin. Long lines of visitors waited their turn and made their way worshipfully into the shrine. Soldiers standing at attention guarded the chamber in which the great man lay; he looked like a wax doll. No one spoke. As we approached the mummy, Steve whispered, "Spooky, isn't it?" One of the soldiers came to life and, glaring at us, hissed, "Shhh!" You were not supposed to speak in this holiest of holies.

That night I said good-bye to Carla. Our leave-taking was

brief and cool. We kissed and exchanged addresses. It was not impossible that we would meet again, but unlikely. I told her how grateful I was for all that had happened between us. She smiled a slow, wise smile but said nothing.

The next morning Steve and I took a taxi to Sheremetyevo Airport. As I stepped into the plane, I realized that I was a different person from the one who had left New York three weeks before. I was a winner.

14

JULIA BOUGHT A new dress in honor of my debut in Carnegie Hall. It was a navy blue silk; she wore dark colors because they made her look less bulky. She had been dieting strenuously so that she would look her best, but she always managed a single fall from grace—a chocolate éclair or sundae—that at one swoop undid a week of self-denial. Her excitement increased as the great day approached. "Remember," she told me, "how we sat listening to Isaac Stern and I said maybe all those people would come to hear you someday, and you said, no, they would all be dead. Well, it's really happening. Who says there is no God in heaven?

"I do," Dad interposed on cue.

"Who's asking you?" Having squelched him, she turned back to me. "Tomorrow we'll get you the tails. We'll go back to where we bought your tuxedo."

The tails came in the same state as the tuxedo: slightly used but looking almost new since they had been rented out only a few times. They cost seventy dollars instead of a hundred and forty new. Julia pointed out that no one would know the difference.

Ruth was accompanying me. We rehearsed every day during the final week. As a result, we developed a sense of each other that made for an almost perfect ensemble. She was sensitive to my every shade of thought. A slight quickening here, a subtle retard there—she never failed to respond. I was not far wrong when I insisted that the two of us breathed as one.

The day arrived. Ruth came early for a last rehearsal. She looked lovely. Lilac was her best color; it went well with her gentle nature. Her eyes shone; her light brown hair was coiled in a bun on top of her head, giving her a Renoir look. I pointed my thumb up twice in approval as I kissed her. "You look special."

"Why not? I feel special. How do you feel?"

"Scared to death. But excited. I want to play my heart out. I want them to hear a kind of playing they never heard before."

"That takes doing."

"Why not? There's only one thing I'm afraid of."

"What?"

"A memory slip."

"How many times have I told you? Think of the harmonies as you play. Then you won't forget."

She maintained that if I analyzed the form and harmonic content of a piece, I would not suffer the dreaded memory lapse. According to her, I relied too much on pure finger memory and luck. Once I knew the underlying structure of a composition, it would stay with me no matter how nervous I was. I, on the other hand, felt that my strong point was fantasy and intuition, which might be frightened away by too much analysis. Too much playing nowadays was intellectual, cerebral. I was all for the supremacy of emotion.

We played my program through once more; it went without a hitch. We reached Carnegie Hall early, so that I would have plenty of time to warm up. There was an air of expectancy in the hall; the prizewinner of an international competition invariably attracted an audience. Promptly at eight I walked out onstage to a wave of applause. I was tense but felt full of energy;

I had taken the precaution of popping one of Eric's pills into my mouth. I launched into the same Bach Partita that I had played in Moscow. Once I was into the music, I became confident. Now nothing could stop me.

After the Bach, Ruth and I played the César Franck Sonata. I had a slight memory lapse in the first movement but recovered so quickly that you would never have noticed it unless you knew the piece. The canon in the finale went particularly well. The wonderful acoustics of Carnegie Hall suited my warm sound; I felt I was making contact with the audience. During the intermission Amos Schein appeared in the greenroom and embraced me. "My Strad never sounded better!" he exclaimed enthusiastically. According to him, I was terrific.

The second half of the program consisted of several warhorses: three Paganini Caprices and Saint Saëns's Rondo Capriccios. Also Ravel's *Tzigane*, which Carla had brought to my attention. I was doing the kind of bravura playing that I hoped was in the tradition of Heifetz. For the encores I offered two of the delicious miniatures of Kreisler and Sarasate's spectacular *Carmen Fantasy*. The audience shouted for more. All in all, my debut could not have been more auspicious.

The postconcert party was, naturally, at Amos Schein's. It was crowded and noisy. Since I had played his Strad, he felt he had a direct hand in my success. However, success was not complete until the review in the *New York Times* said so, and this would not appear until the following day. Fortunately one of Schein's guests was able to call the editorial room of the *Times* for a summary of the review. This was Ed Newman, a successful artists' manager who looked the part: he had a plump, round face with a long black cigar stuck between his lips and a manner that was both jovial and assertive. "It's a rave!" he announced in a loud voice as he put down the phone. The news had an electrifying effect on the gathering. Schein was in seventh heaven. He had so often been disappointed in his protégés that he took my success as a personal triumph.

Julia returned to the suit of armor from the Battle of Agincourt. "Those knights couldn't have been very tall," she observed to Schein.

"European men," he answered, "have grown three or four inches in the last five hundred years."

"You mean Sir Launcelot was a shrimp?"

"Are you disillusioned?"

"Of course. I thought he looked like Gregory Peck."

"I'm sorry I told you the horrible truth."

She shrugged. "You build up a dream; then someone takes it away. That's life." She made a face.

Dmitri Stamos arrived late. He enfolded me in a warm embrace. "You play beautiful tonight. My congratulations."

"I tried to remember what you taught me," I said.

"Some things can be taught; others you must be born with." He shook his mane and was cloaked in his usual dignity. I was happy that our relations were as cordial as if the encounter on Long Island had never taken place.

I noticed that Steve, sprawled on the sofa against the wall, was eyeing us. Did he know anything or suspect? There was no point in wondering. Since neither Stamos nor I would talk, Steve would never discover the truth.

Stamos felt the moment called for serious advice. "When you make money," he admonished me, "there is much temptation. Drugs. Women. Liquor. You must never forget who you are and why you are put on this earth. I have students who have every gift, but they are weak, they lose their heads. Where do they end? No place. You belong on top, and that is where you must stay. You must never allow anything to take you away from music."

I nodded to show that I appreciated his concern. He had given me a solid musical foundation, and I had every reason to feel grateful to him.

I stayed at the party after my parents left. When I came home, they were waiting up for me. As was Julia's custom at important moments in her life, she invoked her personal friend in heaven. “God has been good to me. I prayed to Him that I would live to see this night, and He heard me.”

For once Dad did not contradict her. He embraced me. “I’m proud of you, my boy. We’re both proud of you.”

Julia couldn’t resist having the last word. “I knew all along you’d make it. I said so from the beginning.” She cast a reproachful look at her husband to emphasize that he had not always shared her faith, then turned back to me. “And you look so handsome in tails. You were born to wear them.”

Later, as I prepared for bed, the starch suddenly went out of me. I felt totally drained as I dropped down on the bed. Lying on my back, hands clasped behind my head, I stared into the dark. My parents spoke as if my career were in the bag. Didn’t they realize that the hard part had just begun?

II

1

THE PLANE TO London was full. I sat back in my seat and puffed on my cigarette with half-shut eyes. For the past year I had been flying first class and found it considerably more comfortable. Besides, I needed the extra room for Mr. Schein's Stradivarius, which rested on my lap. This was my fourth trip to London, but I still had not been to the British Museum or the Tower. My tight schedule left no time for sight-seeing. I got to know only three places in the cities I played in: the airport, the hotel, and the concert hall. These brought problems enough.

Each concert seemed a little more difficult. When I was young, playing the violin seemed to be the most natural thing in the world. I had only my parents to please, and my teacher. Now I had the whole world on my back: critics, managers, presenters, conductors, and the audience. I had become a cog in the intricate machinery of the concert industry, whose chief aim it presumably was to present great artists playing great music. Beneath this goal was the good old law of supply and demand, profit and loss. Someone once said that only amateurs talked about art; artists talked about money.

The difficult part was to maintain my playing at concert pitch. This required hours of practice, as well as enough time to study new works and to perfect my technique. But my crowded schedule made this virtually impossible. What with the constant traveling, the constant worry over things that might possibly go wrong, and the constant interruptions I could not foresee, I often felt I was caught in a huge conspiracy to keep me from playing my best.

My life, I realized, was tied to the violin. No allowance was made for my being tired or out of sorts. The customers had bought tickets and expected a top-notch performance; it was up to me not to disappoint them. I was not free to relax the tension that held me together as I poured my heart out in front of one audience after another. True, I loved doing this; it gave me a sense of being alive that nothing else could. Over and above this was the sheer joy of making music, of drawing the marvelous sounds from the violin. But it was damn difficult. I remembered how wonderful it had seemed, in my boyish daydreams, to be a concert artist. Well, it *was* wonderful but not quite in the way I had imagined. There was a price to pay, and it was high.

I sometimes had the feeling that I did not deserve my success. I could not shake off a sense of impending disaster; any day now my luck would change and I would be exposed as a fraud. This of course was a new version of the dream that had left me standing naked in the center of the stage, exposed to the laughter of the crowd. The feeling persisted in spite of my every attempt to shake it off. I was learning that emotions were neither logical nor subject to reason. The trick was to control them, but that was more easily said than done.

I held the Stradivarius firmly against my knees. By now it was worth almost a million and much too precious to leave my sight. Mr. Schein had let me have it on permanent loan and would probably allow me to play it for as long as I wished. Or for as long as I stayed in his good graces. My sponsor thoroughly enjoyed his role as a patron of the arts and had extended himself on my behalf again and again since the first time when he paid for my trip to Moscow. The only thing he asked in return was that I play occasionally at his parties, a request I was only too happy to comply with. There were few people in the world to whom I owed so much.

I glanced at Ruth in the window seat beside me. She had dozed off, her head resting lightly on my shoulder. I took care not to look out the window, so as not to be reminded that I was in the air. I hated flying; it was the only part of my career I did not enjoy. True, statistics proved that it was safer to fly than to drive a car, but being on the ground was natural, while flying through the air like a demented bird was not. Only one little screw in this complex machine had to go wrong, and it would all be over. I could not possibly be the only one on the plane who felt this way, yet we all flew. Gone were the days when an artist traveled leisurely by train or boat. Concert giving in this jet age was organized on a tight schedule that barely left you time to breathe. I should have been born in the nineteenth century.

Ruth stirred. The blanket had slipped from her shoulder; I put it back, taking care not to wake her. She had turned out to be a wonderful friend, always there for me when I needed her. She listened to me by the hour whenever anything troubled me, and she was the perfect accompanist, supplying the necessary background without ever obtruding her own personality.

The trouble was—and I felt enormously guilty about it—that I was no longer in love with her. Truth to tell, she bored me, whether we made music together or love. Her life revolved around me and my career; she depended on me to supply the excitement, the energy. But I too needed to be stimulated, I too needed excitement, and this she no longer gave me. She was too even-tempered, too predictable; I could tell what she was about to say before she said it. I didn't know what I was looking for, but I knew that whatever it was, she didn't have it. The realization saddened me because in the beginning there had been a real buzz between us. Why had it vanished? Where had it gone?

The fact was that Ruth was pedestrian, and would always be. She was an excellent pianist with fine musical instincts, but she lacked temperament. It was impossible to counterfeit temperament; you either had it or you didn't. How could I tell her that I was now ready for another accompanist? This would be as difficult as telling her that I needed another woman. Yet the moment was approaching, I knew, when I would have no choice. It would be cruel to face her with the truth, but even crueler to go on pretending to feel what I no longer felt.

The pilot announced the approach to Heathrow Airport. I suddenly thought of Eric, the English boy I had been friendly with during the Moscow competition. Whenever I came to London I intended to look him up, but something always intervened. This time I had forgotten to take his telephone number, and I no longer remembered his last name. Whatever had become of him? There were dozens of violinists who were good enough to take part in international competitions, even good enough to win prizes, yet were never heard of again. It took a certain kind of talent to build a following and hold on to it year after year. Without it you didn't stand a chance.

It was Eric who had introduced me to the magic pills. A real service. They were only a crutch, of course, yet without them I could not possibly go through the tensions of a concert season. I had perhaps grown a little more dependent on them than I should have, but my body seemed to have a real need for the stimulus of the uppers and relaxation of the downers. I was also into marijuana. Naturally I didn't tell Ruth about what she would have called my addiction. This was far too strong a term for something Steve and I enjoyed but could certainly live without. As he said, how could you apply the usual labels to situations you wouldn't find in any other profession? Only we could judge what we had to take—and how much—in order to cope.

Ruth opened her eyes and stretched lazily. "Where are we?" she asked.

"About ten minutes away."

"I had such a lovely dream."

"About me?"

"Who else? We were walking along a beach, holding hands. The sea was calm, and there were palm trees. But they didn't grow out of the ground; they just floated above the earth. Very strange."

"Sounds fine to me." The plane was beginning its descent. "I wonder if my manager will meet us at the airport."

"Of course he will."

"Good old Max. Where would I be without him?"

"Exactly where you are now. Darling, don't forget, you're not exactly hard to sell."

"But he sells me in the right places."

"Who wouldn't?"

"And he really seems to like me."

Ruth smiled. "You're so grateful for anything people do for you. It's one of your dearest traits, and it always surprises me."

The plane landed with the familiar thud, and I breathed more easily. Ruth saw to it that we didn't leave anything behind. She led the way to the baggage counter and shepherded me through customs; I let her take charge.

Max greeted us with a big smile on his round face. "You're staying at the Connaught," he announced importantly. This was my favorite hotel. "They were full up, but I managed to get you in." The implication was that he had only to wave his wand and whatever I wished would be done. I reached for my valise, but Max intercepted me. "Never carry anything," he said. "You'll get your arm stiff."

He had a car waiting, and on the trip from the airport he outlined our stay. "You'll rest this afternoon"—his artists never slept; they rested—"and rehearse with the orchestra tomorrow morning. Your first concert's on Wednesday, recital on Sunday.

Tonight we can stop by at the presenter, if you're not too tired. He's dying to meet you."

"First I have to practice."

"I had a piano put in your room. A spinet, but not bad." He turned to Ruth. "You'll like it."

I surrendered to the excitement of being in London. The city had a slower tempo than that of New York, nor was it as hectic as Paris or Rome, but it had a special charm and offered Ruth and me one great advantage: We spoke the language. I loved the clipped staccato I had first heard from Eric, so much more intense than the rhythms of American speech.

Max accompanied us to our rooms. With the air of offering me a wonderful surprise, he said: "Did I fix up a deal for you."

"Like what?"

"Vienna Philharmonic. Three concerts, Brahms Concerto. Plus a recital in the Beethovensaal."

I scowled. "Vienna's out."

"What d'you mean Vienna's out? What kind of nonsense is that?"

"You know perfectly well what I mean."

"They're the most musical audience in Europe, and they want you."

"I'm glad to hear it, but I'm not going."

"There's a whole new generation who weren't even born when it all happened."

"They haven't changed one bit, and you know it. They gassed the Jews then, and they hate the Jews now."

"You're being silly. Lenny goes and has a wonderful success." Like most musicians, he referred to Bernstein as Lenny. "They even love his *Jeremiah* Symphony. Sung in Hebrew yet."

"He wants to go, that's fine with me. But Isaac Stern doesn't go. Neither will I."

Max saw his commission going out the window. "Danny, you're not being reasonable."

"Look, Max, my mother's family ended up in Auschwitz. That wasn't reasonable either. If I had been there, I'd have ended up as a cake of soap too. Let's just say that Vienna and Berlin are off bounds for me. I don't want to play for them or go anywhere near them."

Max looked at Ruth for support and shrugged. "It just makes no sense." He knew from my tone that further argument was useless.

When he was gone, Ruth asked, "You're sure you don't want that engagement?"

"Quite," I replied. That settled the matter.

2

LONDON AUDIENCES WERE more serious than those in New York. For them I could program a Bartók or Prokofiev sonata, which I would have hesitated to do in my own city. Even the showpieces at the end of the concert were weightier: Ravel's *Tzigane* or Szymanowski's *Fountain of Arethusa* instead of the *Carmen Fantasy* or Rondo Capriccioso. My London recital came off without a hitch, except for a few spots where I screwed up. Such momentary lapses in concentration or aberrations of pitch were apt to happen in any concert. The important thing was not to be thrown by accidents but to go right on and hope that the critics hadn't noticed.

Once the final encore—generally a tidbit such as Kreisler's *Liebesleid* or the Tango of Albéniz—was over, the scenario followed familiar lines. The greenroom was soon filled with well-wishers clamoring for autographs or eager to shake my hand. Max, looking flushed and important, kept the line moving. An excitement filled the room, the sense that something important had just taken place. I kept thanking people for having come and was genuinely pleased that they had.

The postconcert party was given by a hostess whose hobby

it was to collect celebrities. "Don't look now," Ruth whispered as we entered the room, "but her diamonds are real." I smiled pleasantly at lots of people I had never seen before, expressed interest in matters that didn't interest me in the least, and looked at Max for a sign that we could leave.

He dropped us at our hotel. Having arranged an interview with the *Times* of London early the next morning, he urged me to get some rest. Before taking off my clothes, I surveyed myself in the mirror and was not displeased with what I saw. Like my dad, I had remained slim, which meant that I looked good in tails; they gave me the broad shoulders that made me look taller. My curly dark-brown hair was no longer unruly. I wore it long, not as long as rock stars, but certainly longer than average. I rather liked my straight nose and full lips; Julia was especially proud of my small ears. All in all, I decided, I passed.

I was much too tense to fall asleep. After several fruitless attempts I turned on the light and went into Ruth's room, which adjoined mine. She was reading in bed.

I decided to come straight to the point. "There's something I have to talk to you about."

"Like what?" She sat up, instantly alert, her gentle gray eyes fixed on mine.

"It's been bothering me for some time, but I didn't know how to tell you. I still don't. I want to be honest with you, yet I don't want to hurt you."

"Be honest."

I decided to come out with it. "Seems to me we're not getting anywhere, you and I. We're sort of marking time with each other."

"What's that supposed to mean?"

"Just what it says." How could I tell her that I was bored with her, that I wanted out? "I—I'm looking for something, I hardly know what." The hurt look in her eyes told me I was on dangerous ground, but it was too late to turn back. Nor did I want to. "I'm dissatisfied with my life. Restless."

"You mean, up to a certain point I satisfied you and now I no longer do?"

I was grateful to her for supplying the right words. "I don't know what I mean. I'm just telling you like it is."

She smoothed her hair back from her forehead before she spoke. "Danny, I love you very much," she said softly, "and the last four years have been wonderful. But I would never try to hold you against your will." She said this with enormous dignity. "I knew something was wrong between us."

"How?"

"A woman always knows. But I thought it would pass. That's what you have to decide: whether this is a passing mood or something more serious.

Her not reproaching me took me by surprise. "You're not going to remind me how much I owe you?"

"It wouldn't help if I did. Besides, you don't owe me a thing. You've made me very happy, so the score is even."

I could not hide my admiration. "You're a very unusual woman," I told her.

"No, I'm not. When you go back to your room, I'll probably cry all night. But tears aren't going to change anything. You're a certain kind of man. When you want someone, you go all out for him, and when you don't need him anymore, you drop him."

"You make me out to be a monster."

"That's how artists are. They're supposed to be special, but they're not."

"All?"

"I don't know all, but I know you. It's like your teacher always says. The world thinks the artist is a great human being, but the world is wrong. He's only a great talent."

I was surprised that she remembered Stamos's remark. "Funny thing, I don't feel like a monster."

She was thoughtful. "When we met, you were nobody and I suited you fine. Now you're somebody and I don't suit you fine. It's as simple as that."

Her words put me on the defensive. "Our lives change," I said, "and we change with it. Is that so hard to understand?"

"I've heard of women fighting for a man, but I'm not a fighter. Besides, I would find it demeaning. I'd rather remember us at our best." She hesitated a moment before asking, "Is there another woman?"

"No."

"Then you just don't love me anymore." She fell silent. Soon she said: "None of this surprises me. I hoped our love would be forever, but I knew it couldn't."

I wanted to say something kind. What? "I know we'll be friends." The remark sounded inane, but I couldn't think of any other.

She shook her head. "Not now. Maybe someday."

"Why?"

"Because I have to free myself from you. And the only way to do that is to make a clean break."

"You mean, you won't play for me anymore?" I didn't want her to, so why was I saying this? My trouble was that I was always trying to please people whether I was able to or not.

"No, it would hurt too much. You'll get yourself another accompanist, and I'll find someone else to work with." She sounded as if her mind were quite made up on this point. "It'll feel strange, but—" She held up her hands, then let them drop. "You must admit, I learned to follow you pretty well. You have your own way of phrasing. I didn't always agree with it, but I followed you anyway."

"Why didn't you argue with me?"

"You were the star; it was up to you to decide. Besides, you didn't like me to contradict you, so I said yes."

"Thanks."

She managed a smile. "We sound as if this were good-bye. That's ridiculous. We still have this trip together."

"And there'll be others," I said gallantly, even though I knew there wouldn't be. Feeling a sudden stirring of guilt, I sat down on the bed and put my arm around her. "I bet you think I'm a heel."

She smiled wanly. "Does it matter what I think? Actually I'm much too simple for you. Not enough class. A nice Jewish boy from the West Side makes it, he wants class. Some phony glamour. I'm not much in that department. Strange, you want very much to be loved, yet you're not very good at loving." She said this as though summing me up.

I kissed her and was grateful that she did not misinterpret this as a prelude to lovemaking. Nothing was farther from my mind. I returned to my room but was too agitated to go to bed. Perhaps a walk would do me good. I dressed and went downstairs.

As I made my way down Mount Street, which was totally deserted, I was assailed by doubts. What had I done? And why had I done it? It seemed to me that the important decisions in my life were not really made by me; they were shaped by something in my nature that pushed me into them whether I liked it or not. I pictured Ruth with her head buried in the pillow, crying her heart out. Was this the way to repay her for our years together? Where was loyalty? Gratitude? Common decency?

I tried to fight off my guilt. In spite of it, I could not help realizing that my leaving Ruth was inevitable. And left me free to move on to the next chapter.

3

THE CITIES OF the world were associated in my mind with different colors, each suggesting a mood. Paris was bright red, London soft gray, Rome deep blue, Venice bright yellow. Lesser cities were represented by pastel shades. And New York, the city of cities for me, was a blazing white. No matter how often I returned to it I was dazzled by my first glimpse of that magnificent skyline, its graceful towers thrusting to the sky in a crazy pattern of steel and glass. No city in the world could ever mean to me what New York did.

This particular homecoming had a special quality because I knew it to be my last with Ruth. Now that I had declared myself, I no longer resented her. On the contrary, my newfound sense of freedom allowed my real affection for her to come through. I very much wanted us to remain friends and knew that, given her permissive nature, this would ultimately be possible. We made no plans for future trips, which underlined the farewell nature of this one.

Now that I was back, I could devote myself to a project that required my full attention: to find and furnish my own apartment. I should have left my parents' place years before but had been too busy establishing my career to do so. The time had finally come to make the change. Predictably Julia objected. "Why does he have to move?" she asked Dad. "I give him home-cooked meals instead of the garbage he'll eat in restaurants. And he's perfectly comfortable here. A nice young man leaves his parents when he gets married, not before."

They had fallen back into their habit of discussing me as if I were not there. "A young man needs a place of his own," Dad said, "whether he's nice or not."

Julia hated to see her argument undone. "There you go, putting ideas into his head."

"He's grown up now, dear. Face it. He's going to do exactly as he likes, no matter what you or I think of it."

"Right on, Dad," I said. I kissed Julia but made no attempt to resolve their argument. For me the wonder was that I had stayed with them as long as I had.

Max helped me look. We found a pleasant apartment on Central Park West overlooking the reservoir. He would have preferred a more fashionable address on Fifth or Park Avenue, but I wouldn't hear of leaving the West Side. Many musicians lived in the neighborhood, and this was where I felt at home.

Besides, the rent was cheaper. Next came the problem of furnishing the place. I had no interest whatever in period furniture; antiques were for people who needed ancestors. I preferred the simple lines of contemporary style. We wore twentieth-century clothes and thought twentieth-century thoughts; why then should we surround ourselves with eighteenth-century commodes? I asked Ruth to go shopping with me, even though I was building a home in which she would have little part. But I knew she was not yet ready to accept the final break between us. Shopping together gave us a pleasant way of putting it off.

The apartment—studio, bedroom, kitchen, bath—turned out much better than I expected. This was clearly a man's place, in soft grays and browns with modern lamps and no frills (no cushions or fancy little tables covered with knickknacks). Since the top contemporary painters were beyond my means, I concentrated on drawings: a lithograph by Käthe Kollwitz, one by Paul Klee, plus a Picasso print that, according to Max, added real class. I took special pride in the white leather sofa that showed up dramatically against a black rug. The main object in the room was the large Steinway grand, not new, that Max found for me at a good price. Once it arrived, the apartment was complete.

My housewarming took the shape of a cocktail party on the first Sunday in November. My guests praised the decor whether they liked it or not and presented me with a variety of gadgets, mostly for the kitchen. Max officiated with the beaming smile of the born majordomo. Steve said he envied me the apartment and drank more than was good for him.

Julia wore her best dress. "A bachelor apartment? What for?" she asked rhetorically. "People today need all kinds of things they never dreamed of years ago. This is progress?" She greeted Dmitri Stamos like an old friend and asked him if he was proud of his pupil. He went through his repertoire of dramatic gestures—hands sailing through the air, eyebrows racing up and down as he tossed his leonine mane—to indicate exactly how proud. Dad hovered over the hors d'oeuvres, which came from Zabar's, and talked to Ruth, who was extremely quiet.

The Stradivarius rested in the place of honor on the piano, its varnish lustrous against the ebony background. Amos Schein arrived with his young wife, Valerie, wearing the satisfied smile of the patron whose faith in his protégé had been justified. He approved of the Marcel Breuer chairs, the intricate exercise machine that was guaranteed not to stiffen my muscles, and the bed with resilient slats instead of a mattress. "Much better for the back," was his comment. Valerie smiled pleasantly and cultivated an expression of wide-eyed innocence that didn't fool me for one moment. She had obviously been around. She ignored me during the party; it was only when she said good-bye that I became aware of what seemed like more than a passing interest on her part. Was it the look she gave me, or the pressure of her hand on mine, so slight that I might have imagined it? Or was there a secret body language between people that told the real story?

Sure enough, Valerie phoned the next day to thank me for the party. From there she came to the point in the most natural way. "I'm going to visit a friend in your building. Could I stop by for a little while and you'll play something for me? I'd love it!" There was that little girl sound of wonder in her voice, as if at any moment she were to make big eyes and say, "Oooh, isn't this marvelous?" I sensed the imperious will behind the facade.

"It could be arranged, Mrs. Schein," I said in my pleasantest manner.

"Oooh, don't call me Mrs. Schein. You've been Danny to me for so long, it's time I was Valerie to you."

I hung up, more than a little disturbed. There was clearly no reason for the visit except that she was looking for trouble. She was pretty; she was spoiled; she had married Mr. Schein for his money and was now ready for a little excitement. Was I expected to supply it? Why hadn't I told her I was busy? Could it be that I too couldn't resist trouble?

The room needed a little straightening since I had the habit of dropping discarded shirts and socks on the floor. They disappeared into a closet. I showered, shaved, put on a white pullover and the latest addition to my wardrobe, a jacket of maroon velvet that managed to look both elegant and casual. I decided to be as reserved with her as possible.

She arrived on time, wreathed in a cloud of perfume. She wore one of those exaggeratedly short skirts that were all the rage that season and over it a fitted plaid jacket that showed off her curves. Her honey blond hair fell in ringlets to her shoulders; she looked deceptively young and sweet. "Ooh, I never visited a musician before," she simpered. "What's it like?"

"Take my word for it, musicians are very dull."

"Really? Why?"

"They spend so much time practicing they don't have a chance to develop other interests."

"In that case"—she gave me a provocative smile—"I'll stay only a little while."

"What would you like me to play for you?"

"Oh, you don't really have to."

"But that's what you came for."

"Did I?" She managed to sound amazingly like a little girl. "I don't know the first thing about music. If you must know, neither does my husband. He pretends to like it because it's the right thing to do."

"You can like it without knowing very much about it."

"I don't mind listening to it if there's nothing else to do. But I can always think of something."

"Like what?" I asked, grinning.

She hesitated an instant before she said, with the same little girl fervor, "Like putting my arms around someone I like and holding him tight." With that she walked up to me quite shamelessly and did just that.

I knew what I ought to do—grasp her firmly by the wrists and push her arms back to where they belonged—but I didn't do it. How could I resist a pretty woman who embraced me without the slightest hesitation or embarrassment? That kind of willpower I simply did not have.

She steered me to the bedroom and with an assortment of oohs and ahs helped me take my clothes off. Then she threw off hers. Her hunger for sex was the kind that follows a long period of abstinence. She desperately needed someone to arouse her, and it was apparent that Amos Schein was not the one.

I felt immensely flattered to be the object of her desire. Also, I admired her directness. Most people I knew waffled their way through life. She knew what she wanted and let nothing stand in her way. Her urgency was too intense for me not to respond. She was the opposite of Ruth, for whom sex had been an act of love and tenderness. Valerie knew nothing about me as a person, nor did she care to know. She wanted me solely for her own gratification. Her orgasm was a mixture of ecstasy and torment: She moaned, she dug her fingernails into my back, she whispered all kinds of endearments in my ear that I knew she didn't mean, and she trembled with passion. We practically came together. After my years with Ruth it was wonderfully exciting to experience a totally different kind of woman. I thought of Valerie's perfume as the fragrance of mimosa, even though I had only the vaguest notion of what that was like.

Two of her expressions remained in my mind: when we lay in each other's arms after the first rapture. The little girl way she murmured "Oooh, let's do it again!" and, after our second orgasm, the way she whispered, "You beautiful thing, you."

I didn't mind being reduced to a thing. It was easier than being a person.

4

THE APPROACH OF my performance with the Philharmonic worried me. There ought to be a law, I always said, against giving concerts in New York. Not that New York audiences were more knowledgeable than those of London or Paris; they were only more fickle and spoiled. And the critics were sharpening their knives, ready to pounce. Every appearance in my hometown, I was convinced, took ten years off my life. But there was no way I could escape the ordeal.

I was lucky to have a manager wholly devoted to me. Max would go to any trouble to get me an engagement and see me through it. Yet even this friendship, I could not but be aware, was based on dollars and cents. My management, National Concerts, Inc., was as tough an agency as all the others, and would look out for me only as long as my account showed a profit. The concert industry was as competitive as any other; only the strong survived. This was the law of the jungle, and it worked for Carnegie Hall no less than for General Motors or IBM.

I had wanted so badly to be a famous artist, admired and loved by the world. Why had I never suspected that a public career was so much more difficult than I imagined? You traveled from city to city playing your program, and you wondered if the public would go on liking you from one season to the next. What if they deserted you as soon as a new star sailed across the horizon? What if your agency called one morning to inform you that you had been dropped? No wonder Mischa Elman had felt, at Jascha Heifetz's debut, that it was a hot night. He was right. In the early days of my career I had worried about having a memory slip or that my trousers would fall off when I came onstage. I now had more substantial fears to worry about.

I was certainly not the first one who had single-mindedly pursued an ambition only to discover, when he attained it, an emptiness within. It was simply that I was no longer able to hide this from myself. Something untoward had occurred inside me that was darkening my view of the world. I needed something else to drive it away.

One of my major problems was falling asleep at night. I might be feeling tired and relaxed and make a special effort to get to bed early. The minute my head hit the pillow my sleepiness vanished; a thousand thoughts raced through my mind. I fell into a vague apprehension that was not focused on anything specific; I felt afraid without knowing what I was afraid of. After tossing about for an hour, there was nothing for it but to take a pill. I knew this would leave me feeling groggy the next morning, when I would need another pill to pick me up, but I was desperate to get some sleep, and this the little green and black capsule could give me.

But sleep was not always the answer. I was increasingly disturbed by menacing dreams. Sometimes Steve stood on the rear platform of a train pulling out of the station. He gestured frantically for me to hurry. I tried to run, but the road was covered with tar, my feet stuck fast, and the train left without me. "Too late . . . too late . . ." The words rang a mournful refrain in my ear.

It was Steve who opened up a path out of my doldrums. One night in December he introduced me to cocaine. The drug seemed to be precisely what I was looking for; my one regret was not to have discovered it sooner. I watched spellbound as he chopped up the tiny white grains until he had reduced them to the proper consistency. He arranged them neatly in several fine lines and rolled a twenty-dollar bill into the shape of a straw. "Wouldn't a dollar bill do as well?" I asked, to which he replied scornfully, "Are you comparing a single to a twenty?"

Following his instructions, I inserted the rolled bill into my left nostril and snorted deeply, sucking up one of the lines. My nose burned a little; otherwise I experienced no immediate effect. Soon my head began to feel light, but I attributed this to my imagination rather than to the drug. Steve instructed me to rub some powder on my gums. A coolness spread through my mouth, as if I had rinsed it with novocaine. Then the powder began to work its spell. I was suddenly charged with energy and enfolded in a curious sense of well-being. In that frame of mind I could achieve anything I wished. Doubts, misgivings, regrets, self-reproaches were swept away as if by magic. I loved everyone: my parents, my former teacher, my patron, Steve. A deep peace spread over me; my thoughts were racing but seemed extraordinarily clear. This was an exhilaration such as I had never known before.

The coke loosened our tongues, permitting us to say things we never would have said under normal circumstances. I was usually reserved about my feelings; indeed my tendency was to reveal as little about myself as possible. Suddenly I didn't mind confiding in Steve. "I always had a feeling," I told him, "that I liked you more than you did me. This somehow gave you the upper hand. I hated for you to have it."

Although Steve was as far gone as I, personal confessions were not his style. He grinned contentedly.

"Now I can tell you," I continued, "I was always a little jealous of you. You were taller and better-looking and better dressed. Besides, you had a way with women that I didn't." I remembered the scene at the swimming pool in Moscow. "And you were ahead on some hidden points too."

Steve remembered too. "I told you, it only looks bigger." He laughed. "If you want, we can measure them."

"No, we'd have to be fourteen for that. But it would be fun to have a double date and fuck in the same room. Then we could compare notes."

"The Romans already thought of it. They had a feast in honor of Saturn where they got together and screwed like mad, each one watching everybody else. A saturnalia, they called it."

I was ready for the next confession. "Strange how mixed up I am in my feelings about you. You're my best friend, but at the same time you're a competitor. We're at the same point in our careers; we play for practically the same fee and attract the same audience. If you tell me you got a good orchestra engagement, d'you suppose I'm happy about it? You can bet your ass I'm not. And if you get a cancellation, you think I feel terrible? Sure I'm sorry for you, but better it should happen to you than me."

My frankness induced a similar mood in Steve. "Don't you suppose I feel pretty much the same way? I'm jealous of your double stops and octaves. And don't think I didn't feel it when you won first prize and I came in fourth? But there's one big difference between us. I don't mind being the way I am. You do. For some reason you feel you ought to be perfect. Why don't you learn to accept yourself the way you are? With all your faults. Then you won't go through those ups and downs of yours; you'll sail on a more even keel."

When our high began to wear off, I hated to see it go. The regret resembled what I felt at the end of sex when I tried to make the orgasm last a little longer. "How about another line?" I suggested.

Steve put his foot down. "No, we've done enough for tonight. Don't forget, both of us have to practice tomorrow. We're entitled to a bit of fun once in a while, but only so much and no more."

He was right, I told myself, and was glad that he hadn't given in. For once I was satisfied with myself and the world. It was a wonderful feeling.

5

EACH ENCOUNTER WITH Valerie deepened my feeling of guilt toward her husband, yet I seemed incapable of extricating myself from the affair. I was well aware that what I was doing was thoroughly dishonorable, and if left to my own devices, I would have vastly preferred not to do it. But Valerie had no intention of leaving me to my own devices. Her telephone calls were insistent, and each rendezvous led inevitably to the next.

For me she was more than a good sex partner. She was an extraordinarily attractive woman who had chosen me rather than another. The effect on my self-esteem was little short of miraculous. At first I dreaded the prospect of facing Amos Schein. As the weeks wore on, however, I found myself behaving toward him as I always had. I was properly respectful and friendly and found myself playing the deceiver with an adroitness of which I had never thought myself capable. At the same time I despised myself for doing this so well. I hated to see myself as a monster of ingratitude toward the patron who had befriended me, yet what else was I?

I wondered if my qualms would diminish as I got to know Valerie better, but I never got to know her better. What if, behind the little-girl facade, there was no one to know? Her sexual nature was clearly her most interesting side. Of interest too were her complex feelings about her husband. She had been a salesgirl at Saks Fifth Avenue when he found her, divorced his middle-aged wife, and introduced Valerie to a life of affluence. After spending her first twenty-three years as a nobody, she now sat on the boards of several charities, collected antiques, and gave dinner parties. What more could she want? She had every reason to be grateful to Amos Schein, yet she managed to accumulate a long list of grievances against him and thoroughly enjoyed her resentment. "He seems so kind and thoughtful," she confided to me, "but wait till you get to know him. A cold fish, and what a temper if he don't get his way. A bully if ever there was one. The bottom line, that's what interests him. How much it'll cost and how much he's gonna get out of it. He likes to own things, and I'm one of the things he owns. Or thinks he does. Yuck!" She made a face.

"Are you sorry you married him?" I asked. I tried to work up sympathy for her, but not for one moment did I feel that she was the injured party.

Her grievance, it turned out, sprang mainly from Mr. Schein's attempts to curb her extravagance. He lectured her on her shopping sprees and threatened to cancel her credit cards. How, Valerie wanted to know, could a person live without credit cards? He enjoyed showing her off to his friends in the high-fashion outfits she favored, yet he grumbled when the bills arrived. What did he expect, that top designers gave their things away free? "Doesn't he know," she asked rhetorically, "that if you don't want to go around looking like shit you have to pay for it?"

Despite my bouts of conscience, I enjoyed my sessions with Valerie. She was sensitive to the ebb and flow of my desire, showed endless ingenuity in arousing me, and explored the byways of passion as eagerly as the main route. One morning, as we were in the midst of our protracted foreplay, the telephone rang; I had forgotten to shut it off. Mr. Schein's voice came booming into the room. "Danny, my boy, I'd love to hear how the concerto is going." I was preparing the Beethoven for my concert with the Philharmonic. "I'll come by tomorrow at eleven and you'll play it for me." He hung up.

At the sound of his voice I had automatically turned away from Valerie. It was as if I had been caught red-handed. My erection died.

"What a horse's ass!" Valerie cried. "Once His Majesty decides to honor you with a visit, he just knows you'll be there."

"He's right. I will."

"Of course. And kiss his behind as usual."

"What d'you expect me to do? I need him; he doesn't need me."

"That's where you're wrong! Don't you suppose he gets a kick out of being the patron of a famous violinist? It's an ego trip for him. After all, what does he have? Money. What d'you have? Talent. You without him still have your talent, but he without you has only money. Big deal!"

"If he ever found out about us, he'd never forgive me."

"He can't find out. I see you only in your apartment, when I'm supposed to be visiting my friend Louise two floors below."

I sighed. "I don't know, but I keep having nightmares about it."

"Don't be morbid. A person shouldn't be morbid, I always say."

"And a person never knows what may happen next, I always say."

"That's because you're a pessimist and I'm an optimist."

"That's because I'm a realist," I shot back, "and you're a—" I stopped, looking for the word that would fully describe her.

"What?" she challenged me.

"A natural tease and flirt," I said, and kissed her.

"Some people would say," she added, "a natural bitch."

"That's only because they're jealous of you," I countered gallantly.

She shrugged a shoulder. "Maybe they know what I'm really like."

"What you don't realize," I said, "is that if he got angry with me, he could take his Strad back. Then where would I be?"

"You'd buy another."

"My Philharmonic concert is five weeks away. Strads aren't that easy to find anymore, and they cost a fortune. Besides, I couldn't play a concert on a violin I wasn't used to. Believe me, your husband could get me into deep trouble if he wanted to."

"So you have to keep sucking up to him?"

"No, I just have to stay on the right side of him. You forget, I owe him a lot. If he hadn't been there to give me a hand, I would never have made it."

"Don't be a fool. If it hadn't been him, someone else would have done it for you."

"But he was the one, and I'm paying him back by fooling around with his wife. Makes me feel like a heel."

"Christ, you and your Jewish conscience! Drives me up the wall."

She tried to coax me back into making love, but to no avail. The sound of Mr. Schein's voice had driven away the sexy mood, and in spite of all Valerie's efforts, my erection would not return.

"Talk about my Jewish conscience," I said, "you're lucky you were born without one."

"Know what?" A satisfied smile crossed her lips. "I don't miss it one teeny bit."

5

THE FOLLOWING MORNING Amos Schein arrived punctually at eleven. "How's my young genius?" he asked in his friendliest manner.

I acknowledged the compliment with a respectful smile and ushered my patron into the studio.

"Are you in the mood to play for me?" Mr. Schein asked.

"I'm always in the mood. That's my trouble."

I offered him a drink, which he turned down. "Too early in the day. Gives me acid." He took a sugar-free Pepsi instead.

There seemed to be no reason to prolong the preliminaries. I took the Stradivarius from its usual place on the piano and tuned up. "Of course," I said, "it won't sound right without the accompaniment. You have to hear the harmony."

"That's all right. I'll imagine the background. Besides, without the orchestra part I can concentrate on your playing, which is what I came for." He sat back in the armchair and motioned to me to begin.

I launched into the concerto, filling the room with the rich, warm sound of the Stradivarius. When I came to the songful second theme, I remembered what Dmitri Stamos had told me so many years before: "It must sound as if the heavens are opening." Once I was into the music, my awkwardness in Mr. Schein's presence left me. The sound enfolded me, protecting me from the disruptions of the world. I was afloat in a magic universe where I was safe and happy, where no one—not Valerie, not Mr. Schein—could drag me down to earth.

He had time to hear only the first movement. When I finished it, he exclaimed, "Bravo!" and applauded vociferously. "You're in great shape, Danny. You're playing on the fourteenth, no?"

I nodded.

"Good," he said. "We'll have a little party for you after the concert."

I returned the violin to its usual place. But I spun around at Mr. Schein's next words, which he uttered almost casually. "But I must ask you to stop fooling around with my wife."

A hot flush tore through me. Could it be that I had heard him correctly? "W-what?" I mumbled, and stopped, overwhelmed.

"You heard me," Mr. Schein said evenly.

I felt myself go red. "How—how can you say such a thing?" I blurted out, doing my best to sound indignant yet realizing that I hadn't succeeded.

"I thought you were going to say you didn't know what I was talking about," Mr. Schein said affably. "I'm glad you didn't. It so happens that I know everything: when she comes to see you, how often, and so forth. So I'm just telling you, lay off."

The shame that descended upon me did not permit speech. I stood silent, hanging my head like a small boy called up before his teacher.

"It's a nice way to pay me back after all I've done for you." Mr. Schein continued in that incredibly polite manner. "I don't expect gratitude in this world, but neither do I expect a stab in the back."

Guilt crushed me. My cheeks felt hot; my eyelids burned. I had to defend myself, yet how could I? "It was not my fault," I finally said weakly.

"That's right, blame the woman. It's what Adam did in the garden. I must say, you're not much of a gentleman."

I would have understood his losing his temper and slapping my face. It was his calm that unnerved me. "I'm not blaming anyone," I managed to tell him. "I'm only saying it was not my fault."

"You're a very foolish young man, Danny. What if I decided to take the Strad away from you? Don't think it didn't cross my mind. What a pickle you'd be in."

My heart stopped; my throat went dry. I stared stupidly at my patron.

"I intended to leave you the instrument in my will. Do you realize what you'd lose if I changed my mind? And you're ready to risk all that for an hour of pleasure. How stupid can you be?" Mr. Schein shook his head dolefully.

It struck me that my patron was not as angry with me as he had a right to be. He was minimizing my share of the blame in order to transfer most of it to Valerie. What he needed was a victory over her, and this he had achieved by catching her red-handed. In some crazy way he was even enjoying her transgression. For once he had her where he wanted her.

"You don't have to tell me about my wife," he continued a little more emotionally. "Once she makes up her mind, there's no stopping her. What she wants is a divorce and a handsome settlement, but she's not going to get it. No way!" he blurted out venomously. "I have my own ways of punishing her. I'm holding on to her no matter who she sleeps with. Do you know what they used to do to a woman caught in adultery? They stoned her to death. It says so in the Bible. They still do it in Arabia. Here we take her to a psychiatrist. Fat lot of good that does her."

I kept staring at Mr. Schein, trying to fathom the workings of his mind. Why would he want to hold on to Valerie if he knew she was unfaithful to him? He must have read my thoughts, for he said, "You're wondering what keeps us together? Believe it or not, anger can be as strong a bond as love. Valerie and I need each other. I need her to torment me; she needs me to catch her and punish her. And we both need someone in our lives to outsmart." His lips curved a smile at once scornful and shrewd. "It's as though she had a drinking problem or were hooked on drugs. She'd have to go on doing it so that she could be caught."

For an instant he was lost in thought. He finally turned back to me. "Don't worry," he said. "I'm not going to take the Strad away. I've invested too much time and effort in your career to want to ruin it now. And don't try to defend yourself. I know exactly how it happened. She was strong, and you were weak. She knew what she wanted, and you were stupid enough to give in to her. From here on, though, you'll have to stay away from her and keep your mind on your music. I know you won't go near her again. That stupid you're not."

I wanted to blurt out, "I promise," but no sound passed my lips.

Mr. Schein's manner softened. "You still don't understand how I feel about you. I never had a son, and when you came along, you filled that empty space. I was proud of you and still am, dammit, even though you've disappointed me more than I can say. But a father forgives his son. That's what he's for." There was a catch in his voice. He was revealing a side of him I had never suspected. He had always been decisive, controlled; suddenly he was gentle and vulnerable. "You've fulfilled everything I ever hoped for you. Even more. In spite of this"—he sought the proper word—"unpleasantness, I'm glad you're in my life. I'm glad I found you and helped you. I really am."

I finally found my voice. "I'm sorry, Mr. Schein," I burst out "More than I can ever say." I stopped, not knowing how to go on. Then I said: "I won't see her anymore, I promise. She's coming here tomorrow. It'll be good-bye."

"Good. You can tell her everything I said. In fact I want you to." The vengeful smile flitted across his lips. Then he retreated into his shell and became formal as he held out his hand. "Thank you so much for playing for me. I enjoyed it no end. You'll have a big success with the concerto." He shook my hand, walked to the door, and turned. "Tell me who you want at the party. Make a list," he said, and left.

I threw myself facedown on the couch. I had a splitting headache. Shame and rage in turn swept over me. It was terrible that I had done what I had. But how had the old boy found out? A mad thought raced through my mind. Could it be that Steve had snitched on me? But why would my best friend betray me? Was I becoming paranoid? This was clearly not the first time that Mr. Schein had caught Valerie in a compromising situation. Could this be a game they played with each other? He was obviously suspicious of her to begin with, and she was obviously driven to justify his suspicions. It was a game in which

I had become a not-so-innocent pawn. Once he suspected the truth, the rest was easy; there were a thousand private detectives in town whose job it was to spy on people and report their comings and goings. Amos and Valerie . . . what a couple! New York was certainly full of crazies.

Beneath the layers of self-reproach that weighed me down was a sliver of satisfaction. I was glad the affair was over. I had entered it reluctantly and stayed in it reluctantly, in spite of the pleasure Valerie gave me. The price was too high. Now I was my own man again. No more hiding, plotting, and worrying. No more deception and guilt. And no more married women ever again! The thought threw a solitary shaft of light into the darkness that enfolded me. What a wonderful thing it was to be free!

The following morning I described Mr. Schein's visit to Valerie. She was furious. "What d'you expect me to do?" she cried. "Kill myself?"

I had thought she would be overwhelmed with anguish that her husband knew everything. Instead she was defiant. "I don't care if he does know. He only got what he deserved."

"I promised him that I wouldn't see you anymore."

"There you go, kissing his ass. All he has to do is snap the whip, and you go to pieces."

Her contempt did not ruffle me. "I intend to keep my promise," I said evenly.

"Oh, you do, do you?" Her voice was scathing.

"Look, it's wrong for me to go around sleeping with another man's wife."

"You didn't seem to think so until you were caught."

I decided to disregard her sarcasm. "And it's ten times as wrong to do this to someone who's been very kind to me."

"And who could take his precious little violin away from you if he felt like it."

I was not disposed to contradict her. On the contrary, I decided to give her all the ammunition she needed. "Well, it's a consideration," I said slowly, as though the idea were eminently reasonable.

"That's right, you'd give me up for a violin."

"It's not just a violin; it's a Stradivarius."

"You bastard. I've a good idea to smash it over your head." She took a step, menacingly, toward the piano.

"If you did that I'd—" I stopped.

Valerie planted her hands on her hips defiantly. "What would you do?"

"So help me, I'd bash your head in."

"And spend the rest of your life in jail? Ha-ha."

"It would be worth it," I muttered between my teeth. At this moment I hated her. I wanted her out of my life.

Valerie sidled up to me and curled one arm around my shoulder. "Darling, let's not quarrel. Just because my husband talked rough to you is no reason for you to get all steamed up."

"Oh, yes, it is."

Her free hand parted my dressing gown and, groping its way into my shorts, began to stroke my penis. "I could stand a little fun," she said.

"Valerie, this isn't the right time. I'm not in the mood."

"What if I put you in the mood?" She continued to manipulate me, but there was no sign of response. "You mean, you can give me up just like that?" She sounded incredulous rather than hurt.

"Yes." She had always been the stronger one with me; it was her will, not mine, that had shaped our relationship. Finally I was making the decision, and she had to accept it. She suddenly seemed to realize that I meant what I said; she withdrew her hand and stepped back. "Very well, if that's how you feel." She thought for an instant and added, "It'll be strange, though, not to see you anymore."

"You will. But only with your husband. We'll nod to each other and say, 'How nice to see you.' And we'll mean it."

As she passed the violin on her way to the door, she twanged the E string. Its bright, metallic sound sliced the air. "To think what a guy'll do for a fiddle."

I smiled but didn't answer.

She stopped at the door. "Aren't you going to kiss me goodbye?"

"Of course I will." I came over to her and gave her a peck on the cheek.

"Yuck!" she exclaimed. "That kind you can keep for Aunt Minnie."

I shrugged. "Sorry, that's how it's going to be."

"It was fun," she said, and chucked me under the chin as she left.

I shut the door behind her and was relieved that she was gone.

6

MY CONFRONTATION WITH Amos Schein left me profoundly shaken. I hated to think that I had been willing to deceive my patron and that only when he caught me had I realized how shoddy my behavior was. Nor did I feel better about myself as an artist. I was working as hard as ever but found it more and more difficult to capture a certain spark in my playing. My technique, as always, was impeccable; it was the spirit that eluded me. I had always been able to shake off the world and its concerns when I was practicing, to lose myself in the music. This was becoming increasingly difficult. The real world had a way of intruding. What had been my private domain was no longer so, and I knew of no way to make it so again.

In addition, my place in the music world was no longer as secure as it had been. For a few years I had been the newcomer, for whom brilliant things were foretold; now the novelty had worn off. Each season brought a new crop of competition winners who became potential rivals. The greater their success, the less was left for me. I had spent my early years as an artist worrying about getting to the top. Now I worried about staying there.

At this time I began to coach again with Dmitri Stamos. Our sessions supplied a bright spot in an otherwise dreary landscape. My former teacher and I now met as friends and colleagues. In following the ups and downs of my career, he enjoyed vicariously what he himself had never achieved. We both had left far behind us the memory of that unfortunate night on Long Island; it was never mentioned. Stamos, approaching seventy, was as flamboyant as ever; his voice, gestures, and manner had lost nothing of their drama. He listened carefully to my playing, corrected some matters of bowing and phrasing, and asked for a cleaner attack in certain passages. Otherwise he had only praise. "Your sound is special, Danilo. Not often we hear such a sound nowadays." He gave me a searching look. "How is otherwise with you?"

"Takes a lot to keep going. It's not easy."

"For artist it is never easy. You must keep growing; you must understand more and more."

"I try."

"It is not enough to try; you must achieve. Never let career spoil you. It is very easy to be spoiled. Fame, money, applause . . . only one thing is important: the music. Always remember this."

We could have been back in the studio overlooking Grant's Tomb, with Steve waiting for me in the student lounge. I was swept by a wave of affection for my old teacher and was happy I could turn to him.

The Scheins gave their usual lavish party after my concert with the Philharmonic. Schein was most friendly. He obviously was not inclined to surrender his position as my patron because of what had happened. I dreaded having to face Valerie, but she held out her hand in the most natural way. "How nice of you to come," she said, as if she had never seen me before. She had been so busy preparing for the party that she never got to the concert.

Unfortunately the festive mood was dissipated the next day by the reviews. The critic of the *Times* noted a certain falling off in my playing. The *Daily News* mentioned problems of intonation, while the *New York Post* liked hardly anything about the evening. I knew how unreliable were the opinions of critics; some artists were careful never to read their reviews. Still, there was something daunting about seeing such negative opinions in print. I had never been treated so shabbily in my native town and was devastated.

My mood was not improved when my agent called to say that the head of National Concerts, Inc., wanted to see me. Max tried to sound cheerful. "Don't forget to butter him up. Make him feel he's terrific. That's what he likes to hear."

The office of C. Myron Rollins was on the twenty-ninth floor of a new tower on Fifty-seventh Street. He was finishing a telephone conversation when I was ushered in. There was no receiver in his hand; he spoke into a box from which the rejoinder emerged. Rollins had all the trappings of the successful executive: slightly gray at the temples, a Giorgio Armani suit with discreet tie to match, and bland regular features like those that graced the ads for Dewar's whiskey. He did not know much about music; his job was to sell it, and selling was one thing he did know about. He regarded his artists as a bunch of irresponsible children whom he had to protect, except when they misbehaved or failed to fill the hall. Dmitri Stamos liked to say that God in his delusions of grandeur thought he was C. Myron Rollins.

"How are you, my boy?" he said, extending his hand. He motioned me to an armchair in front of his desk.

I sat down. "Fine . . . fine . . ." I replied, trying to inject into the words the assurance I did not feel.

"Sorry about those reviews, but don't let them upset you," he said brightly. "Everybody gets them at one time or another. I didn't hear you because I was in London, but I'm told you did fine. The critics have to find something to tear down. They think that's what they're paid to do."

I murmured agreement.

"You have to understand," he continued, "that we're not having an easy time of it here. The country's in the doldrums, and this of course affects our business." Rollins belonged to the new breed of managers who favored such phrases as "the concert industry" and "the music business." He bent his fingers and studied the exquisitely manicured nails. "I'm always hearing what a great manager Sol Hurok was. Of course he was. But the time was right for him, as it isn't for us. Even he used to say, 'If people won't come to a concert, there's no way you can stop them.' And he was active long before the customers stayed home at night to watch TV. The streets were safe; it was no problem to take the subway from Brooklyn or the Bronx to Carnegie Hall. Imagine, during Mischa Elman's first season in New York he gave twelve concerts in the old Hippodrome. Twelve in one season. Can you believe it? The old concert public died or moved to the suburbs. And the young one wants rock."

I wondered where this was leading. Rollins finally came to the point. "With all these problems it's not easy for an artist to maintain his standing. The public doesn't know what it wants. One season it goes for a certain artist; the next it prefers someone else." He brought his hands together, curving the fingers into a little chapel. "You're still pulling them in, my boy. Not quite as much as when you first appeared, but that's to be expected. We've been studying the figures, and they tell us it's getting to be a little harder to sell you. I therefore decided to ask for a lower fee. We were getting fifteen thou for you. For next season I'm making it twelve. That should keep it from dropping any further. I hope you understand why I have to do this."

He stopped, waiting for me to respond. I remembered Max's injunction to tell him only what he wanted to hear, but I was too upset to follow it. "Maybe one of the problems, Mr. Rollins, is that you have too many artists on your roster. If you had fewer, you might be able to sell each one more easily. This way your soloists compete with one another as well as with other managements."

Rollins smiled unpleasantly. "Thank you for telling me how to run my business. I already told you," he added pointedly, "that we're in a recession. Until it lifts, our industry is going to be in trouble."

"I don't see that Pavarotti is suffering much. Or Itzhak Perlman."

"You're talking about superstars. They're in a class by themselves. If you'll forgive my saying so," he added testily, "you're not quite up there with them."

"I know that, and I wasn't suggesting that I am. Of course, if they didn't demand forty, fifty thousand for one concert, there'd be more for the rest of us."

"They charge what the traffic'll bear, which is how things work in our world. The public is obviously willing to pay whatever they ask."

"Which only makes it harder for the rest of us." The words rushed out before I reflected that the conversation was clearly not to Rollins's liking.

"Danny, we're not discussing them; we were talking about you," Rollins was now visibly annoyed. "Specifically, your fee."

I wanted to placate him but didn't know how. "What choice do I have? I've got to accept what you offer me." Clearly I was no match for Rollins. I wished Max had been there to fight for me. But what could Max do? He'd have to obey the boss just as everyone else did.

"You do have a choice," Rollins said, recovering his composure. "We're not the only management in town. If you're not happy with the way we're handling you, you can always look elsewhere. Your contract is up this year. After that you're a free agent."

Through some fatality I had managed to bring our talk to the very outcome I wished above all to avoid. Hiding my discomfiture as best I could, I said, "I'd face the same conditions no matter where I went, Mr. Rollins. And I do have one big advantage at National Concerts. You've been behind me ever since I began; I feel at home here." This, I thought, ought to win the bastard over. To make sure, I added, "I'm perfectly satisfied with the way you people are handling me, and I've no wish to look elsewhere."

"I'm glad to hear it." Rollins rose as a sign that the interview was over. "I knew you'd be sensible." He held out his hand.

On my way down I thought of all the things I might have said. Why hadn't they popped into my head when there was still time to say them? The prospect of having my fee cut infuriated me, especially as I repeated the conversation to Steve.

"Bloodsuckers!" he cried, outraged. "Parasites! They live off our talent; they take a cut every time we play; they know we can't do without them. Except go to another management and be treated worse. Fact is, no artist reaches his public without a go-between. Writers need their publishers; painters need their galleries; musicians need their management. Otherwise we're sunk. And they're clever enough to make us feel they're doing us a favor, when the truth is they need us just as much as we need them."

The more we contemplated our situation, the worse we felt. Unquestionably what we both needed was a change of pace. "How about some health food?" Steve asked. This had become our code name for cocaine. I was all for it. In short order I threw off the depression that had followed my encounter with Mr. Rollins. "Fuck him!" I announced grandiloquently, and stretched out on Steve's couch.

"I've a brief message for him," Steve responded with equal fervor. "Just two words. Drop dead!"

"As far as I'm concerned, his outfit could collapse tomorrow."

"Why not tonight?" Steve asked.

"Even better," I said.

"Then you could come over to my management."

Euphoric though I was, the prospect did not appeal to me.

"No, yours is just as bad. Why can't we form our own? As things stand, they control us. They tell us where we play, how often, how much we get. If we had our own outfit, they couldn't kick us around anymore. We'd be the boss."

The more Steve considered the possibility, the more attractive he found it. "I'll be president, as I'm more practical than you. You'll be vice-president."

This was not altogether to my liking. "No, I'll be president, and you be vice-president."

Steve found the perfect solution. "Tell you what, I'll be president, and you'll be chairman of the board. Both equal."

This suited me fine. We shook hands on it and took another snort. Time expanded as we floated through a luminous world where neither Mr. Rollins nor anyone else could ever cause us grief.

7

AMOS SCHEIN TELEPHONED. I had not spoken to him since the night of my concert and was delighted to hear from him.

"Do you like ballet?" he asked.

"Very much," I replied. This was not true. People jumping about on their toes for a whole evening was, I thought, a little too much. But I knew that his question was the prelude to an invitation, and I was not going to turn it down.

"We're taking some friends to *Swan Lake* tomorrow night. I was hoping you'd come with us."

I was totally unprepared for the scene of enchantment that unfolded before me the following evening. A fairy-tale castle made the perfect setting for the haunting theme in B-minor that opened Tchaikovsky's score. The swan maidens descended on the scene gracefully rippling their arms. From the moment their queen, Odette, appeared I fell under her spell. A slight but commanding figure in her white tutu, she seemed to float above the stage in defiance of the law of gravity, each lyrical movement flowing into the next. From where I sat she seemed like an ethereal vision from some other world.

The action of the ballet proceeded in a straight line to the climax, where the spell of the evil magician was broken and the mournful theme of the opening reappeared triumphantly in the major. There were many curtain calls and bravos as the prima ballerina, Natalia Kohanskaya, took her bows, very much the star. I joined in the cheering. The Scheins were giving a party for her after the performance. I could hardly believe that I was actually going to meet her.

She turned out to be an animated young woman with the flat chest and boyish figure common to fashion models and ballerinas. To my surprise, she spoke perfect English. "I thought you were Russian," I said.

She smiled. "If Alice Marks of London could become Alicia Markova, why couldn't Natalie Cohen of Brooklyn become Natalia Kohanskaya? Once you sound like a ballerina, you become one."

"It's as easy as all that?" I asked her if she had ever heard me play.

"No more than you saw me dance," she replied. "I mean, before tonight. We get so caught up in our own thing we have no time for each other. Either I'm performing or touring. It must be the same with you. Were you ever at a ballet before?

"No. I didn't think I'd enjoy it."

"Did you?"

"I was crazy about it. Especially you."

"Thank you."

"I don't hear any Brooklyn in your speech," I said. "In fact you sound vaguely foreign."

"Oh, that . . ." She threw back her head and laughed a low, musical laugh. "That's affected."

Her frankness was refreshing; she was forceful and direct. Her dark eyes were too large for her thin face, so that she wore a look of perpetual wonder. Her features were small and dainty, except for the chin, which jutted forward in an assertive way. Hers was not a kind face, but it was full of personality. There was nothing fragile about her. On the contrary, her gestures were decisive, even imperious. Having created Natalia Kohanskaya, she played the character to perfection. She sat at one end of the room, receiving the homage of her admirers. When they came up to her, she held out her hand to be kissed. It was a queenly gesture, as much of an affectation as her accent, and I loved it.

"Magicians in ballet," she said to me, "are always changing someone into somebody else. In my case the magician was George Balanchine." She spoke of him with reverence. "He had a single ideal, perfection. Nothing less would do. There are people who touch your life and transform it. He was one of those."

I brought her a plate of food and noticed that she ate very little. "Aren't you hungry after a performance?" I asked.

"I could eat a huge steak, but I won't. It's not good for you after you've danced. Besides, I'm always dieting. It's hard enough to stay on your toes without carrying extra pounds. And no dessert." She picked at her lobster salad. "What I'd really like is a chocolate sundae."

At the end of the evening I asked to take her home. She lived in one of the new apartment buildings on Fifth Avenue. When we reached her door, she held out her hand to me. Instead of kissing it, I bent forward and gave her a peck on the cheek, which in the music world was little more than a handshake.

She accepted it as such. "Thank you for bringing me home," she said, "and for being such a charming companion."

"May I see you again?"

"If you like." She made it sound as if she would be available whenever I had the time.

"When?"

"Call me and we'll make a date."

"Are you in the phone book?"

"No. Write down my number."

I felt my breast pocket. "I don't have a pen."

She rummaged in her bag and brought out pencil and paper. As she wrote down her number, "You won't lose it?" she asked. The question was meant to show humility, but it was also an admonition.

"What d'you think?"

Her eyes held mine for an instant; then she entered the house. I walked down the avenue in sheer excitement. It seemed to me that in some mysterious way I had been waiting for someone like her to enter my life. She was different from any woman I had ever met. She was not gentle and kind like Ruth or permissive like Valerie. On the contrary, she was rather haughty and remote, but she posed a challenge that I found wonderfully exciting.

Our first dinner took place early in December. I consulted Max about the proper restaurant; he thought the Four Seasons had just the right degree of elegance. When I suggested it to her, she dissented. "That's for tourists. I know a little French restaurant on Fifty-sixth Street near Eighth Avenue. It's not at all chic, but the food is good, and the checkered tablecloths remind me of a bistro in Paris."

At dinner she did most of the talking, at least at first. Mostly about herself; more accurately, about her work. "Audiences differ so much," she told me. "One night the house can be full, but it's completely dead. They sit on their hands, as though to say, 'We paid to see you; amuse us.' No matter how hard you try, they won't give. The next night—maybe it rained and they had trouble getting there—they warm up to you from the start; they respond to every move you make. I love an audience like that. Is it the same in the concert hall?"

"Pretty much. I try not to think of them. I try to lose myself in the music. That's when I do my best—when I'm up there playing for myself and they're just there listening in."

"It's different for me. I dance for them, I want them to respond. I have to feel they're following everything I do, sharing what I feel. Otherwise there's a terrible emptiness onstage. When they cheer me at the end, that's my reward. Plus the check I'll receive. The one pays the rent; the other warms my soul and pays for all the heartaches, not to mention the other aches and pains."

She spoke about her childhood in Brooklyn. "On Sundays we'd go rowing in Prospect Park. I can still see the lake and the white marble pavilion where we'd have an ice-cream soda. To me it seemed like a little palace. Then there would be a concert at the bandstand. The old flower garden had a staircase covered with violets and morning glories. I'd imagine myself dancing up the stairs, trailing lots of veils like the Sugarplum Fairy in *The Nutcracker.* Always I saw myself dancing, but when I wanted to go to ballet school, my parents objected. They thought a nice Jewish girl should play the piano, not dance. I begged and cried until they gave in. I'll never forget the first time I stood on my toes. I felt so light, so . . . airy. As if I were about to fly off the earth. I didn't want to go to school or study my lessons or practice the piano. I wanted only to dance. It's still the same today. Isn't it wonderful when you end up doing the only thing you ever wanted to do, and earn your living at it into the bargain? The only trouble is"—she thought for a moment—"as Porgy said, 'It takes a long pull to get there.' "

I had the impression of an extremely strong will hidden behind her casual manner. At one point in the conversation I called her Natalie.

"The name is Natalia," she corrected me.

"No, that's your stage name," I said. "The real you is Natalie."

"Not so. We all begin somewhere, but over the years we outgrow that self and become someone else. Which one is real? Who's to say?"

"What we start out with is real. Everything we add later is a put-on."

"You're wrong." She sounded altogether sure of herself. "What we add during the journey becomes part of us. It makes us into the person we become. You're not the little boy from—" she stopped.

"Manhattan," I interpolated.

"Wherever. You're not that little boy anymore. You're a well-known musician now, and an artist. Some things about you go back to that little boy, of course. Others don't, and they're just as important, if not more so."

I thought about that. "The difference between us is," I finally said, "that I live in the past much more than you. I'm always looking back. That's natural."

"Natural? It's not natural to dance on your toes, yet I made it part of me until it became natural. No point telling me it's artificial. Don't people realize that I'm artificial by nature?" The idea seemed to amuse her.

"Okay, you win. It's obvious you don't want to be Natalie, so there's no use my trying to force you."

"You couldn't. I know who I am and what I want out of life, and I won't let anyone change my mind."

At the end of the evening, as we stood outside her apartment house, "May I kiss you good night?" I asked.

She considered my request. "I'm not saying no, but not a long one, please." She offered me her lips. "Those long, wet kisses in the movies give me hives."

I did as she asked. "May I see you again?"

"Of course."

"When?"

"Not too soon. I don't want you to become a habit."

"What d'you call too soon?"

"I dance again next Thursday. You could take me to supper afterward."

"That's a long way off."

"Very well, next Tuesday." She gave me an inviting smile and went off, poised and graceful, every inch the ballerina.

When I described the evening to Steve, "Artificial by nature?" he said, and chortled. "I like that. She sounds like a tough cookie to me."

"She is," I replied. "Maybe that's why I like her."

8

NATALIA FASCINATED ME. She was constantly in my thoughts. In my imaginary conversations with her I was witty, assertive, in every way her match, but the instant I came into her presence my self-assurance vanished. I became inept, tongue-tied, or almost so.

In the next month I saw *Swan Lake* four times and came to know every detail of her performance. What astonished me was how much of her role she improvised. The basic structure was carefully laid out; she never departed from it. But the details, especially in the transition passages, depended to an amazing degree on the inspiration of the moment. Never having been a balletomane, I was unable to judge the fine points of her dancing. But I responded, like the rest of the audience, to the expressive power of her gestures, the lyric line of her adagio, above all the charm and grace she infused into her role of Odette. I sent her a dozen and a half roses. Her comment was: "Should be fifteen."

"Why?"

"The Russians believe an even number is bad luck."

"You're superstitious?"

"Of course. Luck rules our lives. I'll do anything to avoid bad luck.

"But you're not Russian."

"I have a Russian name, don't I? That proves I am."

"What kind of logic is that?"

"Logic has nothing to do with it. You have to feel these things. It's the feeling that counts."

"I see I can't win with you."

A slow smile traveled from her lips to her eyes. "Don't even try."

She gave me tickets for her performances. On the night of my fourth *Swan Lake* I had to practice the Sibelius Concerto and arrived at intermission. She took me to task for it.

I was amazed that she had noticed. "How did you know I wasn't there?"

"My seats are in the fifth row. I can't help noticing when they're empty."

"You mean to say that's all you have to think about while you're dancing?"

"No, I'm thinking of my role, but I also notice what's going on around me. Matter of fact I'd be in deep trouble if I didn't."

"With me it's just the opposite. When I'm onstage, I try to shut out the audience and lose myself in the music."

"Then why are you up there if you're not playing for them? When I dance, I'm communicating something, I have to have someone to communicate it to."

"I'm communicating—or trying to—with Mozart or Beethoven."

"No, you're not. You're communicating with the ones who bought the tickets. If you didn't, they wouldn't come back to hear you."

"I see I can't win with you."

"I already told you, don't even try."

Our evenings followed pretty much the same pattern. I would take her to supper after her performance; occasionally one or two members of the company came along. Their talk was exclusively about the dance world. The great names of the past were much invoked: Nijinsky, Karsavina, Diaghilev, Balanchine. Mostly they gossiped about other dancers, especially Nureyev, Barishnikov, Gregory, Kirkland. Since they always referred to them by their first names, I was not always sure whom they were talking about. They kept at it till well past midnight, when I saw Natalia home. Since she never asked me up for a nightcap, we parted at her front door. She seemed to have no desire to carry our relationship a step further. I complained to Steve. "She's a cool customer, I'll say. I'm about ready to give up."

"Don't tell me you're falling in love with her."

"I could, with a little encouragement. But she makes no move. She acts as though she's above all that."

"Maybe she is. You have to realize, dancers are strange people. Their main love affair is with their own bodies. Everything else is secondary."

Natalia's indifference only whetted my desire. As I watched her onstage, her body inflamed my imagination; I imagined her, gently yielding, in my arms. There was no point, I told myself, in trying to rush her. She was clearly too set in her ways to be swept off her feet; I would have to be patient. Meanwhile I continued to send her roses—fifteen instead of eighteen—and went on hoping.

I had my first sign that she was not indifferent to me on the night I played in Carnegie Hall with the Cleveland Orchestra. The ballet company was in Washington that week, but she took the trouble to fly in for the occasion. I had been hoping she would, and when she phoned to say that she was in New York, my spirits zoomed. I played the great theme of the Tchaikovsky Concerto like the love song it is and made it soar with the intensity of my emotion. The finale became a wild peasant dance that conjured up figures of drunken muzhiks, arms akimbo and legs flying out from under them. The audience responded enthusiastically to my mood, but I had eyes only for the second box on the left. She was shouting, "Bravo," and I managed to send her a smile as my eyes traversed the sea of faces before me.

She was waiting for me in the greenroom. "I had no idea you were this good," she said, and kissed me on both cheeks.

"What did you think I was?"

"It's hard to imagine what a friend is like onstage. The real you comes out when you're standing in front of an audience. It's a very nice you."

"Nice? I hope it's more than that."

"You suddenly throw off the covers under which you hide. Suddenly you're saying, 'Look at me, world! This is what I really am.' "

"And what was your reaction?"

"I liked what I saw."

I spent the necessary half hour in the greenroom accepting the congratulations of my well-wishers. When I arrived at the Scheins, all the guests applauded; now they could proceed to supper. Natalia was helping herself to chicken salad when I came beside her.

"I'm famished," I said. "I never eat before a concert."

"I can't before I dance, of course, but why do you have to go hungry?"

"My head isn't clear on a full stomach, and I must have my wits about me when I'm up there. So many things can go wrong if you don't watch out, and even if you do."

"Nothing did tonight, that's for sure."

"There were a few rough spots, there always are, but on the whole it went well. Maybe because you were there."

"Really?" She seemed pleased at my remark.

I helped myself to a generous portion of roast beef. "Protein, to replace lost energy."

The party was memorable because of its aftermath. As we stood at her front door, Natalia suddenly said, "How about a nightcap?" and led the way into the lobby.

She lived on the eighteenth floor. The living room was extremely feminine, with shaded lamps and small cushions on the sofa. A Chinese rug presented an intricate pattern of blue flowers against a saffron ground; the windows were shrouded in silk curtains to match. Since street sounds were muted, the room seemed totally shut off from the world. Natalia poured me a scotch and soda and took a Diet Pepsi for herself. "Calories," she said. "Everything in the world is chock-full of calories. Even, I suspect, the air we breathe."

When she cuddled up to me on the sofa, I put my arm around her and kissed her, but it was without bravado and without the erotic images that had surrounded her in my imagination. She attracted me, but for some indefinable reason she also intimidated me. I had never made love to a woman whose reputation was greater than my own. With Natalia it was she who was the star, not I, and she was not disposed to let me forget it. At the moment, true enough, it was the woman who concerned me, not the artist, yet I found it difficult to separate the two. Thus my initial response to her was an ever so slight withdrawal. I did have the presence of mind to slip my tongue between her lips. From then on it was easier sailing.

Abruptly she jumped up from the couch, cast off her shoes, and danced around the room in her stockinged feet. When she reached the center of the room, she balanced herself on her left foot and, with the right extended, executed a pirouette. Then she actually danced out of her clothes.

She stood naked before me, exhibiting herself with a kind of childlike pleasure. Her body had nothing of the voluptuous female about it. It was beautiful in an androgynous way, with tiny breasts and very little curve at the hips. Indeed she could almost have been a boy. As she rose on her toes, she seemed to take off. For a moment it amused her to mimic the jerky movements of a marionette; then she became a mechanical doll.

Her performance put me at ease. I went to her side, laughing, clasped her in my arms, and held her tight. Only then did I realize how much she meant to me. This was not a one-night stand. On the contrary, I felt that I could love this woman for the rest of my life. I loved everything about her, but I was also conscious that in some strange way relationships were not easy for her. Even as she surrendered to me, part of her held back. The act of giving herself seemed to repel as much as it attracted her; she had to conquer something in herself in order to overcome the repulsion.

On the one hand, she was the woman I desired, a flesh-and-blood creature who lay beside me and was as real to me as anyone could be. On the other, she was the ethereal creature I had glimpsed the first night I saw her in *Swan Lake*, who floated over the earth by defying all the laws of gravity. I was fascinated by this dual impression, which only served to make me more aware of her. Her body was her instrument in the same way that the Strad I played on was mine. Yet it had been disciplined to the needs of her art for so many years that she had lost touch with its simple pleasures. Now that we were in bed together, her partial withdrawal only whetted my appetite. I would have to win her over again and again. The effort, I knew, would make her more precious to me.

Only when I was in her did we achieve something of the wonderful intimacy of lovers, yet as my climax approached, I became increasingly aware that she was unable to share it with me. She moaned with desire, she pushed frenziedly against me, but fulfillment eluded her, her face expressing more pain than pleasure. I came alone, and she suddenly stopped. She didn't finish; she simply left off.

We lay in each other's arms. Finally, I said, "You didn't come."

"It's like a door opening, waiting for me to step through. I get closer and closer to it, but just as I'm about to make it, the door shuts." She shrugged, as if to say, "What can I do?"

"That's because this is our first time. These things'll clear up as you get accustomed to me," I said with greater assurance than I felt, knowing that in some essential way I had failed her.

She smiled but said nothing. Suddenly she said: "You know, passion originally meant suffering. Like when we say St. Matthew Passion. Balanchine wanted to choreograph that, a dance combining pleasure and pain."

She lit a cigarette and, after turning on her back, lay blowing smoke rings into the air. I took her hand and interlaced our fingers. Kissing her, I moved my lips across her neck to her ear. "I love you," I murmured.

"How sweet," she whispered back, and gave me a slow smile.

But I noticed that she did not say, "I love you too." I pressed the tip of my tongue against her earlobe and said, "What little ears you have."

"The better not to hear you, my dear."

I do not know why I held myself responsible for Natalia's difficulty, but I did. I wanted to be the perfect lover and give her the same satisfaction that I achieved. She obviously had a problem, and I needed to solve it. But how?

The first step was to consult Steve. He had obviously given much thought to the subject and fell immediately into the role of marriage counselor. "There are three things you must do," he pontificated, "and you must do them all. First, penetration. Once you're inside her, you have to push for dear life, as if you were trying to come out the other end. That'll give her a much better start. Second, a pillow under her ass. You'd be surprised how much that helps. And third, twice as much foreplay. The area behind the clitoris is very sensitive. Play it for all it's worth, molto legato and pianissimo. This problem is not as rare as you think. I've always solved it, and so can you."

To my amazement, Steve's method worked. By the fourth or fifth time we were together Natalia enjoyed our lovemaking almost as much as I did. In *The Sleeping Beauty* the prince awakens his beloved with a kiss. Could it be that I too was awakening Natalia? She was gradually learning to give in to her feelings, and I began to hope that she was falling in love with me.

9

I ADMIRED NATALIA enormously for her total dedication. Her life revolved around the dance; every facet of it absorbed her. She spent four to five hours a day in practice at the barre and was the most disciplined person I had ever met. She ate no sweets, drank very little, hardly ever smoked. Apart from her work, she was fascinated by people and could gossip endlessly about her colleagues, their love affairs, the ups and downs of their careers, their problems and foibles. She was surrounded by a coterie of homosexual dancers with whom she maintained close friendships and had in addition a corps of groupies who worshipfully ministered to her every whim.

My love for her was tinged with anxiety. I wanted to be with her all the time, hear her voice, look into her eyes, hold her in my arms. It seemed to me that I had been waiting for her from as far back as I could remember, that I had dreamed about her even before I knew her. I could not imagine there would ever come a time when I did not feel this attachment. That I had found her at last seemed nothing short of a miracle.

My infatuation brought its own doubts. Did she love me in return? And how well did she love me? I wanted desperately to be sure of her, yet how could I be? I was experiencing an emotion I had never known before, quite different from the calm affection I had felt for Ruth. My love for Natalia filled every corner of my life, uncertainty only intensifying the excitement she aroused in me.

She was a creature of moods. She could be kittenish and coy, but also imperious and aloof. All the more precious, then, were the moments when she dropped her defenses, stopped playing the star, and became a real person. Those were the moments when I found complete contentment with her, or at least came close to it. Because I did, I began to think more and more about marriage. If she were to belong to me, if we had a home and a life together, my doubts would give way, I was convinced, to the joy of complete sharing. I had never before seen myself as a husband; suddenly the image took on a compelling attraction. I needed peace of mind to be able to devote myself to my work, I needed someone who would always be there for me. I had achieved most of the good things in life. I needed only one more—happiness; and this, I decided, only Natalia could give me.

All this seemed perfectly logical to me when I was alone. But when I came into her presence, the thought of asking her to marry me no longer appeared to be so reasonable. Indeed it became something of an impertinence. I was being too impatient, I thought, and was pushing the relationship faster than I should. She needed time to come over to my point of view, and it obviously made no sense for me to try to rush her.

Dancing, she told me, was the only thing she really cared about. "If anything happened so that I could never dance again, I don't think I would want to live."

"Why imagine such things? You'll probably go on dancing till you're past sixty."

"Margot Fonteyn did. But it's important to know when to stop. A dancer shouldn't continue after her powers are gone. Muscles age with the years and grow weak; there comes a time when you have to say good-bye. I only hope it'll come for me later rather than sooner. What'll I do then? What all the great ballerinas did after they stopped dancing. I'll teach. Somebody said, 'He who can, does. He who cannot, teaches.' "

"Not true. I got a tremendous amount from my teacher."

"I'm sure my students will get a tremendous amount out of me. You can't be on the stage for a lifetime without having a lot to pass on to a young person. Of course there's only a certain amount that can be taught: technique, tradition, style. But not talent. You can't teach anyone to be a great artist. That's a mystery."

"What do you suppose makes the great artist?"

She thought hard. "A combination of things. They don't often come together. First, of course, is technique, the sheer physical ability to do the thing. To execute a fouetté or jeté like Ulanova or Danilova, you have to have perfect control. They say Nijinsky seemed to stop in the middle of a leap and hang suspended in the air. He didn't, of course, but he gave the illusion that he did. In any case, that's the physical part. Then comes the emotional. You have to be able to make the audience feel what Giselle, Odette, Aurora are feeling. You have to say something to which people will respond. When a great artist comes onstage, something happens in the house, like a charge of electricity. That's the mystery, call it talent, charisma, genius. It's the quality that takes hold of an audience and makes them come back for more. All the great performers have it."

"Do you?"

"Silly question. If I didn't think so, would I be onstage?"

"I sometimes wonder if I do."

"You have to believe that. Otherwise how can you go on? The night I heard you, you seemed very much to have it."

"I sometimes think I had it for a while, now I'm losing it."

"We all go through moments like that. That's why you need the audience to applaud you, to make you feel they love you."

"What about the money?"

"That helps. If you make a lot, it proves to you they really appreciate you. And lets you put away something for the future, when you won't have your audience anymore. Some great artists died awful poor. You have to be prepared."

"I may have some doubts about me," I said, "but I've none about you, Natalia. You have it, whatever it is."

The next time I saw her I was finally able to come to the point. "Were you never in love?" I asked. "That seems impossible."

"Let me think. A few times. But I never let it get out of hand."

"What does that mean?"

"I never let it interfere with my work. My dancing came first. When love threatened to take over, I let go."

"Didn't you miss a lot?"

Her chin jutted forward. "You have to make a choice. I chose my work and never regretted it. That way I was never disappointed, as I might have been if I had chosen love."

"But isn't there something in you that needs it?"

She gave me one of her slow smiles. "You think everyone is made for love? You're wrong. Some people are better off without it. Loving someone isn't easy. If you must know, it can be a nuisance. When you love someone, you give him the power to make you miserable. For an artist that can be dangerous."

"You mean, an artist doesn't have the right to be married and have a family?"

"Some great ballerinas did very well without it. Markova, for example, and Danilova. Others didn't. Fonteyn loved her husband very much. Ulanova even had children. It all depends on the person."

"What about you?"

"I take it you want an honest answer."

"Yes."

She was thoughtful. "It wouldn't be easy for me to adjust to a husband. I'm not the marrying kind. To begin with, I don't want children. And I don't relish having someone run my life for me. That would only get in the way."

"So there's no point my asking you to marry me?"

"Why, Danny!" She laughed. "When did that idea occur to you?"

"When I met you, I began to realize that if you were mine, I'd finally be at peace. For the rest of my life. I'd have everything I could wish for. Only one thing is needed to make that dream come true: for you to feel the same way."

Natalia took my hand and pressed it to her heart. "You dear boy! You are a dear, you know. The trouble is, we're not quite ready for all that. I mean, I'm not."

"Meaning?"

"A pretty house in suburbia, with two cars in the garage and two kids in the kitchen . . . it's a pretty sight on TV commercials. But it's not for everyone."

"All you're saying is that you're not ready for it now. But you might be a year from now. I'm willing to wait."

She was suddenly serious. "I don't think I'll ever be."

"I'll take the chance."

"Danny, I don't think you understand. The thought of someone coming too close frightens me. Basically I'm a loner. I need breathing space; otherwise I feel I'm choking. Marriage would destroy my breathing space. It's not for someone like me."

"You mean, I have to give up that house in the suburbs."

She nodded. "I'm afraid so."

"What about love?"

"No objection, as long as it leaves me my breathing space."

"I thought you were enjoying our friendship."

"Of course I am, in my own way. But don't expect too much from me, or you'll be disappointed. Above all, you mustn't make demands. When that happens, I feel I have to run." She smiled. "And since I'm a dancer, I can run pretty fast."

"I'm beginning to see . . . it all has to be on your terms."

"How else?"

"Shall I tell you something? It doesn't make me want you any less. You can see I'm crazy about you."

"I don't mind, as long as you leave me my space."

"I'll try to remember." I grinned and pulled her to me. She let me.

10

My involvement with Natalia made me much more subject to abrupt changes of mood. I might rise to a high level of optimism where everything looked rosy, or suddenly drop into a depression in which the world became a dark, unfriendly place. I had always tried to keep my mind uncluttered by emotion so as to free it for my work. Yet it was now becoming more and more difficult for me to concentrate on my practicing. I realized that I would not achieve the repose I needed until I had solved my problem with Natalia. In the meantime it was simpler to pop an amphetamine into my mouth when I was low or do some cocaine when I was too tense.

The remarkable thing about my relationship with Natalia was

that it never seemed to move forward. We seemed to be engaged in a subtle battle of wills; the more demanding I became, the less she gave, and the less she gave, the more demanding I became. I took revenge in my imagination for the anguish she was causing me, yet when I was with her my resentment vanished, I was aware only of how much I needed her. Also, I could not escape the notion that for all practical purposes I was getting nowhere with her. The thought was maddening.

I had a recurrent dream in which a rowboat we were in capsized, throwing us both into the water. I managed to scramble back into the boat and began to row away with fiendish joy, leaving her behind. In another dream we were wandering through the desert, guided only by a torn map I held in my hand. A storm came up and enveloped us in clouds of sand. Too exhausted to continue, Natalia sank to the ground, while I pressed on alone. I smiled my way through several fantasies of this kind, in all of which she needed me desperately but could not find me.

I was insanely jealous of the men who had preceded me in her life and plied her with questions about them. She resisted my inquiries. "I already told you," she would say, "I live in the present. The past is a closed book. I try not to think of it." On the other hand, she was only too happy to remember the beginnings of her career. Balanchine she continued to revere. "He was my ideal of what an artist should be. Absolutely convinced that what he did was right and refusing to compromise even one inch. He knew how to deal with the world—you have to if you're going to have a career—but he was never blinded by it, never corrupted."

Matters came to a head between us one night in September, when we attended a benefit for some musical cause. Since I still had not learned to dance—my sense of rhythm, I insisted, was in my hands, not my feet—Natalia spent the evening dancing with Steve. She danced with wonderful abandon, her hands floating in the air in front of her as she snapped her fingers in rhythm, lips parted in a smile of sheer delight that was matched by the expression on his handsome face. I could not wait for the evening to end and sulked all the way home. She pretended not to notice but vented her annoyance when we reached her apartment. "What's wrong with you tonight?" she asked.

"How should I feel when I watch you flirting with Steve all evening? Am I supposed to enjoy that?"

"I'd have been perfectly happy to dance with you if you knew how. I guess it's my fault you never learned."

"I had more important things on my mind. Anyway, you didn't have to dance every dance with him."

"Why not? He asked me. Besides, I'm a dancer, which mean I love to dance. Any objection?"

"You're also a flirt and a tease. You had a wonderful time leading Steve on while I sat watching."

"You know what you are? A spoiled brat!" her voice rose several pitches. "Baby has to have his way or there'll be hell to pay. One would think you'd be more mature."

"You're the mature one, I suppose. Can't forget for one moment that you're the great Kohanskaya. A star is a star is a star." I spat out the words.

"Jealous little bastard, aren't you! I sometimes wonder why I put up with you. After all, I never trained to be a nursemaid. I didn't expect I'd ever have to be one."

The temperature in the room rose steadily as insults flew back and forth. Natalia had a talent for aiming her barbs at my most vulnerable spots. Sooner or later she was bound to shift her attack from the man to the musician. "How in hell d'you expect to be a mature artist," she shrieked, "if you have the mentality of a six-year-old?"

Her sneering tone cracked my self-control. She was wiping me out, and I was not going to let her. Bending down, I seized the first object that came to hand—a ceramic ashtray—and hurled it with all my might in her direction, but not before a final shred of reason deflected my aim ever so slightly. It flew past her, banged against the wall, and split in two. The sharp crackle of the breakage brought me to my senses. I stood quite still, staring at her as I gasped for breath.

She bent over and picked up the two halves, one in each hand. "You must be out of your mind," she said.

"I'm sorry. I could have hit you."

"No, you couldn't. I'd have ducked. Remember, I'm fast on my feet." Her manner suddenly changed. "I'm sorry too," she said. "I shouldn't have egged you on. Sometimes I think I'm not good for you."

I met her halfway. "I'd rather it were you than anyone else."

"Maybe you shouldn't love anyone. Maybe you should stick to your violin. At least it doesn't talk back to you."

"I can't make love to my violin. No, that's not true. I do make love to it. But I prefer making it with you. Do I have to choose?"

"Yes, there is always a choice."

"Well, I'm not giving up either the violin or you."

"I could answer that, but I won't. We've had enough trouble for one night." She glanced at her watch. "It's late, and I've a rehearsal in the morning."

I could not bear to leave at this point; I had to redeem myself. "Can't I stay a little longer?"

"Darling, I can't let you stay over. You know I don't sleep if there's someone in my bed."

"I'm not asking to stay over. I only want to hold you in my arms a little while, until I'm sure you've forgiven me."

Impatience crossed her face. "If I let you stay, you know it'll be more than a little while."

I hated to beg for her love, but I did. "Half an hour at the most, that's all I ask."

She was about to refuse but thought better of it. "Very well," she said wearily. She led the way into the bedroom and threw off her clothes.

Whenever I lay down beside her, I was gripped by desire. I reveled in the softness of her skin, knew every curve of her body, and basked in its beauty. This time, however, my passion collapsed against the wall of her indifference. I realized that she was humoring me because she knew this was the quickest way to get rid of me, and I could not make love to her on those terms.

Nor could I accept her compliance, knowing that I had forced it from her.

I realized that I was making myself ridiculous. The thought crushed me. Abruptly I turned away from her and buried my head in the pillow. There was a burning behind my eyelids, as though tears were gathering. God, was I going to be a crybaby on top of all the humiliations the evening had inflicted on me? I was suddenly shaken by a series of sobs. A hot shame poured over me as I tried to stifle them, but my shoulders shook and gave me away.

Natalia put her hand on my shoulder; it felt wonderfully cool. "There, there . . ." she murmured. After a while she said: "Danny, why don't you go home and get some sleep? Tomorrow things'll look different."

I dressed, kissed her good night, made no further attempt to excuse myself, and left. It was only after I got home that the full impact of my behavior swept over me. I had lost my temper not because of any single circumstance; the real reason lay in the nature of our relationship. Because she was keeping me in a state of suspense, sooner or later there had to come a moment when my uncertainty spun out of control. Because of her, I was neglecting my work, my playing was off, I could not sleep or eat or think straight. This state of affairs could not possibly continue. Either she married me and gave me the serenity I needed, or we would have to part.

I also knew that I was not going to fall asleep that night until I had had it out with her. It was much too late to telephone her, and she would never forgive me for waking her. I struggled against the temptation but knew at the back of my mind that I would end by giving in. I finally picked up the phone and dialed her number.

"Danny?" The drowsiness faded from her voice. "It's almost three in the morning. Are you mad?"

"I just had to speak to you."

"It couldn't wait till tomorrow?"

"No."

"As usual, thinking only of yourself."

"Cut the crap and listen."

"Okay, I'm listening."

"We can't go on as we are. I need a wife; I need a home."

"So what do you want from me?"

"I want you to be my wife and make my home."

"Danny, we've been through this before. You're a dear, and I'm terribly fond of you, but I'm not ready to be your wife, or anybody else's for that matter. Now can I go back to sleep?"

"The trouble is, you don't love me enough."

"I love you to the best of my ability. If that's not enough for you, it's your problem, not mine."

"Don't you see what you're putting me through?"

"I wish you'd see what you're putting me through. I've a rehearsal at nine in the morning, it's practically the middle of the night, and you're complaining that I don't love you enough. Young girls dream of having a lover who'll be crazy about them. They don't suspect that such a lover can end by being a pain in the ass."

"Natalia, be serious."

"Danny, listen. I can function only within the limits of what I am, and what I am is not in love with you as you want me to be. Waking me from a deep sleep and arguing with me about it isn't going to change a thing. To satisfy you, I'd have to change the way I feel, the way I think, the way I live, and that obviously isn't going to happen. It's pretty clear that I can't give you what you want, and you're not going to squeeze it out of me by force. You have every right to want it, but I'm simply not the right person to want it from. I'm doing all the wrong things to you and vice versa. Since neither one of us is going to change, the sensible thing is for us to say good-bye now, before we've caused each other more harm. You'll get over me, believe me, and find someone who's right for you. Now may I go back to sleep? Please . . ."

Totally defeated, I hung up and surrendered to my rage. God damn her! She was a heartless bitch, and I had been a fool to get mixed up with her. There wasn't a shred of humanity in her. She was a dancing doll without a heart, and I hoped I never saw her again.

I knew I was much too agitated to fall asleep. I popped a pill into my mouth and turned in. When that didn't work, I took another. I finally calmed down and grew drowsy. The train began to pull out of the station. She stood on the back platform and let out a shrill, mocking laugh. I ran as fast as I could, but the train was faster. I stopped running and, breathless, stared after it. I had come too late. . . . I had missed it. . . .

11

WHEN MY ANGER abated, my longing for Natalia returned, settling into a gnawing pain that gave me no peace. I had to see her, talk to her, reason with her. I had to make one more attempt; this time I was sure I'd persuade her. At the same time I was terrified that another try would be futile. Thus hope alternated with despair in ever more rapid succession. When I struck bottom, I revived my spirits with two amphetamines, which I washed down with a shot of vodka. My strategies to get Natalia to change her mind converged on a single point: I had to see her again, and soon!

A visit from my manager did not improve my mood. He told me that my bookings for the following season were definitely down.

"I can't understand why," I objected. "I got good reviews."

Max's round face puckered into his I-hate-to-remind-you expression. "A few not so good."

"So what? Everybody gets them."

"Don't forget, there's a recession in the country. A number of orchestras have folded; others are in trouble."

"Maybe if my management worked a little harder."

"That's what every artist says. If only management worked a little harder, everything would be okay."

"But why should my bookings be down? I try, I work hard."

"You have to realize, Danny, giving concerts is a business. Like any business, it has its ups and downs. You've had it pretty good till now; you've no right to complain if there's a slump. And while I'm at it, let me give you some advice. Your playing has fallen off lately. Maybe your mind's been on other things; maybe you're not practicing enough. In any case, get yourself in hand, my boy. You need to." Max patted me on the back affectionately, as though to indicate that his admonition need not be taken too seriously but was not to be disregarded either.

Max's visit left me in even worse shape than before. My preoccupation with Natalia returned in full force, yet I seemed incapable of settling on a course of action. On the one hand, I told myself that I must forget her. A moment later I found myself wanting desperately to phone her. Torn between the two, I veered back and forth; whichever choice I settled on, I at once gravitated toward the other. Thus I lay helpless on my back as the hours passed, unable to practice and unable to reach a decision.

I finally decided to get some air; I forced myself to get up, shave, and dress. I remembered that I hadn't eaten all day and heated a can of soup. The thick liquid spread a pleasant warmth through my body. I felt as if I had just emerged from a long illness. When I came into the street, the stars were already out. They looked much less bright than they had when I was young, probably because there was more pollution in the air. The city had that vague sense of expectancy that hangs over it in the early evening. The trees in Central Park were beginning to blossom. I strode along briskly, breathing deeply and enjoying the sense of physical movement. I needed more exercise than I was getting and wondered if I should join a health club. I walked along Central Park to Columbus Circle and from there to Fifth

Avenue, where I turned north. When I reached Seventy-sixth Street, I crossed to the park side and sat down on a bench op posite Natalia's house.

I remembered the first time I had been there, the night of my concert with the Philharmonic. How different my life had been then. I had been carefree, sitting on top of the world; then she had come along and spoiled everything. Why had I allowed her to do this? Clearly because I couldn't help myself. The notion that we were masters of our fate was pure bullshit. We were like the puppets in a Punch and Judy show, with someone behind us pulling the strings. We went through the motion of making decisions, but the whole game was decided for us well in advance. This was our fate, our destiny, call it what you would.

I wondered if there was any point in trying to see her. If the doorman announced me, would she let me come up? I was not sure. In our last conversation she had sounded pretty much as if she were saying good-bye. I didn't like to barge in on her, but this was probably the only way I would get to her. And this was precisely what I was going to do.

Having reached a decision, I relaxed. It was a mild evening; the air was fresh with the fragrance of Central Park. With its caravan of automobiles, Fifth Avenue displayed the simple elegance it wore so well at night. I watched as a man and woman drove past in an open carriage, holding hands. Tourists, no doubt. Who else would pay for a drive in a carriage? A woman in evening dress came out of Natalia's house; the doorman hailed a taxi for her. I looked up, counting the floors to Natalia's apartment. The windows were lit; she was home. Was she alone? If not, who was with her? Would it be Steve? The thought sent a twinge of anger through me. Snake in the grass. My best friend indeed!

A damp wind blew from the park; it was growing cooler. I roused myself, crossed the avenue, and entered the building. The man at the desk knew me. He rang up. "She said to come up. Apartment Eighteen-F."

The corridor leading to the elevator was lined with mirrors. I glanced at my reflection. I was wearing a sports shirt and leather windbreaker; my hair was tousled. I smoothed it down and tugged at the windbreaker so that it lay better around my shoulders. My eyes glowed; they were tense. I took a deep breath to relax. By the time the elevator reached the eighteenth floor I had myself pretty well under control.

Natalia was waiting for me at the door and held out her hand. "What a surprise!" she said.

I kissed her and entered the apartment. The first thing I saw, when I entered the living room, was Steve sprawled on the sofa. Without greeting him, I wheeled around to Natalia. "Why did you ask me up if he's here?"

"Why not?" She was all innocence. "He's your friend, isn't he?"

"Sure! With such a friend I don't need enemies." I put all the venom I could into the words.

"Did you come here to make yourself unpleasant?" Natalia asked.

"I was hoping to see you alone."

"I can ask Steve to leave if that's what you want."

I remained silent, as though considering her offer. At that point Steve interposed with "I'm not ready to leave."

"Boys, stop fighting." She sounded like a teacher admonishing a class. "You're both over twelve. Why don't you act it?"

I decided to assert myself. "I'm in love with you, and I come by to find another man in your room. Is that supposed to make me happy?"

"If you must know, that's why I asked you up. I wanted you to find him."

"And why, may I ask?" I sat down in the armchair facing the sofa.

Natalia drew a sigh. "I've explained it all to you before, but I'll do it again. I'm very fond of you, Danny. You don't think so, but I am. And I like your friend Steve too. But I'm not ready to sign my life over to you, or Steve, or anyone else. Once you get this through your skull, you'll have no problem with me. I'm not ready for love or what you call love. I'm in love with my work and my career."

"With yourself, you mean." I interrupted. "Let's not forget the most important item."

"So what? I've a perfect right to. In any case, I'm not ready to be your wife. I am ready to be your friend, but you won't let me. It's all or nothing as far as you're concerned. A sure sign of immaturity."

"A psychologist yet"—I sneered—"on top of everything else."

"You can say that again. A little bit of psychology wouldn't hurt you either, believe me."

Steve suddenly intervened. "Why don't you lay off her? You can't strong-arm her, Danny. She's more than a match for either one of us."

I turned to face him. "Fine friend you turned out to be. You know how I feel about her, so what the fuck are you doing here?"

"Watch your language, man."

"Asshole!" I spit out, and realized in a flash that I had just repeated the first word I had ever spoken to him. Long ago in the students' lounge, with Steve telling jokes to Ruth and her friend and sending me down the wrong corridor. The memory sent a wave of fury through me. I sprang up and with one leap swooped down on the sofa. I grabbed him by the armpits and pulled him to his feet, and before he could gain his balance, I punched him in the jaw as hard as I could.

Steve staggered back, dazed for an instant. Then he shot forward, seized me by the shoulders, and, thrusting his foot behind my ankle, pulled with all his might. We went down together and rolled over on the floor, with me locked in his viselike embrace. I managed to free my right arm and pushed it against his chin, forcing his head back. But he did not relax his grip. We rolled over again to the middle of the room, Steve holding me tight while I thrashed about to free myself. I suddenly felt a sharp pain in my right arm and forgot all about the struggle. "My arm!" I cried. "My bow arm!"

Steve instantly let me go. I flung away from him. "Get up, you idiots!" Natalia commanded. "I wouldn't believe this if I didn't see it with my own eyes. Two of our leading violinists putting on a wrestling match."

We stood up and, somewhat sheepishly, dusted ourselves off. I rolled my shoulder to make sure nothing was amiss. The brief tussle had rid me of my anger. There remained only sorrow at Steve's betrayal. Besides, I felt foolish.

Steve recovered his equanimity. "We should try this more often," he remarked smoothly, pinching the front of his trousers to restore their crease. "We might get better at it."

"There's some white wine in the fridge," Natalia said. Steve went to fetch it, but I felt an overwhelming need to get out of that room. I went to the door.

Natalia followed me and put out her hand. "I'm sorry it didn't work out, Danny. Believe me, I'm not a bad woman and you're not a bad man. We were just bad for each other."

I noticed her use of the past tense. Taking her hand, I looked into the immense dark eyes that dominated her fragile face. I remembered my first glimpse of her as she floated above the stage in *Swan Lake.* She had danced both Odette and Odile, the two contradictory sides of her nature, going from one to the other without warning. It seemed to me that my overwhelming sorrow at losing her was part of a much larger regret at the way my life had shaped up.

"Someday," she said, "you'll stop being angry at me. Then we'll be able to be friends."

But I didn't want her for a friend. I wanted her as my lover. Instead of answering, I left.

12

THE DOORBELL RANG. I answered it. "Steve!" I cried, caught off guard. "What are you doing here?"

"What d'you suppose?" When I didn't answer, "Aren't you going to ask me in?" he said.

I stepped aside to let him enter. He settled in an armchair. "I want to talk to you."

"So talk." I sat down on the sofa facing him.

"You're being very unfair to me."

"You don't say!" I underlined the sarcasm by clasping my hands.

"You feel I took her away from you. Don't you realize that no one takes anybody away unless they're ready to be taken? You upset her with all your talk about love and marriage. She isn't that kind. Instead of letting up, you pressed her, so she gave up on you. Now you blame me for your mistake."

"You know I'm crazy about her," I said bitterly, "so what d'you do? You move in and take over. There's such a thing as loyalty, Steve. You never felt it, and you never will."

"If you enjoy making me feel like a heel, go ahead," Steve said. "You're the one to talk. Amos Schein helped you no end, and you repaid him by having an affair with his wife. That's loyalty?"

"You know damn well I didn't want to. She forced me."

"Bullshit! I don't think either one of us has any principles, but at least I'm honest about it. I don't hide behind a moral tone." He returned to the main theme. "You have to understand there are people who can't accept love; they're afraid of it. She's one of them. Once you fell in love with her, you lost her. I don't make that mistake. I'm as casual as she is."

"If you hadn't appeared," I said morosely, "she might have come around to my way of thinking."

"That's where you're wrong. Her way of thinking is part of

her personality. She needs it in order to lead the kind of life she wants. It leaves her free to devote herself to her dancing, which is what she really cares about. She had to escape from your brand of loving and used me as an excuse. If it hadn't been me, it would've been someone else."

"But it was you."

"Pure accident. As far as I'm concerned, I have one big advantage over you. I'm not in love with her, just as she's not in love with me. We've never even mentioned love. I'm there to give her a good time, and that's it."

In spite of myself, my anger began to ebb. I wanted to believe what Steve was telling me; it somehow lessened the hurt of Natalia's rejection. "You know how to get around me," I said at length. "I shouldn't even be talking with you. No matter what trick you pull, you find an explanation for it, and I'm stupid enough to believe you. Until the next time. By now I almost expect it."

Steve threw me his most fetching smile. "I must say it gives me a kick to make love to someone you made love to. Maybe it's my way of getting closer to you. Did you ever think of that?"

"No, I don't think of such things."

"You always were a prude."

"Trouble with you is you have no shame. An alley cat if there ever was one."

Steve grinned, delighted at this description of him. I turned away, disgusted, and realized where the problem lay. Now that I had lost Natalia, I simply could not face the prospect of losing Steve as well. The truth was, I was dependent on him in a most fundamental way, and he knew it. As a result, we never met as equals. In any confrontation between us I was defeated before I began.

"I sometimes wonder," he said, "why you put up with me."

"Because, outside my parents, you and Natalia happen to be the only two people I really care about."

There was another reason for my forgiving Steve, which I barely admitted to myself. He was my cocaine buddy. I had begun to do the drug by myself, but it was more fun to share a high with him. During the weeks of tension with Natalia I had grown more and more dependent on coke; it was the only way I could get through the wild mood swings of that period. But I didn't always know when to stop. Steve was the restraining influence I needed to keep me from bingeing. When he said, "Enough!" I listened.

My talk with Steve ended in total reconciliation. According to him, any other outcome would have been childish. I needed all the support I could get at this point, and there was no one to whom I could talk as freely. Nor was I jealous of him any longer. He was able to make me see that if Natalia preferred him, it was only because his nonchalant attitude suited her far better than mine did.

At about this time Steve introduced me to the cocaine parties of his friend Tim Bosworth, a TV producer who lived in a loft in SoHo. Most of Tim's guests were TV types for whom it was just as important to guard their secret from the world as it was for Steve and me. Thus they were in a state of continual tension to hide their addiction, a tension from which they relaxed at Tim's. In this convivial setting it was altogether acceptable to snort, smoke, or inject coke (as well as heroin and Quaaludes). Our habit united us into a tightly knit us-against-them group. Our host was a handsome, freewheeling man who liked to surround himself with a lively crowd. He created the proper atmosphere. Also, he was generous in providing liquor and the precious white granules that rested in several bowls scattered inconspicuously throughout the room.

I felt much less comfortable in these surroundings than Steve did. As far as I was concerned, cocaine was a private experience not to be shared with a group of strangers with whom I had very little else in common. I suppose I would have felt the same way if the bond between us were simply that we were all black or Jewish or gay. There had to be something more personal, more inclusive for me to be able to come close to people. I went to Tim's because Steve did, rather than from any impulse of my own. My best moments with drugs came in the more secluded atmosphere of Steve's apartment or mine.

Steve was convinced that the high induced by coke went exceedingly well with sex. Combining the two, he believed, would bring him to the highest level of ecstasy: nirvana! Tim's loft lent itself to such flights of fancy. A tiny bedroom at either end made it possible for two people to become very cozy. This was a perfect setup for Steve. As long as the girl was his type—a fairly inclusive category—he was ready for adventure.

I, on the other hand, found it a little more difficult to make immediate contact with a stranger. Nevertheless, I was willing to experiment and found myself in one of the cubbyholes with someone named Ellen. She had dirty-blond frizzly hair, was attractive, and was also quite high. "My trouble is," she confided, "I don't have an ego. It's tough going through life feeling like a lump of shit. When I was a kid, I read a story about a boy without a shadow. Well, I go through life without an ego."

"You shouldn't," I said, to reassure her. "You're charming."

"That's not enough. Charm cuts no ice." She clearly had no intention of letting me strengthen her ego.

"What does?" I asked, reflecting that mine wasn't so strong either.

"Money, lots of it."

"Not always," I objected. "Look at the people who are loaded and still have problems."

"I should have their problems." She made herself comfortable on her back and took my hand. "I want you to love me, darling," she said.

"I do."

"I want you to give me a good time."

"I will."

"And I want you to be gentle with me because I'm very sensitive."

"I promise."

"Okay. Fuck me, darling. Fuck me good."

I did. Drugs seemed to slow my responses. As I was always hoping to make sex last a little longer, I should have been delighted. I wasn't. There was something not quite natural about my climax. The fact that I didn't really care about Ellen may have contributed to the unsatisfactory outcome. I liked sex too much, I decided, to be casual about it. Besides, as Steve pointed out, it was a mistake to have sex with someone whose problems were obviously worse than your own.

He was leaving the next day on a concert tour of South America, for which I envied him. I had only three concerts scheduled in Ohio, after which I would be free for several weeks. What, Steve wanted to know, was I going to do with myself while he was away? "You haven't had a vacation in ages," he said. "This is the perfect time to take one."

"I would, if there was someone I really wanted to go with."

He made a gesture of distaste. "Are we back to that again? Pull yourself together, man."

I drove him to the airport the following afternoon. "Come back with a good batch of stories," I told him.

"I will. If they're not true, at least they'll be funny." He embraced me. "And for God's sake, Danny, be careful."

He didn't specify what he meant, but I knew.

13

NATALIA'S DEPARTURE USHERED in the first major depression I had known. I shuttled from one mood to its opposite with what I came to think of as roller-coaster speed. I might awake in the morning in a cheerful frame of mind, feeling that I had my whole life ahead of me. Suddenly, for no apparent reason, the landscape darkened, and I was plunged to the bottom of a black pit from which it seemed nothing could rescue me. These mood swings were of a violence such as I had never known before; they appeared to follow a mysterious rhythm of their own that left me utterly drained. I grew restless and apprehensive, unable to shake off the vague anxiety that weighed me down. Suddenly I felt strangely isolated from the world, surrounded by an infinite aloneness. I might escape it temporarily when I was with people, but it was there waiting for me when I returned to my empty apartment.

Unfortunately my work made it necessary for me to be alone for a good part of the day, leaving me particularly vulnerable to upsets. The slightest disturbance made it more difficult for me to concentrate on my practicing. I usually began with a series of technical exercises—scales, trills, arpeggios, double stops, harmonics, pizzicato passages. These had become so many empty gestures that I went through mechanically. Where, I wondered, was the verve, the drive that had carried me through the first part of my career? Irretrievably gone.

In this disturbed state I needed cocaine more and more to soften the feeling of rejection that Natalia had left me with. My dependence sneaked up on me, as it were, so that I was not too sharply aware of it; I watched the changes in me as from the outside. There were times when every pore in my body became a gaping hole hungry for a snort. I fought against the temptation just as years before, in my adolescence, I had fought against the desire to play with myself, knowing all the while that in the end I would give in. It needed only a few sniffs of the drug for an immense peace to descend upon me, lifting me to a heartwarming high that brought back my confidence in myself. Magically the problems that weighed me down vanished, the dark corners lit up. Life was worth living again.

I had always been what Steve called a health nut, taking care not to miss my daily quota of vitamins and yogurt, plus a vigorous workout on my exercise machine. In addition, I jogged in Central Park. How did I reconcile all this with my growing appetite for coke? I didn't. The two occupied separate compartments of my brain, neither interfering with the other, so that I was able to take my wheat germ in the morning and do a few lines of cocaine at night.

Unlike Steve, I had no intention of frequenting the tiny park on Broadway where drugs were sold at night. What if I ran into someone who knew me? Since I would barely admit my addiction to myself, I was certainly not ready to let others in on it. Instead I had Steve's dealer come to me. The man was only a phone call away and could be summoned whenever I ran out of supplies. I was spending more on drugs than I should, especially at a time when my earnings were down, but the credit card style of life to which I (along with everyone else) had become accustomed made it quite painless to be extravagant.

At the same time I grew increasingly impatient with the professional duties that hemmed me in. There were concerts it was politic for me to attend, parties at which it was good for me to be seen, persons I had to contact for one reason or another. These chores formed a dead weight that I resented more and more. How could I free myself from obligations that wasted so much time and energy? Through coke I shook off the restraints that dragged me down, I achieved a semblance of freedom. Small wonder I reveled in it.

An invitation arrived for a dinner at the Scheins'. I hated to go but knew that my patron would be offended if I didn't. What if he had also invited Natalia? The prospect of seeing her upset me very much. I thought of phoning and telling Mr. Schein that I couldn't attend if she did. But no, it would never do to make him choose between us. I agonized over the possibility that I might be seated next to her—what would I say to her?—and arrived at the Scheins' in a state of deep agitation.

She wasn't there. I put on my most casual manner and asked the host if she was coming. "No," he said. "She's on tour with the company. They're dancing in Boston; next stop is Montreal. She's taken a house for a month on Cape Cod, near Truro. That's the town before Provincetown, at the tip of the Cape."

I breathed a sigh of relief. At the same time a sliver of regret passed through me. It would have been exciting to see her. . . .

The evening unfolded without incident. Valerie wore a slinky black dress that showed off her figure, and I remembered the first time she lay naked in my arms. At her right sat a pompous conductor from Vienna. Since I did not intend to play there even if I were asked, I did not have to impress him. Dmitri Stamos sat on Valerie's left. He was his usual flamboyant self, the bright spot in an otherwise interminable evening. He was a true people pleaser: You put him at a dinner table, and he gave.

The next day Julia called to complain that she had not seen me in weeks. I visited my parents that night. They were aging. Julia was a little fatter. My father looked tired; deep furrows lined his face. He had had to give up smoking and soothed his longing for cigarettes by sucking on nicotine-flavored lozenges. He was clearly in awe of what he considered my success. Yet my happiest years at the violin, I now realized, had come when he was teaching me. Those had been the years when no one other than Julia expected anything from my playing. I did not have the heart to tell him that the career he so envied hung like a dead weight around my neck.

It astonished me how far I had grown away from my parents. Wasn't that the inevitable part of becoming an adult? At the same time I was aware of how much I owed them. They had been wonderfully supportive of my ambition. I remembered Julia's taking me to my first lesson with Stamos and giving up a new fur coat in order to buy my violin. As soon as I came into their presence, I felt like a child again. It oppressed me that no matter how free and easy I was with them, there was so much in my life I didn't want them to know about.

Dad was disturbed over the collapse of communism in Eastern Europe. "It was a wonderful idea, believe me. The trouble was with the people who were supposed to make it work. Socialist man, it turned out, was just as selfish and greedy as capitalist man. But you *can* change human nature. It just takes longer than we figured. Like a million years."

For an instant I wished I shared Dad's interest in politics. I had never been concerned, really, with the world around me. The struggle of the masses for a better life was an abstraction that had nothing to do with me or my work. I had a vague notion that I would have been a better person if I worried more about mankind. Why didn't I?

Julia had prepared chicken soup, her remedy for all ills of the body, mind, or heart. She lost no time in facing me with the invariable question: "So when do we have a wedding?"

I responded with the stock answer: "As soon as I meet the right girl, Mom."

"I want grandchildren."

"When the time comes, you'll have them."

Dad came to my rescue. "Stop bothering him. A fellow doesn't marry because his mother's after him."

Julia fell into her old habit of discussing me as if I weren't there. "What he really needs is to raise a family. If he had a wife and kids to worry about, he wouldn't be so self-centered. Or so moody. He'd settle down to the real problems of life." Back to me. "I never did like that ballerina of yours. Stuck-up bitch. Thought that just because she could stand on her toes the whole world must cater to her. What you need is a nice Jewish girl who'll make you a good wife. As a matter of fact I know someone . . ."

I let her burble on. How could she know what I wanted out of life if I myself didn't know? It was enough that she loved me.

I had to go to Dayton for an appearance with the local orchestra. For once I didn't look forward to the concert. If I had to play in Ohio, it should have been with the Cleveland or Cincinnati orchestra. Besides, my management had accepted a lower fee. It was the tail end of the season, and I certainly was not in the right frame of mind for this particular performance. It occurred to me that a concert artist's career was like an actor's: The show had to go on whether he was in the mood or not.

I arrived in Dayton the evening before the concert. The rehearsal was scheduled for the next morning and went quite well. I was playing the Mendelssohn Concerto, an old war-horse of mine. The conductor knew the score and followed me without any problem. I hated conductors who tried to impose their own ideas on the soloist. This one didn't.

I went to my hotel after the rehearsal. It was my custom, on the day of a concert, to take an afternoon nap, but I was unable to fall asleep. I had a premonition of disaster so vivid that I could almost taste it; I was afraid, I didn't know of what. I remembered my old fears before a concert, that my trousers would fall down or that I would forget the music. This was a different kind of fear, without a specific object, an anxiety I could not escape. I finally dozed off, but my somber thoughts pursued me even in sleep.

When I awoke, I ran off some exercises on the violin, showered, and dressed. As always, I liked the way I looked in my tails. I was not as handsome as Steve, but I was certainly passable. My regimen of health food and exercise had helped. Should I take an amphetamine to steady my nerves? I had a better idea. I would bring along my cocaine kit and take a few snorts before I went onstage. Just enough to make me feel good.

I arrived at the hall on time, went to the artist's room, and tuned up. The orchestra began with the *Coriolanus* Overture, one of my favorite pieces. I put down my instrument, took the kit into the men's room, and locked the door. Chopping up a small dose of powder, I took several snorts. By the time I came out the orchestra was in the final section of the overture. The concerto was next.

I went onstage in my customary manner, walking quickly to the center as though to say, "Look at me, people! I'm eager to play for you and love you all!" The orchestral introduction was extremely brief, only a measure or two; I swung into my solo, an exuberant melody on the E string that sang out with all the ardor at my command. The passage work that followed demanded nimble fingers. I sailed through the movement, tossed off the cadenza, and took the coda with a kind of reckless brilliance that made the audience burst into applause even though it was not customary to clap between movements.

The Andante, elegant and tender without being profound, ideally suited my style. There followed the Vivace, in which I could show off the spiccato or "bouncing bow" for which I was vastly admired. Not far after the opening came the disaster I had vaguely envisioned. My mind went totally blank. For a second I didn't know where I was or what I was doing. I gazed down into a dark, bottomless abyss, suspended helplessly in time and space. Then, as suddenly, my experience as a performer asserted itself. I jumped into the next measure and continued triumphantly to the end.

The interruption passed so quickly that most of the audience did not even notice it. Only someone who knew the piece thoroughly would have been aware of my slip. Nonetheless, I was devastated. Nothing like this had ever happened to me. I covered my consternation by acknowledging the enthusiastic applause with an exuberant smile and pumping the conductor's hand as if my life depended on it, but I was completely wiped out. I went to the postconcert party as in a trance. No one mentioned the disaster, and I had no way of knowing if people really had not noticed it or were merely being polite.

I returned to New York in a dark mood. Max's phone call did not help matters. It seemed that one of the critics had noticed my mishap and mentioned it in his review. "What happened?" Max demanded.

I hated to confess but had no choice. "I just blanked out."

I must have said it so tragically that Max hastened to console me. "What's the big deal? It happens to the greatest."

"I know, but it never happened to me before. I swear, I've played that piece a hundred times."

"You've only two more concerts this season, so practice, my boy, practice!"

I considered the prospect and knew that I could not face it. I hesitated for an instant, then plunged: "Max, I'm afraid we'll have to cancel."

Max hated to see his fee going down the drain. "Wait a minute, Danny, you're being emotional. You know canceling is not good for an artist. Gives you a bad name."

"It never harmed Michelangeli or Caballé," I countered. "They both cancel more concerts than they play."

"You're talking about world figures, Danny. When you're one, you can cancel as much as you like. Not now."

"Look, Max, I've never missed a concert in all these years. Just this once won't upset anything. I'm tired, I need a rest, and when I'm feeling this low, it's no time for me to play. Please, Max, try to change the dates to next season. Give them one excuse or another. If they won't postpone, just tell them I can't."

Max knew when to yield. "Okay, Danny, but don't make a habit of it, please. I've enough *tsurris* as is, believe me."

I breathed more easily. The danger, for the time being, had been averted.

14

I BECAME AWARE of a curious apathy in myself, a surrender of will that made it pleasant for me to drift along, letting things happen to me rather than making them happen. It was suddenly easier for me not to make my mind up about anything, allowing chance—or fate—to push me in one direction rather than another.

This indecisiveness manifested itself in small matters as well as in large. Steve's friend Tim Bosworth invited me to one of his parties. Did I want to go or didn't I? I shilly-shallied for two days and finally decided to attend. Once there I remained curiously detached from the evening, completely the outsider. I ran into Ellen, the girl I had become friendly with the last time. Her

"Hiya!" was impersonal, the greeting of a stranger, as was mine. I managed to disentangle myself from her and, gripped by a vast restlessness, wanted to escape from the crowd, the noise, the spurious gaiety. Yet I stayed, unable to tear myself away. What held me there? A need to fuel my disgust? Or simply a self-destructive streak hidden deep inside me? I could not decide.

The feeling of uprootedness had become chronic. Wherever I found myself, I felt I ought to be somewhere else. I used so much energy going up and down my internal roller coaster that I had not much left for moving forward. Clearly I was coming apart at the seams; I needed either a psychiatrist or a change of scene. The second choice was more attractive. Steve had left me his car. The time had come to use it.

Where to? The whole world beckoned. It made my choice more difficult. Go west? I should have liked to visit Los Angeles but had no intention of motoring that far. South? June was not the time for Palm Beach. North? The Canadian Rockies were too far away. I decided on Quebec. Why there? I had played several concerts in Montreal but had never been to Quebec. Besides, I remembered from my seventh-grade history class that a decisive battle had been fought on the heights outside the city. Between Generals Wolfe and Montcalm, both of whom were killed. As a result of Wolfe's victory, Canada passed from French dominion to British. Was it worth dying for such a prize? Not if you were the corpse.

I found it extraordinarily difficult to prepare for my trip. It was as if my wish to go were balanced by an almost equally strong desire to avoid going. Finally, however, the last-minute chores were out of the way and I was ready to leave. I called Steve's dealer and laid in an adequate supply of cocaine. On the first Monday in June I drove up the West Side Highway, open to adventure. I had meant to start out in the early morning; what with one thing or another (mainly my habit of procrastinating), most of the afternoon was gone by the time I got under way. It was one of those early-summer days when the city is too muggy for comfort. I was encumbered by a minimum of luggage, and Mr. Schein's precious Stradivarius was securely strapped to the backseat. I intended to practice one or two hours every day.

Soon the trees on either side of the road began to rush past me in an endless procession. Poplars, oaks, hemlocks? I realized I did not even know their names. I had never been an outdoor type; my idea of communion with nature was an occasional walk in Central Park. All the same, the open road framed by a tapestry of green lifted my spirits. "Still stands the forest primeval . . ." Who wrote the line? It sounded great.

The journey through Connecticut was pleasant. There was a wooden bridge over the Housatonic, and I remembered that this was Charles Ives's river. I had an impression that all New England churches looked alike. The fresh air whetted my appetite; I stopped for dinner at a roadhouse outside New Haven. It suddenly became clear to me that I wasn't going to Quebec at all. I didn't give a hoot about General Wolfe or Montcalm. I was going to turn off at Hyannis, motor along Cape Cod to Truro, and see Natalia. The decision had been taken deep inside me without my being aware of it. Truro was where I wanted to be, no ifs or buts about it.

Once my true goal revealed itself, a great excitement swept over me. It occurred to me that before I proceeded any farther, I had better find out exactly where she lived. I telephoned Amos Schein. Fortunately he was home.

"You follow the highway past Truro," he told me, "until you come to a hotel called Colonial Inn. There are several houses just beyond. Hers is the first. You can phone and tell her you're coming. Information will give you the number."

I decided not to; it would be more exciting to surprise her. I would simply ring her doorbell. The more I thought about it, the more attractive the prospect seemed. But I also needed to bolster my courage. At the next gas station I repaired to the men's room with my kit and chopped up a line of coke, so that by the time I reached Hyannis I was enjoying a good high. I rejoiced in my change of plan and had absolutely no doubts about its outcome. My mind was racing as it trotted out all the old arguments to persuade Natalia to accommodate herself to my wishes. I stepped on the gas until I was doing ninety; it seemed to me that the car was skimming over the road without really touching it.

As the flat landscape of the Cape sped past me, trees gradually gave way to dunes. I decided I needed a final infusion of courage (I had reached that ebullient state where you go on doing coke because you still have some) and was reckless enough to chop up a line right in the car, without bothering to seek the privacy of a washroom. From there on I was sufficiently exalted to see how well I could zigzag from one side of the road to the other without coming to grief. That I didn't, proved beyond doubt that I was an infallible driver. Zigzagging accorded perfectly with my ebullient mood. Fortunately no traffic cops were nearby to appreciate my performance. It was past eleven when I finally hit Truro. Tiers of stars were scattered in milky galaxies across the New England sky, and the air was heady with the smell of the sea. In my feverish interior dialogue I forestalled all Natalia's objections and triumphantly overcame them. I arrived at her house, parked the car, and, my heart beating wildly, rang her bell.

"Who is it?" Her contralto voice came clear and firm from the other side of the door. I would have known it anywhere.

I tried to sound utterly sure of myself. "It's me, Danny."

"Who?" She flung open. "My God! What are you doing here?"

"I was in the neighborhood and thought I'd drop in."

"Some joke. Come in," she commanded, sounding peremptory rather than friendly.

I entered a large room filled with summer furniture. Two of her ballet buddies were sprawled on the wicker couch. In a more serious vein I added, "I wanted us to have a talk."

Indicating her friends, she said, with the barest hint of irritation, "Can't you see I'm not free?"

I stood my ground. "No matter, I still want us to talk."

She resigned herself with a sigh. To her guests she said: "If you'll excuse us . . ."

They pulled themselves to their feet and ambled out of the room. Once they were gone, Natalia turned fiercely on me. "You barge in on me, you disrupt my evening, and you expect me to put up with it?"

"I do."

"Why?"

"Because I love you. Because I want us to get back together again. Because this time I know it'll work." I spewed out the words before she could stop me. My next move caught her by surprise. I bounded over to her, threw my arms around her, and pulled her to me in a tight embrace. Before she could object, I bent forward and pressed my lips against hers. A wonderful elation poured through me, unaffected by the vain beating of her fists against my chest. Finally I let her go.

She stared at me in disbelief. "You must be out of your mind!" she cried.

"Really? Just because I kiss you I'm out of my mind?"

"You're stoned out of your mind. Otherwise you wouldn't behave like this."

"What's the difference whether I am or not? I want you back, and I'm going to get you back."

She put her hands on her hips, challenging me. "You think so?"

"I know so."

She suddenly decided to sit down. "Danny, we're not going to have a serious talk while you're high. Why don't you get yourself a good night's sleep and come back tomorrow? Then we can talk."

"I'm not going anywhere. I'm going to sleep right here."

"Danny, there's only one guest room, and Paul is staying there. Carlos sleeps on the sofa in this room. There's nowhere else, so you can't stay here."

"I'm not going anywhere," I repeated doggedly.

"Danny, you're trying to force my hand, and you know I don't like to be forced."

We were locked in the old battle of wills; it was as if I had never been away. "Just find me a mattress," I said, "and I can sleep on the veranda."

"The issue is not whether you can sleep on the veranda. The issue is that this is my house and I don't want you to stay here."

"I'm not going to let you send me away."

Since I was being obstinate, she had to be more so. "Danny, you can't stay here if I say no. And I'm saying no."

"I'm not leaving. What are you going to do about it?"

"One simple thing. I'll call the police in Provincetown; they'll come and put you out."

"You wouldn't do that."

Her eyes took on that flinty look I remembered so well. "Oh, yes, I would! You know me well enough to know I would. I'd rather you didn't force me to, but if I have to, I will."

We were back in our old pattern, I imploring, she refusing. In the face of that refusal my bravado collapsed. Even though I had been fortified with several lines of coke, I was helpless against her rejection. I stared at her in silence.

"Now be a dear and leave," Natalia said, "and I'll see you tomorrow."

"I didn't think you'd be like this," I finally said.

My capitulation made her defend herself. "You leave me no choice. You arrive unexpectedly and try to take over my life. What am I supposed to do? I don't want to be unpleasant. Believe me, I don't enjoy it. But I'm a certain kind of person, and you must deal with me in a certain way. If you don't, I strike back. I'm sorry."

"Okay, have it your way," I said wearily. "Where can I get some sleep?"

"The Colonial Inn is down the road. They'll take care of you. And I'll give you breakfast in the morning."

I turned and without a word went back to the car. I remembered what high hopes I had had when I left it, and felt like crying. I also felt like doing some coke. Instead I followed the road to the hotel. I remembered from a previous visit to the Cape that Truro had a high cliff overlooking the ocean. It would solve all my problems, I reflected, if I drove Steve's car off that cliff. But how could I do this to my best friend? It was his only car.

When I reached the Colonial, I faced another disappointment. Except for a single light over the sign on the road, the place was completely dark. I decided I was much too tired to go looking for another hotel. Where would I find one at this hour? There had to be an empty room where I could rest. I went up the stairs and, instead of going into the lobby, tiptoed along the veranda that extended in front of the building. I tried the first door I passed. It opened. I went in and found myself in an empty bedroom. Without bothering to undress, I flung myself on the bed and fell into the dreamless sleep of exhaustion.

15

MY EYES OPENED on a room flooded with sunlight. I surveyed my unfamiliar surroundings, trying to remember where I was, and became aware that I was not alone. Two policemen sat opposite the bed; behind them stood a chambermaid. "She found you here," one of the men said, "and called the manager. He called us."

I was too bewildered to speak. "We found your car in the parking lot," he continued. "You forgot to lock it, and the motor was running."

My God, the Strad! To think that I had left it in an unlocked car. The realization hit me with the force of a physical blow. "My violin!" I cried in the greatest agitation. "What did you do with it?"

"It's safe. You're lucky someone didn't walk off with it."

"When can I have it back?"

"When the time comes." There was something ominous about the way he said this. "Why didn't you register?"

"The office was closed for the night, and there was no one around. I was dead tired, so I went into the first room I found and fell asleep. I can register now."

"We also found drugs in your car. We're very strict in these parts about possession. That's why you're under arrest."

I stared at him, trying to absorb the import of his words. How could I have been so careless as to leave my supplies in the car? How had I gotten so high? If only Natalia had let me stay over, none of this would have happened. The bitch!

"You owe the hotel fifty-five dollars for the room," the officer said. I pulled three twenty-dollar bills from my pocket and handed them to the chambermaid. "Come with us," he ordered.

I followed the officers to the police car parked in front of the hotel. A strange thing happened to me once I got in; my sense of reality collapsed. It seemed to me that none of this was really happening to me; I was dreaming it. Or it was happening to someone else who looked like me, while I watched from a safe distance. A wall of total bewilderment hemmed me in; I felt nothing.

"You from New York?" the officer who was driving said. It sounded like a statement rather than a question.

"Yeah."

"We get a lotta folks from New York this time of year. They bring us a lot of trouble."

"They also bring you a lot of money," I observed.

"Sure, but it ain't worth the trouble. They're either Commies, fags, or potheads."

I remembered that I had a small bag of cocaine hidden in each of my back pockets. They would certainly find these when they searched me at the police station. As I was alone in the backseat, my first thought was to throw them out the window. But no, they could see my every movement in the little mirror over the driving wheel. Fortunately the lower half of the car was outside their field of vision. By sitting low in my seat, I managed to slip the incriminating little bags out of my pockets and into my shoes.

Nothing more was said till we reached Provincetown. The jail was in back of the city hall. I was duly photographed and fingerprinted. I intended to falsify my name, but they already knew it from my driver's license. It was obvious that Provincetown had never heard of me, something to be grateful for. I was led into a dingy cell with a toilet seat, a bunk, and a wooden bench against the wall. I sat down, planted elbows on knees, and buried my face in my hands. According to the standards I had grown up with, jail was the ultimate disgrace (except, of course, for those who had been arrested for their politics). No one I knew had ever been in jail; it was no place for decent people. What would happen to my career if the story got out? I would never live it down. How would I face my parents, my sponsor, my manager, my friends? I sank down to the nethermost level of depression; my despair rolled itself into a bundle of hate for Natalia. This was all her fault! I'd never have seen the inside of this cell if she hadn't turned me out.

On the bench opposite me sprawled a drunk who slobbered to himself over and over again, "She'll be coming round the mountain when she comes. . . ." He was too far gone to take notice of me. I stared at the wall of vertical bars that separated my cell from the corridor. The more I tried to figure out what had happened to me, the less sense it made. I had been on my way to an innocent summer holiday. How had I ended up in this miserable hole? The silence was punctuated by a mixture of noises from the street. I leaned my head against the wall, shut my eyes, and lost track of time, lost also my connection with the world. Would I ever get out of this filthy cell? How? When?

A guard came by with a cup of coffee and a stale roll on a tin tray. The hot liquid revived me. I realized how hungry I was and softened the roll by dipping it in the coffee. It tasted wonderful. The guard left me with a new problem. "You can make one phone call," he announced. "I'll be back and take you to the phone." He followed this with a bit of friendly advice. "They're strict around here. Get yourself a good lawyer."

Whom would I call? This was a difficult decision. My parents? How could I possibly tell them what had happened? Besides, what could they do? My sponsor? Never. Steve? He was in South America. Ruth? I hadn't been in touch with her for months. She would help me if she could, I knew, but there wasn't a thing she could do. I decided to try to reach Stamos. After what had happened between my teacher and me, I didn't need to be ashamed of my predicament with him. He would understand.

The guard returned and led me to a phone. I dialed Stamos's number. What if he was out of town? My heart sank. I was lucky; he answered. "Maestro . . ." I still called him that from my student days.

"Ah, Danilo . . . how goes it?"

I told him what had happened. There was a long silence; then he asked, "You have someone to help you?"

"No."

"How far it is?"

"You can fly to Boston in forty-five minutes. Then there's a small plane to Provincetown."

"Good. I come tomorrow morning."

"Thank you, Maestro." He would never know how relieved I was at the prospect of seeing him.

Next came the problem of bail. The judge set it at fifty thousand. Unable to post bond, I faced the possibility of being locked up for several days. I was desperate. "Your Honor," I asked, "why can't I post my violin as surety?"

"Your violin?" He looked puzzled.

"Your Honor, it's worth much more than fifty thousand."

The judge, a Yankee with a bony nose and sallow complexion, looked incredulous. "How can a fiddle be worth that much?"

"It would fetch over half a million on the market," I declared with conviction.

The court clerk glanced at me with new interest, not sure whether I was a liar or a loon. His Honor, not convinced, shook his head vigorously. "Accept a fiddle as bail? Out of the question!"

I realized at once that I had made a serious mistake. Up to this point I had been just another nobody from New York. Now I was somebody, which lessened my chances of keeping my misadventure a secret.

I was led back to my cell and locked in for the night. What I needed more than anything else was a fix, and I needed it badly. Fortunately I had a little bag of coke hidden in either shoe. Without my kit I could not prepare a line properly; I lacked the razor blade to chop up the powder and a surface to chop it on. No matter. My teeth would do the chopping. I dipped one finger into the packet and sucked off the little white grains. They had a slightly bitter taste that soothed my craving. This was not the right way to enjoy cocaine, but it would do.

Dinner consisted of some watery beef stew and another hard roll, with which I sopped it up. As at breakfast, never had food tasted so good. Then I lay down on my bunk. Time floated around me, gentle and remote. I flavored it with vain regrets for my life. If I hadn't gone to the Moscow competition and met the English boy who taught me to perk up my nerves with amphetamines, I wouldn't have fallen into the habit. Not true. There must have been something deep inside me that predisposed me to this kind of pleasure, an appetite that was waiting from way back to attach itself to whatever came along. It was what Steve called the addictive personality. Once the appetite had found its object, it grew. Yet I didn't regret my addiction, which had brought me so many happy hours. What I regretted—with an intensity that spread through me like wildfire—was that I had been caught at it. A single misstep now jeopardized everything I had worked so hard to attain. How could I have been so blind to the possible consequences of my behavior? As well ask how I could have been so reckless as to leave the Stradivarius overnight in an unlocked car.

My thoughts began a desperate race at the back of my head. It seemed to me that I had been locked away in this filthy cell forever, and always would be.

I finally dozed off. A woman followed me, her face heavily veiled so that I could not see her features. She did not walk as normal people did but jumped from one spot to the next, advancing so fast that I could not keep up with her. We argued strenuously, I did not quite know what about, but it was clear that I could not convince her. I awoke the next morning as though from a long tussle that left me exhausted.

The guard brought the news that I had two visitors. I hurried out to face Dmitri Stamos and Amos Schein. My teacher threw his arms around me and locked me in his embrace. "Danilo!" he exclaimed. "*Caro mio.*"

I tried to tell him how much it meant to me that he had come but couldn't. My emotions ran away with me; tears filled my eyes.

Mr. Schein's handshake was reassuring. "Don't worry, Danny," he said, "we'll get you out of this." Not a word of reproach, for which I was grateful. "I called my lawyer in Boston. He's on his way."

Mr. Schein went off to speak to the judge. I was left alone with Stamos, who said, "Something I must tell you. Better you hear it from me than from someone else. The *Times* learned about this, I do not know how, and printed it this morning."

My heart stopped. "What did it say?"

"What it could say? Concert violinist arrested."

I cringed. "On the front page?"

"Of course not. Why it should be on front page? It is small item inside."

Small comfort. It seemed to me that the entire structure of my life was crashing down around me. Steve and I had been so careful to keep our habit a secret, and now the whole world would know. My old dream of being left naked on the stage, exposed for all to see, had finally come true. It had begun as a dream and ended as a blow of fate.

Back in the cell I dropped on my bunk and tried to empty my mind. I was shattered. I wished I could awake from the bad dream my life had become. If I could only stop thinking, stop feeling, stop being. . . .

Mr. Schein returned in the afternoon. "I had a long visit with the judge," he told Stamos and me. "I explained to him who you were. It helped that you were never in any trouble before. In fact it helped very much. He finally agreed to give you a suspended sentence and release you in my care. I promised to get you to a rehab center and keep you there until you're cured." He shook his head appraisingly. "It could have been worse."

The next morning the judge delivered his sentence. He also gave a little speech that expressed his feelings about summer visitors, the ones the policeman in the car had called Commies, fags, and potheads. I also suspected that a fourth category was included in the judge's diatribe, New York Jews. "You people come here every summer and disrupt our way of life. Our way of life is a wholesome family life. You people think it's all right to disrupt it because you're paying your way. That's where you're mistaken. Believe me, I'd pass a law if I could that would make our town off bounds for the whole lot of you. We don't need you people."

I breathed deeply when I stepped into Main Street; I was a free man again. By this time Mr. Schein's lawyer had arrived from Boston; we had a Cape Cod lunch consisting of the most delicious lobster I had ever tasted. Amos Schein seemed delighted with the successful accomplishment of his mission. "When I was at college," he said, extracting a white slab of lobster from a pink claw, "a prof of mine used to tell us, 'You spend the first half of your life trying to get your name in the paper, and the second half trying to keep it out.' Well, Danny, I see you've now started on the second half."

He patted my forearm and smiled. I managed to smile back and tried to feel a little less terrible.

III

1

I ARRIVED AT Hillcrest in the grip of an immense rage. Against myself, for messing up my life. Against Natalia, for causing my downfall. Against fate, for having played a dirty trick on me. Curiously enough, my anger did not include Steve, who had introduced me to cocaine in the first place. I had enjoyed our sessions together too much to turn against him now.

Although I was in no mood to notice it, my surroundings were not unpleasant. The main house was a rambling villa adorned with balconies, gables, and stained-glass dormer windows in the ornate style favored by the rich in the early years of the century. Set pleasantly amid the rolling Connecticut hills, it commanded a view of well-kept lawns as far as the cye could reach. The swimming pool, of Olympic size, nestled behind the house. My fellow inmates were friendly enough, although in my first days at Hillcrest I tended to disregard them. At that point

I was too preoccupied with my own problems to pay much attention to others.

Nor did my first impression of the director, Dr. Howard Nelson, improve my mood. He was a tall, blondish man with regular features and intense blue eyes that seemed to be trying to bore their way inside you. His large frame and broad shoulders invited confidence, yet I very much resisted the idea of sharing my innermost thoughts with a stranger. I happened to be an intensely private person.

"Well, how do you like it here?" he asked.

"Do I have to be polite or can I say what I feel?"

"By all means, be honest."

"I don't."

"Why?"

"I don't like to have my life regimented."

"Why not say structured?"

"Call it what you like, it's not my style. I live alone; I'm used to spending most of the day alone. Here I don't have the space I need."

The good doctor smiled. "At Hillcrest we believe in sharing. We try to make you feel part of the group."

"My situation is very different from theirs."

"How?"

"They came here of their free will. I came because of a court order. That makes a big difference."

Dr. Nelson had a way of curling his fingers around his chin as if he were carefully considering what you said. "What does it matter how they came here? The point is that they're here. With a problem they can't solve by themselves. Free will, Dan, is a much more complicated subject than you think. If you asked them, I'm quite sure the answer would be that they had no more choice about coming here than you did."

At my next session with the doctor I tried to be less hostile. He began by telling me that I might have trouble adjusting to Hillcrest. "You've always been treated as a star, and we don't believe in the star system. Here nobody gets special treatment because everybody is equal."

This put me on the defensive. "My work depends on my feeling special. People come to hear me play because I sound different from other violinists."

Pursing his lips was another of the gestures that showed he was carefully considering what you had said. "We try to stress the similarities between people rather than the differences. You may find that you're not as different as you think."

When he referred to my addiction, I protested hotly. "I'm not an addict. I did coke with a friend once or twice a week, purely for recreation. This hardly makes me an addict."

He smiled. "You remind me of the woman who keeps saying her daughter is just a little pregnant. There's no such thing as being only partially addicted. You got into trouble with the law as an addict, and you were sent here because of your addiction."

"A label is only a label. Just because you attach it to something doesn't make it so."

"When you label a problem," he countered, "it helps you to recognize it. That's the first step to dealing with it. At the moment your problem is denial. You simply deny what's too painful for you to face."

"Is this what you're supposed to teach me?"

"It's one of the things."

"How long is this lesson supposed to take?"

"That depends on you. I don't have a magic wand that I can wave over you and turn you into someone else."

"Why would I want to be turned into someone else? I'm quite satisfied to be me."

"You'll resist my suggestions and waste a lot of time arguing with me. Once you admit that I may know what I'm talking about, you'll make progress."

According to the doctor, the antidote for my denial—and self-deception—was for me to try to be relentlessly honest with myself. That meant I had to stay tuned to reality all the time.

I struck back. "Since you ask me to be honest, Doctor, I can tell you the truth. I don't like you."

"Why?"

"It turns me off to be with someone who knows all the answers."

The smile returned. "Every profession has its drawbacks. The French call it *déformation professionelle.* A sandhog get pressure in his ears; a psychoanalyst sounds as if he knows the answers."

"And your job is to change me?"

"No, that's your job. I can only provide a bit of guidance along the way. My first job, I would say, is to rid you of the notion that the world revolves around you."

Again he was putting me on the defensive. "An artist has to feel that about himself or he can't function as an artist. Maybe you'll cure me of wanting to play the violin. If that's the price I have to pay for your cure, I'd rather not."

"There's no cure for talent."

"I'm glad to hear it."

"I would only try to cure you of whatever might harm your talent or destroy it. That's why I'd want to free you of your addiction. Believe me, in the long run it could be most damaging."

I did not care to pursue this line of reasoning. Instead I told Dr. Nelson that I was worried about my parents. "I should see them, but I don't really want to."

"You're afraid they'll reproach you for what happened."

"Could be."

"I say, call them. The sooner you get it over with, the better you'll feel. They may not be as judgmental as you fear. In fact they may surprise you."

I phoned Julia and suggested that she and Dad come to Hillcrest the following morning. She surprised me by arriving alone. She threw her arms around me; I was glad she did. When she released me, "My poor boy!" she cried, and burst into tears.

"Come off it, Mom, I'm not dead yet." It struck me that as

far as my career was concerned, I might as well be. "Where's Dad?"

"Your father has a bad cold. He wasn't up to coming."

A bad cold in July? This sounded to me like a flimsy excuse, but I decided not to make an issue of it. Dr. Nelson would probably have said that I was being unduly suspicious.

Julia took my hand and intertwined her fingers with mine. "You were never like other boys. They played ball or rode their bicycles while you stayed home and practiced. You really had no boyhood."

"I was doing what I was meant to do."

She seemed not to have heard me. "Your father and I keep asking ourselves, What did we do wrong? We tried our best for you. Where was our mistake?"

I was stung to the quick. "What kind of thinking is that?" I demanded.

"That's how parents are. If something goes wrong, they blame themselves. They feel the trouble came because of something they did or failed to do."

"But I was doing fine until this thing happened."

Julia took out her handkerchief and dabbed her eyes. "Maybe you had the wrong kind of friends. Steve I liked, but that stuck-up ballerina of yours I couldn't stand. All this happened while you were visiting her. It figures. Once you fall into the hands of the wrong woman, you have no end of sorrow."

I certainly was not disposed to contradict.

"Why did you leave Ruth? A sweeter girl never was. And she really loved you. She was too good for you, I guess."

Again I did not contradict. Julia threw me a look full of reproach. "My mother used to say, 'Small children press the knee; big ones press the heart.' She was right." Julia shook her head significantly. "Imagine what your father felt when he opened the paper and read the news. Now the whole world knew."

"Mom, did you come here to cheer me up or to make me feel worse?"

She raised her hands and let them drop. "A mother thinks she knows her own child. It turns out she doesn't know the first thing about him. What will all this do to your career?"

"I haven't spoken to Max yet." Why hadn't I? Was I afraid he would tell me something I didn't want to hear?

Julia fell back into the magical kind of thinking that came naturally to her. "It was an evil eye, nothing else. Things were going too well for you, so someone put a hex on you."

"Mom, stop talking nonsense. I just got high and went haywire. Could happen to anybody."

"But it didn't happen to anybody. It happened to you."

"Stop worrying. The whole thing'll blow over, you'll see." I said this with a conviction I didn't feel.

Julia dropped her arms, as though the strength had suddenly gone out of them. "We're in God's hands. It will be as He decides. I try to understand Him, but it's no use. He doesn't answer my questions."

I accompanied her to the bus that took visitors to the train. "Tell Dad I'd like to see him."

"He'll come as soon as he can."

I kissed her and stood watching as the bus moved off. What grief my behavior must have caused my parents. The realization hung heavily upon me. Would it ever lift?

2

DR. NELSON PRESENTED my situation to me in black-and-white terms. "At this point, Dan, you stand at the crossroads. You can either kick the habit or let it conquer you." This was not exactly what I wanted to hear, but I was sufficiently objective to know that it was good for me to hear it. "The task ahead of you is not an easy one. But if you were able to master the violin, which took a lot of discipline, you should be able to handle this too. No one can do it for you. All I can do is guide you from time to time. The rest is up to you."

Having given me a few days to adjust to Hillcrest, Dr. Nelson decided that I was ready for group therapy. The prospect of confessing my problems to a group of strangers was most unattractive. "It's like undressing in public," I said.

He smiled. "Undressing with others may teach you an important lesson."

"What?"

"That, for all the differences, you're more like others than you think."

I had no particular desire to get to know my fellow patients. Dr. Nelson put me down as a "loner" whose response to people was as inadequate as my relation to reality. The cause? I considered it to be my natural shyness, but he blamed my acute fear of being rejected. According to him, this went hand in hand with my tendency to be self-centered, which had been fostered by my life as an artist. I did not care for these labels, but they fit too neatly for me to be able to disregard them.

My first experience with group therapy was not particularly happy. Six or seven of us sat in a circle and talked about ourselves. Dr. Nelson explained that there was only one rule: "Tell it like it is. No dressing it up or aiming for effect." When he was called away, as happened occasionally, a woman named Sheila directed the discussion. (We used only first names.)

At one point she turned to me. "When a newcomer joins the group, we ask him how he happened to get here. Would you like to tell us?"

I choked up. Was I to tell them about my zigzag drive along the Cape, my run-in with Natalia, the two policemen in my room the next morning, the jail cell in Provincetown? The thought froze my blood. I covered my confusion. "Perhaps some other time . . ."

Sheila did not press me. "Very well," she said, and turned to the next person.

When I mentioned the incident to Dr. Nelson, he said, "You're being uptight about this, Dan, but you'll get over it. No one in the room would be shocked in the least if you told them exactly what happened to you. Every one of them has a story that's different, yet they're all part of the same story."

When the session was over, I stayed on to talk to Sheila. A woman in her fifties, she was a commanding presence in her impeccably tailored suit, with dark eyes that were very bright and expressive, and a single streak of gray running through her overly black hair. She was a well-known designer of women's clothes who ran her own business. "When the pressure gets too much for me," she told me, "I have to take a break. Which means going on a binge. Three or four days of drinking. I realize these have to stop, but when I try to stop them, I don't seem to be able to. Funny thing"—her eyes flashed, and when she smiled she was extremely attractive—"your mind tells you the sensible thing to do, yet you don't do it."

In the next days I spent as much time as I could with Sheila. I had finally found someone at Hillcrest who interested me. Besides, by this time I was starved for female companionship. She was the first woman I had known between my mother's generation and mine. I thought her face was beautiful, the features large and striking as though carved in stone, eyes deep in their sockets over high cheekbones, a wide mouth and determined chin. It was a dramatic face, full of character, like the face of some actress out of an earlier time. "You have a man's mind," I told her. "Razor-sharp."

She bridled. "That's supposed to be a compliment? Sorry, I don't take it as such. It's a myth that men have better minds than women. They spread the idea, of course. You should know the men I come up against in my business. Most of them are weak sisters unable to make their minds up about anything. The stronger sex, indeed! It makes me laugh."

I listened, fascinated by the strength of will behind the words. I was sorry I had not met her when she was twenty years younger.

"A lady to see you, Dan."

My heart skipped a beat. I dreaded the encounter; what was the point? As I hurried to the waiting room, anger swept over me.

Natalia stood near the window. I made no attempt to go over to her. Had she come to tell me how sorry she was? A fat lot of good that would do.

She sat down. "Aren't you going to say hello to me?" she asked.

"Hello."

"I know, you're mad as hell. You have a right to be."

"You can say that again." I took a chair opposite her.

"I'm sorry I behaved the way I did. I wouldn't have if I had known how it would turn out."

What was I supposed to say—"Thank you so much for telling me"? I knew only that she had hurt me more than anyone I had ever known. I stared at her, remembering what she had meant to me, remembering that she had left my life in ruins. Why was I sitting in this armchair facing the bitch as if we were about to have a drink together? I said nothing.

"You're giving me a hard time, Danny," she finally said. "I don't think you should."

I looked into her eyes and saw the steely expression with which she had ordered me out of her house that fatal night. "You don't think I should?"

"I know I hurt you very deeply. But I came here to see how you are and to hold out my hand to you."

"Thanks. You walked all over me; you kicked my love around like a football; now you come to hold out your hand to me. Am I supposed to dance for joy?" I struggled to retain my composure. "That first night I saw you dance, in *Swan Lake*, you were a dream, an illusion. That's your real role. The human being underneath is someone else. She's not human. How could I have let you treat me the way you did? I find no answer to that question. Perhaps what we call love is a form of madness. An addiction."

"If you had only been reasonable, we could have had a great

time together. But you tried to force my hand, and that didn't work."

"I wasn't after a great time. I was after something meaningful."

"But I told you I didn't share your dream. I told you I couldn't. I was perfectly honest with you from the beginning."

"Even then you had no right to be so cruel. No one has the right to be that cruel."

Coldly she said: "I didn't come here for a lecture."

"It wouldn't do you much good if you did."

"If that's how you feel, I'd better go."

I leaned forward in my chair to emphasize what I was about to say. "What you want, Natalia, is easy forgiveness. That's what you came for. I'm sorry I can't give it to you."

Her features took on the hardness I knew so well. "You're behaving like a spoiled brat, which of course is what you are. Someday you may change your mind about me, and you'll regret this."

"No, I won't. That night, when you ordered me out of your house, something in me died, and it's not anything that can be revived. Or that I would want to revive. Certain experiences are finished, and it's best to get as far away from them as possible."

She stood up. "I'm glad I came. At least I tried."

I rose too. "I suppose I should thank you for coming, but I'm not going to."

"Good luck anyway. And don't worry about your career. Your public will forget about the scrape you got into. A friend of mine, a gifted conductor, got caught coming back from Europe with drugs. He went right on conducting and tells me he's busier than ever." She went to the door and turned to me. Suddenly she was Natalia Kohanskaya, the prima ballerina. "I'm dancing *Giselle* next season, a new production. If you'd like to see it, you can have my seats."

"Thanks. I don't think I will. I've had enough ballet for the time being." Actually I had had enough to last me a lifetime. I did not go over to kiss her good-bye. As she was about to leave,

"Natalia," I said to the woman I had once loved, "that gorgeous theme in B-minor at the beginning of *Swan Lake*. It's terrific, the way Tchaikovsky brings it back in major at the climax."

She left. I sat down and felt like crying. There came a time when we grew indifferent to those who had made us suffer. It was our final revenge.

Steve returned from his South American tour. He heard the details of my misadventure from Julia, Dmitri Stamos, Natalia, and came immediately to see me. We clapped our palms together in the old way and embraced. He would never know how happy I was to see him.

"The minute I turn my back," he exclaimed, "you get into trouble." He thought a moment. "To tell you the truth, I was afraid you would. I felt it in my bones. Have you spoken to Max yet?"

"No, he's in Europe. Probably signing up some new competition winners."

"Well, until he comes back you won't know where you stand."

The possibilities were so depressing that we decided not to consider them. Instead I described Natalia's visit.

Steve grinned. "She had it coming to her. Of course you might have been a little more grown-up about it."

"I'd like to see how you'd behave to someone who'd kicked you around."

"It was sporting of her to make the gesture. She didn't have to."

"I wasn't buying it."

Steve was suddenly serious. "I feel I'm to blame for the mess you got into. I led you into the habit. Of course I couldn't foresee that you'd go overboard."

"How could you?"

"True, but if I hadn't—"

"How much is anybody responsible for someone else? We'll never know."

"All the same, you and I are not doing coke anymore. Tell me, how are you managing without it?"

"I guess I don't need it as much when I'm not playing concerts. Besides, the shock of my arrest was so great it just drove everything else out of my mind. And in this place they arrange everything so you won't miss it. If I ever do it again, I'll know how to handle it."

Steve shook his head. "You won't do it again. I won't let you. . . . By the way, are you playing?"

"No, there's no music in me now."

"Don't you miss practicing?"

"Not really. Maybe I needed a rest. At the moment I don't feel like doing anything. It's enough just to be."

"Okay. Being has its points too."

"Maybe even more."

I dreaded Max's return from Europe. What if he told me that my arrest had terminated my usefulness? I envisaged the scenario: C. Myron Robbins wanted no part of me; National Concerts dropped me cold; no other management took me. An artist depended on management for his engagements. Once he was dropped, he could have no career. I would simply cease to be a concert artist. What else could I possibly do? It was much too late for me to study law or medicine, even if I had had the slightest aptitude for either profession, and I certainly did not. I saw myself sawing away in the second violin section of some midwestern orchestra or teaching untalented youngsters in a third-rate music school in Paducah. How else could I earn a living?

Now that I seemed to be on the verge of losing my career, it appeared to be the most desirable way of life I could ever have. The unfailing excitement of facing an audience, the thrill of playing the music and being rewarded by their applause: Where else could I possibly find such satisfaction? The regret stored deep within me came pouring out in giant waves. My career had been handed to me on a silver platter, I had held it all in the palm of my hand, and I had lost it. With a recklessness beyond belief I had let it slip away. What madness!

That night, without warning, my craving for the drug returned. My insides exploded, I broke into a sweat and felt nauseated, my head felt as if it were about to roll off my shoulders, and my nerves became so many sharp needles piercing my brain, clamoring for a fix. There was only one way I could get my hands on some coke, and that was to persuade Steve to bring me some. I lay wrestling with the temptation to call him, resisting it with every fiber of my being yet knowing all along that I would end by giving in. The question was only when. Finally, at about two in the morning, I woke Steve up and begged him to do as I asked.

He was outraged. "Are you out of your fucking mind?"

"Just this once, Steve. Please! Come up in the morning, and I swear I'll never bother you again."

"Danny, listen to me. There's no such thing as just once, and you know it. This is your opportunity to kick the habit, and I'm not going to let you mess it up. To make it easier for you, I'm gonna stay clean too."

"Why's it so much simpler for you?"

"Because my chemistry's different from yours. If you don't make the most of this chance, you'll be hooked for life."

"Just this once," I persisted. "What harm can it do?"

"Danny, I'm not bringing you any cocaine. I'd never forgive myself, and I already have plenty not to forgive myself for. Take a sleeping pill and read awhile, and in the morning you'll talk to your doctor. Now go back to sleep."

I gave up arguing, as I knew he was right. There was only one road to follow: to grit my teeth and bear it. In the morning I decided not to confess my lapse to Dr. Nelson. How could I tell him that all his preaching had done me so little good? However, once I came into his presence, denial seemed foolish. I described what I had gone through.

He listened to the end. Then he told me, "You mustn't expect too much of yourself, Dan. I think you're doing quite well. In fact I'm surprised your relapse didn't come sooner. If you were an alcoholic, I'd put you on metabuse; with heroin, methadone would help. But there's no equivalent for cocaine, where the problem is mental as well as physical. These attacks gradually grow weaker. I'm giving you a tranquilizer. You may have a bad time for a while, but by Monday you'll be all right. You're a survivor, and survivors don't go under."

Monday was when Max came back. I had to wait three more days until C. Myron Robbins returned from his vacation. Max finally called to lift me out of my despair. "You're a lucky son of a bitch," he announced lustily. "The boss says publicity never hurts, good or bad, unless you rape or kill someone. Otherwise it doesn't matter what the papers say about you, as long as they spell your name right. A million people read that item in the *Times*. Some of them will be curious to hear you play. Baby, you're still on."

I put down the receiver and took a deep breath. Max's news meant that I was being given another chance. This time nothing in the world would prevail on me to spoil it. Nothing!

3

JULIA CAME, AGAIN alone. My suspicions were aroused. "Where's Dad?" I demanded.

"I told you he's not well." She stopped and added uncertainly, "He still has that cold."

"Mom, tell me the truth. What's wrong with him?"

When challenged, Julia found her best defense in tears. They rolled slowly down her face. She blew her nose and sighed. "I didn't want to worry you. He's in the hospital."

"What for?"

"He had a stroke. Thank God, a slight one."

"When?"

"A couple of weeks ago."

"After he read about me?"

"I knew you'd blame yourself. No, it happened a few days before. His blood pressure's been high for years, and he smoked two packs a day. I couldn't get him to stop. There's no point your thinking you made him sick. You didn't."

"I want to see him. We're going right now."

I was scheduled for a session with Dr. Nelson that afternoon, but explained to him why I had to accompany Julia to New York. We reached the hospital shortly before noon.

Dad was lying in a large bed reading the *New York Times.* He gave me a wan smile that was slightly crooked; the left side of his mouth was out of sync with the right. "Danny boy," he said feebly, "I'm glad you came."

"How are you, Dad?"

"A little damaged, but it could be worse."

I sat down beside the bed and took his hand in mine. "Are they taking good care of you?"

"No coffee, no smoking, no salt, no butter. You call that living?"

Propped up by two sprawling pillows, he seemed strangely weak and vulnerable, his face pale, the ruts deeper than I remembered them. He had never been part of the intimacy I shared with Julia, and had always been a little in awe of me because I played the violin so much better than he did. There was a shyness between us that neither of us could overcome. I simply never knew how to tell him how much I loved him. At the moment my love was clouded with guilt. Although Julia had assured me it was not true, I could not shake off the conviction that I was somehow to blame for his illness.

I wondered whether he would allude to my misadventure. He finally did, but indirectly. "We both gave your mother plenty to worry about. Fortunately she's a strong girl." He thought for a moment and added, "You have to be strong too, Danny boy. You mustn't let them get you down."

"I'll be all right, Dad. My management is standing behind me."

His face relaxed, as though this had been the news he had

been waiting for. I nerved myself to my next remark. "I'm sorry for what happened, Dad. It was not my fault. I guess it had to happen."

"As long as it didn't finish you off." He slightly raised the *Times* resting on his knees. "I search the paper for good news but don't find any. The world could be a beautiful place. It's the people in it that spoil it. There was a time when I believed they were getting better. Quite the opposite. They get steadily worse."

Suddenly he looked tired. At parting he made me promise to visit him again soon. "Don't forget your dad," he said.

"Forget you? Not a chance, Dad." I bent over and kissed him.

I decided to visit Dmitri Stamos before returning to Hillcrest. He welcomed me with his customary operatic embrace. "What a beautiful surprise!"

He wanted to know if I was practicing. "Not yet," I told him.

"Do not worry," he assured me. "When the time comes you will begin. Musicians think they must always practice. But to take time off, to ask yourself what music means and how to express what it means, this is just as important. To interpret music, you need combination of mind and heart and fingers. All three must mix together. Only when they mix do we have great artist, and great artist is only kind worth having."

Somewhere in the conversation—more accurately, monologue—I became aware that his attitude toward me had subtly changed since the black day when he visited me in the Provincetown jail. He now saw us both as fellow noncomformists engaged in a ceaseless struggle against the conventions of society.

"It is not easy for me to hide my real self, to pretend I am not what I am. But it is very necessary. Today it is a little easier for person who is different. But when I am young, the world is not ready to accept him. It wants to destroy him, to punish him for not being like everybody else. His only defense is to hide what he is; he must take care that the world does not find out about him. But everything he does to protect himself is a lie, and he cannot escape from it. When I see you that morning in Provincetown, I feel molto simpatico to you. I realize we are both—how that James Dean movie calls it?—rebels with a cause.

I did not contradict. He was obviously speaking out of a deep need to confide, and despite the great difference between us in age and background, I felt very close to him.

"You must go back to Hillcrest for now. But when you come again to the city, you will call me, yes?" I promised.

The trick was to get out of town without laying in a supply of coke. The prospect was enormously tempting. If I did bring some back, it meant that I would not have to suffer through another painful episode of withdrawal. It meant too that I would have the drug at my disposal whenever I needed it. I struggled against the temptation. What strengthened me was not so much Dr. Nelson's admonitions as Steve's promise to give up coke in order to make it easier for me to do so. I managed to get to Grand Central without telephoning his supplier, and regarded my having done so as a triumph of willpower on my part. Once safely inside the train, I sank into my seat exhausted. It was a good feeling.

4

LIFE AT HILLCREST flowed uneventfully, in an atmosphere well insulated against the outside world. My stay there, I felt, was in the nature of an interlude, intended to let me gather up my forces for the next step. The days passed swiftly. I talked to Dr. Nelson, watched TV, attended group sessions as well as the lectures intended to show us the damage inflicted by drugs and alcohol on the nervous system and other organs. The diagrams and statistics were sufficiently melancholy to impress even the most hardened addict. My favorite spot was the swimming pool behind the main house. I had always wanted to learn to do the crawl. Now I had the opportunity.

For the first time in my life I was not playing the violin and had no desire to do so. Instead I listened to music. The library had a fairly good collection of records. Schubert was represented by his Quintet in C and the great C-Major Symphony. I played these again and again, only to discover that Schubert's music, so tender and full of longing, meant more to me at this time than the music of any other composer.

My conversations with Dr. Nelson were challenging. He listened carefully and remembered everything I said. He tried to make me see my life from another point of view. I had always thought of myself as a fairly well-balanced individual, with no more hang-ups than the next fellow. He showed me a different picture of myself, as someone fiercely ambitious and competitive who approached life in a thoroughly aggressive way. It was this that triggered my inordinate need for success and approval.

I objected strenuously. "Doesn't everyone want to get ahead? What else keeps the world moving?"

"It depends on the degree. You're still trying to prove to your mother that you deserve her love."

"Everybody had a mother."

"True, but some of us had her more than others."

"Maybe that's the picture she presented to me."

"That's how you interpreted it. Don't you suppose she'd have loved you if you hadn't turned out a success?"

"I felt she'd love me more if I did. But we're talking about events that happened when I was a boy. I'm grown up now."

The doctor shook his head. "We never grow up. We carry the marks of those early years for the rest of our lives. We grow older, but they remain the same."

Dr. Nelson explained how all these elements within me, hidden away from consciousness, created tensions that accumulated until I desperately needed an escape. This was what cocaine gave me. Only by understanding the forces behind my addiction, the doctor maintained, could I learn to cope with them. He had a novel way of looking at things, and drew connections where I had never suspected any existed. I questioned his pronouncements and, as he predicted, found a curious pleasure in arguing with him. "Why do you resist me so?" he finally asked. "Don't you realize how much better off you'll be if it turns out I'm right?"

Outwardly I did whatever was expected of me, but beneath the facade that helped me face my surroundings a totally different kind of activity went on. The inner me split off from the outer and engaged in all kinds of rebellion. Increasingly I detached myself from the activities of the group. I seethed with chronic doubts and objections that put me in opposition to whatever went on around me; I was being pulled deeper and deeper into a private zone of exile. I alternated between the familiar moments of anger and moods of futile regret, and was assailed by a fear that after what had happened to me I would never again be able to face an audience. When I finally overcame that threat, along with the depression that accompanied it, I became convinced that I was the real cause of my father's illness, and was overwhelmed with guilt despite the arguments I tried to muster against it. All this furious inner debate pursued its course beneath the external calm I presented to the world, and became the reality for which the other was merely a cover.

At this point my roommate, a businessman from New Jersey who was overweight, balding, and alcoholic, finished his course of treatment and was replaced by a more colorful character. Wallingford Nash—Wally to his friends—was an actor in his forties who loved being the center of attention. As soon as he had an audience he was on, and could be lots of fun.

Wally was fond of quoting lines from the plays he had acted in or the poems he had read. He had total recall; once he saw something in print, it remained in his mind. I found it vastly entertaining to hear him enliven an ordinary conversation with a line from Shakespeare or Shaw; he declaimed it as if he were onstage. I marveled at his erudition. Like most people who never went to college, I stood in awe of anything literary. To me Wally's high-flown quotations seemed the essence of culture.

He was sufficiently older than I to take on the role of mentor, and he listened patiently when I felt like talking about something that disturbed me. At the moment I continued to be bothered by the connection, at least in my mind, between my father's illness and my own disaster. Wally tried to free me of my feeling of guilt.

"My dear boy"—this was his favorite way of addressing me—"I can only repeat what your mother told you. Of course your father was upset at the mess you got into, but a stroke is a complicated business. If he were a health nut—you know, someone who lived on raw carrots and brown rice—he wouldn't have had a stroke no matter what happened to you. It's ridiculous of you to consider yourself responsible. We all feel guilty about one thing or another; it's part of the human condition. As Richard the Third says, 'My conscience hath a thousand several tongues.' "

Wally's main effort at the moment went into trying to control his addiction to alcohol. In addition, he was devoted to a cause. "The world," he announced loftily, "is full of professional blacks, professional Irish, professional feminists, professional Jews. I'm a professional gay." He had a long list of famous men, beginning with Alexander the Great, Michelangelo, and Leonardo da Vinci, whose names he trotted out at every opportunity to prove the value of what gays had given the world.

Sunday evenings at Hillcrest were given to socializing and often enlivened by impromptu entertainment. Wally's contribution was on the flamboyant side. He declaimed Marc Antony's address to the Romans and Hamlet's soliloquy, followed by an excerpt from Lady Bracknell's scene in *The Importance of Being Earnest.* A lift of the eyebrow, reinforced by a sudden downward inflection and flip of the wrist, gave her lines just the right flavor of inveterate snobbism. "To lose one parent may be regarded as a misfortune—to lose *both* looks like carelessness. Who was your father? He was evidently a man of some wealth. . . . I would strongly advise you, Mr. Worthing, to try and acquire some relations as soon as possible, and to make a definite effort to produce at any rate one parent of either sex, before the season is quite over."

The evening ended early. By eleven I was comfortably settled in my bed, with Wally in his at the opposite end of the room. He was high after his performance. "How did you like it?" he asked.

"I haven't enjoyed myself so much in a long time."

"I was in several productions of the play. The part I really wanted was Lady Bracknell; I'd have been much better than the girl who played her."

I put out the light. There was a silence. Suddenly Wally said, "What would you do if you awoke in the middle of the night and found me in your bed?"

I thought a moment. "Matter of fact I was in that situation once. It was someone I admired very much. My teacher."

"What did you do?"

"I was too frightened to do anything."

"How did it end?"

"He finally left, and I stole out of the house. I didn't know how I'd ever face him again, but I had to. We never again mentioned what had happened."

"What would you do now?"

"First of all, I'd turn the light on. Then I'd say, 'Wally, come off it,' and throw you out of my bed."

"I feel rejected."

"Sorry, you asked for it."

" 'Oh, lift me as a wave, a leaf, a cloud!' " he suddenly declaimed. " 'I fall upon the thorns of life! I bleed!' "

"Who wrote that?"

"Shelley."

"It's beautiful."

"He and Byron got out of England as fast as they could. England was too stuffy for them. They went looking for a freer life in Italy."

"Did they find it?"

"Sort of. Unfortunately Shelley was sailing in the Mediterranean, a storm came up, and he drowned."

"How terrible."

"He was thirty-one. That's too young to die, especially if you're a genius. Byron burned his body on the beach at Rapallo. I guess you won't find me in your bed after all. I don't go where I'm not wanted."

"Now you're being sensible."

"Good night, Danny."

"Good night."

Busy though he was, Amos Schein found the time to visit me; he wanted to see for himself how I was getting on. I assumed my best behavior and was able to persuade him that I was eating well, sleeping well, and in a much better frame of mind than when I first arrived at Hillcrest. He considered all this to be a sign of progress and was pleased.

Mr. Schein looked quietly elegant in an Yves Saint-Laurent suit. He was in an oracular mood. According to him, people could be divided into two groups. "Not tall or short, white or black, fat or thin, smart or stupid. I divide them," he announced, "into those who know what they want and those who don't. The ones who do look ahead and move forward. Once an experience is finished, they close the book and never look back. The other group do just the opposite. They keep reliving the past, wishing they had acted differently, not knowing where they're going or how they're going to get there. They can be a pain in the ass. I want you to be in the first category. Avoid the second like the plague."

He sat forward stiffly in his chair, his thin body exuding authority. "I never look back. No matter what happens, I take it in stride. You had a good example of how I react in a crisis. I didn't reproach you about Valerie; I didn't raise a stink. What had happened was over and done with. The point was not to be thrown by it. This is how a man of action reacts. I might say, a man of character. He doesn't feel sorry for himself or waste time in vain reproaches. What'll it get him? Because I reacted the way I did, you and I were able to remain friends. Don't you agree this was the wiser way?"

I did.

"Now you too went through an unpleasant bit. I'm glad to see it didn't throw you. I want you to learn from the experience even as you put it behind you. You mustn't brood about it or let it fester. Instead put your mind on the next step, which is to get back to giving concerts. That's what you should be thinking about. You've just a couple of weeks more at Hillcrest. Use them well to prepare for what's ahead."

I shook my head to show that I recognized the wisdom of his advice and walked him to his car. In the nick of time I remembered my manners and said, "Thank you so much for coming, Mr. Schein." I still had not learned to call him Amos.

The car pulled out, and I stood looking after it. I had no quarrel with Mr. Schein's advice. The problem was to apply it.

I WAS CHANGING—to a greater degree than I would have thought possible. At one of the group sessions Sheila again asked me to tell how I came to Hillcrest. This time I was able to do so. I described my disastrous trip down the Cape, my unfortunate visit with Natalia, my arrest, and the night in jail. Confession, I found, was good for the soul. It turned out to be as easy as exchanging confidences with the stranger next to you on an airplane. You spoke freely because you had never seen him before and never expected to see him again.

I gravitated to Sheila whenever I could. I was attracted by her directness of manner, her strong will and clear thinking. She had a way of moving straight to the heart of a problem without wasting time on side issues. She and Wally hit it off uncommonly well since both were fanatics, she as staunch for women's rights as he was for gay liberation. Each harangued the other on his favorite topic, while I listened. "I don't mean to criticize," she told him, "but you people are too eager. You can't push the country faster than it's willing to go. Otherwise you'll find yourselves so far ahead of the public that you won't connect. Your best bet is to fight for civil liberties. Gays are citizens; therefore they're entitled to all the rights guaranteed by the Constitution."

This didn't satisfy Wally. He needed moral as well as legal support for his beliefs. "The straight world has to realize," he insisted, "that gays have a special part to play, especially in the arts. They have a special sensitivity. D'you think Proust would have written the way he did if he had been straight, or Oscar Wilde? Not in a million years."

Since their frame of reference was considerably broader than mine, there was very little I could contribute to their discussions. But the two of them were adding a quality of excitement to my life at Hillcrest. I was more attentive to Sheila than ever. We promised to look each other up after we returned to New York, although I knew that once we were back in harness, neither of us would have much time for the other. She was touched by my attention and teased me about it; I assured her that I had a crush on her, as indeed I did. It never occurred to me that she might misunderstand my meaning. My admiration was completely platonic. It would no more have occurred to me to go to bed with her than it would have for me to make love to my mother (although, according to Freud, this was precisely what I wanted to do when I was five).

In any case, Sheila took to flirting with me and I, always eager to please, flirted back. It seemed a harmless enough game between us until an unexpected turn of events gave the situation another direction. Sheila's roommate departed, leaving her alone in her room for several nights. Which meant that with enough precaution and ingenuity, I could visit her. This resulted in an invitation for which I was utterly unprepared. Delivered casually—"Why don't you come by tonight, say, a little before midnight?"—it nevertheless had the force of a command. Too embarrassed to do anything else, I made a noise in my throat that vaguely signified yes.

I realized that without meaning to, I had led Sheila on until she mistook my affection for something else. It was easy for me to see how I had got into this predicament. The question was, How did I get out without hurting her feelings? What excuse could I offer? What if I simply failed to appear? Whichever alternative I hit on, it left me seeking another, so that my mind began to whirl in that endless circle I had so often encountered. I even considered an actual liaison, but only for a moment. The prospect was too distasteful.

Midnight arrived. I sat on the edge of my bed, still undecided what to do. The one alternative I did not seriously consider was not turning up. That would have been too unfriendly a way out and too cowardly. I finally forced myself off the bed and tiptoed down the hall to Sheila's room. She was reading in bed. She had put on a black lace negligee, which in view of what I was going through struck me as totally incongruous.

My heart thumped as I sat down on Sheila's bed. I gazed at her without a word, trying to look as woebegone as I felt. She shut the book and put it aside. "Aren't you going to kiss me?" she said coquettishly.

"There's something I have to tell you," I said hesitantly, without the slightest notion of what alibi to serve up. At this point I was certain of only one thing: that I could no more muster an erotic mood than fly off the bed.

In her eagerness to be helpful, Sheila decided for me. Looking puzzled, she suddenly said, "Don't tell me you're gay." She said it as if she didn't quite believe it.

A burden dropped off my shoulders; I grabbed the easy way she had opened up for me. I had only to confirm her suspicion to be protected from any further demands. Still maintaining my silence, as though too ashamed to admit it, I slowly shook my head yes.

"Why didn't you say so right away?" she asked.

Now that I had found my role, it was not difficult to fill in the details. "Those things are not easy to say," I murmured tentatively.

"To be honest with you, I thought you might be. Many musicians are, you know."

I was about to say, "Many more are not," but didn't. Why weaken my case?

I could hear the wheels of her mind spinning as she adapted to the new situation. "Dear Danny, it doesn't matter in the least. You and I are good friends and will remain so. We can enjoy each other in any case, if not in one way, then in another."

"Except one" was my unspoken comment.

"I've always believed that friendship is a form of love," she said. I nodded vigorously to show that I agreed. All things considered, the evening was turning out much better than I had expected.

We sat talking in the friendliest fashion, and in the end I gave her a deeply felt good night kiss. When I returned to my room, I tiptoed past Wally's bed with a smile. Wouldn't he enjoy knowing that I had stolen his role in order to save myself? I decided not to tell him.

More and more the split widened between my outer and inner self. There seemed to be no immediate connection between them, as if they were two strangers who happened to inhabit the same body. I could not tell which was the real me, as I gave myself to each in turn. Although it was not apparent from my outer manner, my alienation from my surroundings was complete. I seemed to be participating wholeheartedly in the activities of the group; actually I was retreating into a total withdrawal. I forced myself to go through the routine of Hillcrest. What I really wanted was to lie down in some quiet place and stay put.

I seemed to have fallen into a kind of lassitude where it was increasingly difficult for me to reach any kind of decision, whether in trivial or important matters. I let myself drift through each day, swept along by its various currents rather than trying to shape them. Always eager to please, I gave the impression that I was benefiting from Dr. Nelson's treatment, as on certain levels I undoubtedly was. But I was unable to shake off the feeling that life was a betrayal, a promise never fulfilled. Without being aware of it, I was being sucked into a total depression. Nor had I freed myself from the fierce anger that had thrashed about in me since my arrest. My dark view seemed to be much closer to the actual state of the world, what I recognized as reality.

In this mood I yielded to what I came to identify as downward thinking. I denigrated whatever I had achieved and wrapped myself in a mantle of worthlessness, whether as a man or musician. By looking at myself through dark glasses, I made everything around me fit my desolate point of view. I was too ashamed of these feelings to reveal them to Dr. Nelson; they struck me as the fantasies of an adolescent rebel. I knew I would not give in to them if I could maintain my outer composure. As long as I kept up the pretense, I would be safe.

Julia telephoned with a piece of news that pushed everything else out of my mind. Dad had taken a turn for the worse. I left at once for the hospital.

He had had another stroke, this time a more severe one. The left side of his face was locked into that crooked smile. I sat on one side of the bed and held his hand. "It's all right, Dad, you'll be fine," I said, and knew that he was not going to be. Julia sat on the other side and managed not to cry. She peered anxiously into my father's face. He couldn't swallow and was being fed intravenously. His speech was slurred, but when I brought my head close to his, I had no difficulty understanding him. "Mother tells me you're going to play again," he whispered. "I'm glad of it. I hated to think people wouldn't hear you anymore. You have so much talent. Don't waste it. To waste talent is a terrible thing."

I put the palm of my hand against his cheek and held it there. He motioned to me to come closer. "People say the world is going to the dogs. They're wrong. It's going to be a better place someday. I won't live to see it; maybe you will." He lapsed into silence. Then, out of the blue, he said: "God is just an adult version of Santa Claus. Invented for those who are afraid to stand on their own feet." Exhausted, he shut his eyes.

I bent over and kissed him on the forehead. Julia wept silently as we tiptoed out of the room. I went back to Hillcrest, intending to return in the morning.

He died that night.

6

I HAD NEVER before faced the death of someone close to me. This was something I had to think through, a mystery I had to solve. I hardly knew where to begin, but I did know that I would think more clearly if I got away from Hillcrest for a few hours. One car in the garage was available to residents. I decided to take a spin in the woods. I felt the warm night air rush past my face like a caress. The tall, thin shapes of the forest sped by me on either side, and the road snaked ahead like a ribbon of black velvet. I remembered when Dad had taught me to play the violin, before I went to Dmitri Stamos. His manner was altogether different from the Greek's. Stamos saw it as his duty to pass on to the student a fixed tradition whose laws were immutable; what he had to teach was beyond argument. Dad, on the other hand, was deliciously tentative. He was searching for truths that he was eager to share with you, but he wasn't quite sure what they were. His very uncertainty spurred him on to discover ideas, and it transformed the lesson into an adventure. Which method did I prefer? Actually each had its place, Dad's in the earlier years of study, Stamos's in the more advanced stages.

The arch of trees gave way to open spaces; I was approaching Long Island Sound. The air took on a salt tang, and I soon faced the black immensity of the sea. A few stars were scattered uncertainly across the New England sky, and the stillness was punctuated by the murmurous waves on the beach. I parked the car and sat staring into the dark. Since I barely knew what life was about, why would I understand death? It was, fundamentally, the absence of life, its negation. Or was it a door through which we stepped into another form of being?

Dad had been a sweet, soft-spoken man whose nature it was to submit, and in Julia he had found the controlling force to which his submission made sense. He had endless faith in the power of the mind to solve any problem; she was stronger on faith and intuition. They were well matched, each responding to the needs of the other. Although he deferred to her in all practical matters, there was an area of conviction at the core of him that was not open to outside influence. He knew what he thought of the world, and his beliefs formed a tower of inner strength that could not be toppled.

I gazed at the vastness of sea and sky, each shading into the other without a trace. Dying was simply the act of slipping through that door. Once you did, you floated away on a broad, stately river to an infinitely calm sea. I saw myself finally released from the endless conflict of irreconcilable forces that tore me apart: courage and fear, hope and despair, ambition and indifference, self-love and self-hate. I tried to envisage a world in which I no longer existed. What was so terrible about returning to the sea from which we came, of dissolving in the caress of its waters? The prospect brought me neither regret nor sorrow. On the contrary, the more I thought about it, the more it lured me. The possibility of falling asleep forever captured me in its spell; I would be free at last from the necessity of ever waking up again. I had a vision of myself floating into the nirvana of nonbeing and was enchanted by it. The notion of death as such hardly entered my mind.

Time passed. I finally roused myself. There was no use having a vision if I was to sit in the car and do nothing to make it come true. The point was to act, not hastily or angrily, but in a calm, thoughtful manner, with due consideration of all the factors involved. What struck me about the fulfillment of the vision was how simple it was. It took no heroic effort; it demanded no more than stepping through the door without fuss or fear. What it demanded, really, was that I remove my clothes down to my shorts, cross the deserted beach, and walk into the sea. This I did.

The water was bracing, a little colder than I had expected. I waded in to where it was deeper, the cold sending little arrows up to my thighs and balls. I set out for the serene river. My swimming at Hillcrest had improved my stroke; I used the crawl. Soon I was in over my head and continued in a straight line away from the beach. My motion through the water took on a rhythm of its own; it kept my mind fixed on my goal, permitting neither doubts nor questions. After I reached what seemed to be the right spot, I treaded water awhile; then, using my arms, I dived and pulled as hard as I could. The pressure on my ears increased as I went deeper; the weight of the sea seemed to be resting on my forehead. My head felt as if it had been caught in a vise; I needed air. A flash shot through my brain, followed by a dull pain. I felt consciousness slipping away, leaving a million gallons of water pressing down on me. I blacked out, but my body must have taken over, for when I came to, my arms were desperately flailing the water, pulling me up with all their might. Up, up, up. When I finally reached the surface, I seemed to be about to explode. I sucked in a great draft of air and, splashing frantically, made for the beach.

I floated in with each wave; as it left me behind, it blotted out the lights onshore, plunging me into a total darkness from which the next wave rescued me. I swam purposefully, eager to leave behind every memory of eternal sleep. My body had decided it didn't want to die. As it turned out, neither did I.

I continued my efforts until I made it back to shore. I pulled myself out of the water, staggered up the beach, and dropped down on the sand in a state of total exhaustion. I had the sense of having escaped a terrible danger. A wild joy spread through my veins. I was alive . . . alive. . . . The word beat an exultant refrain in my mind until thought and feeling vanished in a pink haze; I fell into a dreamless sleep.

It was daylight when I awoke. Pearl-tinted clouds floated over the horizon, and I realized I might have been dead by now if my mad scheme had worked. I dressed and, delighted to leave the beach, motored back to Hillcrest. I arrived in time for breakfast; my absence had not even been noticed.

As I sat enjoying a dish of scrambled eggs, it came to me that life was bizarre indeed. Here I was, safely surrounded by the buzz of a dozen conversations, while only four hours before I had had a brush with death. I wrestled with an important decision: What was I to tell Dr. Nelson? My first impulse was to tell him nothing. The sooner I put my suicide attempt out of my mind, the better it would be. Predictably I immediately swung to the opposite extreme and decided to give him a full account of what I had gone through. My night on the beach obviously marked a turning point in my life; it would be a mistake for me to gloss it over. As soon as breakfast was over, I asked to see him and told him everything.

He listened to the end. "It never struck you," he asked, "that death is pretty awful?"

"No. It seemed quite easy. I rather liked the idea of never getting up again."

"You weren't afraid?"

"Not really. Except for the moment when I went down to the bottom and ran out of air."

"Didn't it occur to you that suicide is a form of murder? You're killing a human being, with all his potential, his talent, his mind?"

"All I saw was a door opening and me stepping through it."

"You wanted to be dead, yet when you lay on the beach afterward, you were glad to be alive."

"Oh, very. I had a change of heart."

"Lucky you." He thought a moment, then said, "Dan, you finally hit bottom. Now you have nowhere to go but up."

7

DAD LEFT NO instructions concerning his funeral. I felt that since he had been an atheist, the service should be nondenominational. Julia demurred. "Hitler didn't know from atheists. In Auschwitz your father would have died as a Jew. He should be buried as a Jew, even if he didn't believe in the Jewish God. We'll have a rabbi. He doesn't have to read the whole service, only the main prayer, maybe a psalm of David too."

I was surprised at how many turned up at the funeral. Ruth, I noticed, sat toward the back. I spoke briefly. "My father was a man of few words, but he meant what he said. He lived in his own space and walked to his own beat, no matter what others thought. And he didn't get into anyone's way. He was a man of inner courage, and I loved him very much." Now that he could no longer hear me, I was finally able to say it.

The rabbi intoned the ancient prayer for the dead, *Ayl molay rachamim*—O Lord, full of mercy. Then he read two psalms, first in Hebrew, then in English: "The Lord is my shepherd" and "Hear all ye people, give ear." After the ceremony a number of Dad's friends gathered in our living room. Julia served the spicy cold cuts and coleslaw that he had not been permitted to eat and let herself be distracted by her duties as hostess. It was only after she and I were alone that she gave vent to her feelings.

"The house is so quiet. For more than thirty years there was always someone there. He listened to what I had to say; he made me feel special. Now he's gone, and I'm alone. I listen for the sound of his footsteps, the sound of his voice. But there is only a stillness. That's what makes it so hard to bear." Tears rolled down her cheeks. She wiped them away. "In India they solved the problem much better. They burned the wife together with her husband. Very sensible."

"Come on, Mom, you're too full of life for that."

She shook her head sagely and said, "Still, it's a perfect solution. Of course I have you, thank God, but I can't expect too much. You can't have your mother hanging on your neck; you have to do your own thing. Maybe when you'll give me a grandchild or two, I'll have something to keep me busy. Until then I'm"—she looked for the word and found it—"unemployed."

I kissed her. What else at this point could I offer?

I went back to Hillcrest to finish my time. After I returned, Dr. Nelson made a request for which I was quite unprepared. "Since you'll soon be leaving us, Dan, why don't you give us a little music this Sunday night? Everyone would love to hear you play."

The idea didn't appeal to me at all. "I don't even have my violin with me," I replied.

"I'm sure we could find you one. Or send someone to Manhattan to bring yours."

"I haven't practiced for weeks."

"Dan, I'm not asking you to give a concert. Just some informal music for a few friends. I'm sure you don't have to practice for that."

I was not going to let him force my hand. "To tell you the

truth, I'm not ready to begin playing again. I'm not in the mood."

"What has mood got to do with it? A physician heals because that's what he's been trained to do; a musician plays for the same reason."

"Do I have to?"

"In a way, yes. Your talent is a gift that was given you to share with others. It's not something you hide away for your own pleasure, like a miser counting his money. That's why you should do it."

"I thought I was having a rest."

"But the vacation is coming to an end. You'll be back in harness one of these days. Why not Sunday?"

"Even if I don't want to?"

He changed his tone. "Look, Dan, I don't want to force you. I'll tell the others you don't feel like playing, and that's that."

"No, Doctor, don't do that. I'll play."

"Remember, it's not Carnegie Hall. Just a little music after Sunday night supper."

"For an artist it's always Carnegie Hall," I replied pompously.

He smiled. "You may be a fine violinist, Dan, but you sure don't have a sense of humor."

I called Amos Schein and asked him to send the Strad up to Hillcrest. There were several pianists I could have asked to accompany me, but my thoughts turned to Ruth. Indeed I was glad I had agreed to play because it gave me an excuse to call her. If she consented, it would simplify matters considerably. She knew my repertoire; we wouldn't even need to rehearse. Would she agree? I wondered. She had not paid me a visit at Hillcrest or even telephoned. After the way I had treated her, she certainly had a right to say no. It took me two days to summon up the courage to dial her number. I finally did.

"Ruth, it's me."

Silence. Finally: "How are you?"

"Why didn't you call to find out?"

"Your parents filled me in."

"I've a favor to ask you."

"Else why would you call?"

"That's not a friendly remark."

"It's not meant to be."

"Anyway, the people here would like me to play a few pieces on Sunday night. I haven't played since—since that thing happened. I guess I'm a bit rusty and a bit scared of beginning again. I need some encouragement. Would you give me some?"

"Encouragement?"

I swallowed hard and came out with it. "Would you play with me?"

She was silent. I added, "It would help me a lot if you did."

Still not a word. "Would you?" I asked, and felt myself grow tense.

"Danny," she said finally, "what you're asking me is not easy for me."

"Why?"

"I think you know why. If you don't, there's no point my trying to tell you."

"Still, I'm asking you."

"It's hard for me to say yes and just as hard to say no."

"Then why not say yes?"

"I know you're in a difficult spot. But there are others you could ask. As a matter of fact why are you asking me?"

"Because it's you I want."

"It would have been easier for me if you hadn't asked. I know you've been through plenty, and I hate to turn you down. You're using a kind of blackmail on me."

"Then it's settled," I cried, jubilant. "You're coming!"

I wondered what it would be like to see her again. I had not given her much thought during my involvement with Natalia. It was difficult for me to recapture my frame of mind when I broke off with her in London. That decision had been taken by an earlier Danny Sachs who bore very little relation to the person I now was. I was genuinely sorry for the pain I had caused her, but there was no undoing the past. I only hoped the past would not weigh too heavily between us.

She arrived the following morning. I was more agitated than I thought I would be. Her hair was cut a little shorter than I remembered it; I thought she looked prettier than the last time I had seen her. What I especially liked was to be looking again into her gentle gray eyes. She was clearly tense—she had never been good at hiding her feelings—but calmed down once we began to play. She had brought with her a number of selections that would appeal to people who rarely went to concerts. Indeed the numbers we chose would have fitted into a collection of "Violin Pieces the Whole World Loves": Schubert's Serenade, Dvořák's Slavonic Dance in E-minor, Kreisler's *Liebesleid* and *Liebesfreud*, Sarasate's *Zigeunerweisen*, and the violin arrangement of Chopin's Nocturne in E-flat to which Dmitri Stamos had objected. I wondered how I could have ever thought Ruth's playing dull. It had lovely phrasing and rhythmic bite. Like me, she never lingered over a measure too long.

We were so thoroughly attuned to each other's beat that we could have played the performance without a rehearsal. And it was a great feeling to have my hands again on Amos Schein's Stradivarius. Its singing tone warmed my heart.

It was clear to me on Sunday night that I had benefited from my vacation; I was very much in the mood. Each number on our program was a huge success, and I was generous with encores. There was a special charm about performing in a room instead of a concert hall; no wonder the Europeans were so keen on *hausmusik*. When we finished, the others crowded around me. "My dear boy," Wally intoned, "you're fahbulous!"

Sheila was perceptive. "You really enjoy playing," she said, "which makes it easy to listen to."

Dr. Nelson was extremely pleased. "I'm glad you did it," he told me. "It was good for you and good for us."

In the social hour that followed the concert Ruth and I chatted pleasantly. Since we were not alone, our conversation was fairly impersonal. She told me she had been to visit my father. "He spoke mostly about you," she said. "He was so proud of you."

When I tried to tell her how much I appreciated her coming to play for me, she minimized her contribution. "If it hadn't been me, someone else would have done it."

"But it was you," I replied, "and I'm more grateful to you than I can ever say."

She gave me a skeptical look, as if she doubted my gratitude. I reflected that she had ample reason to do so and did not protest. It struck me that she was much more self-confident than she had been. The years away from me had obviously done her good; she had learned to stand on her own feet.

She had been invited to spend the night at Hillcrest. When we met the following morning, she was markedly less cordial. It was as if she had had a chance to reflect on our situation and had decided to keep her distance. To cover my discomfiture, I kept up a steady stream of chatter, mostly about Hillcrest.

"A place like this gives you a chance to think things over. Also to find out a lot about yourself that you never knew before. It's like a breathing spell that lets you get ready for the next battle."

"Does it have to be a battle?" she asked.

"Doesn't have to be, but generally is."

"I like Dr. Nelson. He seems very knowledgeable."

"He turned me off at first. Acted as if he knew all the answers. But after I got to know him, he didn't seem that way at all."

"Maybe you're the one who changed."

"Could be."

I walked her to the bus that was to take her to the train. I thanked her profusely and finished with "I hope to see you sometime."

Lifting her soft gray eyes to me, she smiled vaguely and held out her hand. I wondered if I should kiss her, but before I could decide, she had turned away and entered the bus. I was sorry to see her go; I should have liked us to have a talk.

8

MY FINAL DAYS at Hillcrest were enlivened by the presence of Patrick O'Hara, a cantankerous Irishman who wrote murder mysteries. His novels, according to Wally, bore not the slightest relation to literature. Indeed Wally insisted that among the different literary genres, the murder mystery was the lowest. O'Hara's novels had only one possible merit: they grabbed hold of you. Once you began a whodunit of his, you couldn't put it down. They illustrated what Wally called the sheer power of action. His characters were continually running somewhere and usually managed to escape.

O'Hara held that all novelists were slightly mad. How otherwise explain why a presumably normal person would hole up in a room to invent stories which his readers, comfortably curled up in their armchairs, knew weren't true? Fiction writers, according to him, had a constant conflict with reality. That was why they drank.

O'Hara came to Hillcrest, he said, for the sake of his liver. He found fault with every aspect of the place: the food, the bed, the treatment, the people. He spent a good part of the day in his room, writing; when he finally did appear, everyone took notice. He was intensely personal in his behavior: He said unpleasant things to people (he called it being honest), picked quarrels with them, forgave some, misquoted others, and seemed to enjoy causing trouble. The point was that it was impossible to ignore him. He was a central force in any group, and when he turned on his Irish charm, he was irresistible.

O'Hara had a dark, heavy beard; he needed to shave twice a day. When he omitted the late-afternoon shave, his jowls sprouted a dark stubble that made him seem to be scowling even when he wasn't. Sheila called him Bluebeard. They took their meals together and seemed to have much to say to each other.

Since O'Hara had difficulty submitting to the kind of discipline imposed by a place like Hillcrest, Sheila became his mouthpiece, defending him against all criticism. Unlike the rest of us, he did not attend the lectures dealing with various aspects of addiction. He stood above such "baby talk," as he called it, and expected the regulations of the rehab center to be eased to suit his personal needs. He had been to Hillcrest several times before but had always slipped back into alcoholism because of one crisis or another. Sheila said that he manufactured his own crises.

The conversation that created tension between O'Hara and Wally started out as a reasonable exchange of ideas. O'Hara expounded his view that a writer must always consider the expectations of his public. Writing, he maintained, is a form of communication, and you couldn't communicate if you didn't think of your communicatees. All this talk against the so-called commercialization of literature was typical of those who couldn't cope with the market. In other words, it was an admission of personal failure.

Wally vehemently disagreed. "The first duty of a writer is to be honest. He's got to say what he really thinks and feels. If his main purpose is to sell, he cheapens art by treating it like a commodity. And he falsifies, because his first aim is to please. Imagine Tolstoy writing that way. If he had, we would never have had a *War and Peace* or *Anna Karenina*. The great writers wrote what they truly felt. Their goal was truth, not royalties."

For some reason O'Hara took Wally's views as a direct attack on himself. "Hogwash!" he exclaimed, and grew increasingly belligerent in his discourse. "You don't know what you're talking about. Why would you? You're not a writer. A writer writes because he wants to talk to people, and he talks to people because he wants them to listen. Why would he tell them things he knows will drive them away?"

"Because art is not created for the marketplace; it's created for its own sake. Oscar Wilde said there was no such thing as a moral or immoral book. A book was either well written or badly written."

"Oscar Wilde didn't know his big fat ass from a hole in the ground. Anyone who gets himself into jail when he should be at the height of his powers is a fool."

Wally was outraged. "You're speaking about one of the great figures in English literature."

O'Hara suddenly decided he had had enough of Wally. He turned on his heel and stalked off, muttering under his breath.

"Don't mind him," Sheila said. "He's in a dark mood today. I can't imagine why."

This was my last night at Hillcrest. Some of us had persuaded Wally to recite a few numbers. O'Hara had vanished early in the evening and had obviously stopped at the local bar for a little refreshment. He came in during Wally's recital and stood at the back of the room, staring darkly before him. At the moment Wally was deep in Lady Bracknell's speech to Jack, who hopes to marry her daughter. "The whole theory of modern education is radically unsound. Fortunately in England, at any rate, education produces no effect whatsoever. If it did, it would prove a serious danger to the upper classes, and probably lead to acts of violence in Grosvenor Square. What is your income?"

Suddenly, with no provocation whatever, O'Hara's drunken voice cut the air like a whip. "Faggot!" he shouted at Wally. "That's what you are. A faggoty faggoty faggot." He barked out the consonants as if it gave him the greatest pleasure to do so.

Wally stopped short. For an instant he stood speechless, staring at O'Hara as though in shock. Then the pasty white of his cheeks gave way to an apoplectic red. "You son of a bitch," he snarled, and practically hurled himself across the room. Before anyone could stop him, he threw himself on O'Hara, who was too befuddled to put up any defense. Grabbing the Irishman by the throat, Wally began to choke him.

Several of us jumped up and pulled Wally away from O'Hara. Wally repeated, "You son of a bitch!" several times. At least he had finished Lady Bracknell's speech.

It was a basic rule at Hillcrest that no patient was allowed to attack another. Unless O'Hara apologized to Wally, as he resolutely refused to do, he would have to leave. He preferred that. The next morning, valise in hand, he went to Sheila to say good-bye and asked for her telephone number.

She was quite firm. "Pat, listen carefully to what I'm about to tell you. I don't know people who use words like *nigger, kike, faggot.* What's more, I don't want to know them. These words have no place in the vocabulary of decent people."

"What makes you think I'm a decent person? I happen to be something much better, a good hater."

"Your trouble is you think what you did was cute. It wasn't. It was ugly and reprehensible."

"Come off it, Sheila. You don't have to put on that tone with me. It doesn't suit you."

"Oh, yes, it does."

"What'll you do if I call?"

"I'll hang up on you, Pat."

"You wouldn't do that!" he said, giving her that sidelong glance from under long lashes that he thought made him irresistible. When he smiled, two dimples appeared on either side of his mouth.

"You know me well enough, Pat, to know that I will. Don't try to pull your Irish charm with me. It's probably got you out of plenty of scrapes, but there's always an exception."

"Stop wasting my time. Your phone number, please."

"I'm in the book, so you won't have any problem with that. But just remember that I won't see you unless you've expressed regret for your impossible behavior. I'm as devoted to my principles as you are to your prejudices, and on that score I'm not prepared to yield."

"We'll see," said O'Hara, incorrigible, and Sheila countered with, "Indeed we will."

I was leaving that afternoon. Dr. Nelson was cordial when I came to say good-bye. "I'm sending my report to the judge in Provincetown. You've made sufficient progress here for the charges against you to be dropped. They want to hear that you've been cured, but that's not a scientific word. There is no cure for living. I think you learned some things at Hillcrest, and I think they'll help you cope once you're home. When things get too heavy, call me and we'll talk it over." We shook hands, and I realized that I had ended by genuinely liking him.

I exchanged phone numbers with Wally and Sheila; we promised ourselves a prompt reunion in New York. By midafternoon I was happily on the train to Manhattan, summing up in my mind what Dr. Nelson had taught me.

First of all, to like myself a little more. Not to be so hard on myself. Not to expect so much. To stay away from perfectionism (except when it came to playing the violin). Not to be so self-centered, or at least to try not to be. He had helped convince me that I could do without cocaine and never tired of reminding me that the drug would end by interfering with my playing. He had pointed out my desire to punish myself by courting failure, danger, and defeat and had tried to cure me of being a loner. He had freed me from the notion that my mishap had caused my father's death (although I still believed there was a connection between the two events). He had lightened the general burden of guilt that weighed me down and had reinforced my belief that I could cope with the future. In short, I had every reason to be grateful to him.

9

IT WAS GOOD to be home again. My Steinway, the white leather sofa, and the black rug looked more elegant than ever, as did the lithographs by Käthe Kollwitz and Paul Klee. I laid the Strad in its usual place on the piano. When I remembered that I had left it overnight in an unlocked car, I winced.

Nothing more vividly summed up the madness to which my addiction had led me.

I called Steve, who came over at once. "Where do I begin?" I asked him.

"Where you left off."

"I don't remember where that was."

"Your first step is to start playing again. The second is to call Max and find out about your concerts."

"You want to know the truth? I can't imagine myself facing an audience again."

"You'll get over your fear, just as you got over it way back when you began."

I had already described to him over the phone my night on the beach. "It changed a lot of things for me," I said.

"Look, more people than you think go through something like that. A certain mood takes over, and it suddenly becomes very attractive to put an end to yourself. No harm in it as long as you don't, and you didn't."

"At the moment it seemed like a swell idea."

"Yeah, but you never stopped to figure out what death is. It's the end. Unless you believe in life after death--and who does, really?—only life here below has meaning. Which means that death is simply the absence of meaning."

"A philosopher yet."

He laughed. "Why not? You and I are alive, and we're going to stay alive. We're going to keep fighting and hoping and sweating it out. That's what it's all about. So there's no point in your dwelling on what happened. That was sick, and now you're well." He sounded as if this were his final thought on the subject; I accepted it as mine too.

I told him about Ruth. "We played as if we'd never been apart. She was terrific. I'd like to get her back as my accompanist."

"Does she want to?"

"I asked her. She said no."

Steve thought for a moment before uttering in his sagest

manner, "Remember one thing. When Natalia said no, she meant no. When Ruth says no, it might just be that she means maybe."

"Thank you, Doctor. Already I feel better."

10

FOR ME, GETTING back to normal living meant getting back to practicing. This presented a problem. I was most ingenious in putting all kinds of obstacles in my way: a snack, a telephone call (or several), reading the newspaper, or a workout in the gym. Anything to keep me from settling down to serious work. I finally asked Steve to help me. He came by with his violin every day and stayed for several hours, during which we played for each other and practiced together.

I was working on two concert programs and needed a pianist. After some hesitation I called Ruth. She listened to my request. "You're making it very difficult for me, Danny," she said. "One part of me wants to help you out. The other part wants to get as far away from you as possible."

"Then why did you come when I called you from Hillcrest?"

"You were obviously in a tight spot, and I just couldn't say no. But now you're asking me to work with you on a new program. That's a long-term project. I have to ask myself if I want anything like that."

"Do you?"

She thought. "For several years I lived in your shadow. In such a setup the woman exists because the man loves her, and when he stops loving her, she stops existing. She has to pull herself together and start all over again. That's not easy, believe me. When she finally achieves some inner peace, she's going to hold on to it, which is what I'm doing. I've managed to put my life together. Why would I do anything that might shake it up again? You tell me."

"Because I'm asking you to."

"Even if it means putting myself at risk?"

"Isn't it possible that I've changed? People don't stay the same year after year. They learn; they grow; they develop. Maybe I'm a different person from the one you knew."

"No, Danny, I don't think you're different. Of course what you've been through left its mark. All that stuff in the newspapers must have been very painful for you. But would you act differently toward me from the way you did then? To be honest with you, I don't think so."

"You're not giving me much of a chance to convince you."

"I loved you very much, Danny, and was deeply hurt when you decided to break it off. I don't intend to let myself be hurt again. It's as simple as that."

"Then you won't play for me?"

"I hate to say it, but I'd rather not. I'm sorry, but this is how I feel."

The conversation left me depressed. Ruth's rejection was nowhere as cruel as Natalia's had been, but it was rejection nonetheless. I was suddenly thrust back to the night on Cape Cod when Natalia turned me out of her house. I needed to shake off the dark mood; the simplest way to escape it was through a fix. All at once the weeks of recovery at Hillcrest were swept away; the pores of my body became so many gaping holes, each hungry for the sense of well-being that a line of cocaine brought.

For once I did not call Steve. He had sworn not to let me slide back into the habit, and I knew that he meant to keep his word. Instead I called his dealer and arranged a purchase. It was only when the two little bags of white powder lay on my table that I calmed down. I sat there looking at them, and summoned up a big No! from the depths of me. I was not going to give in. My stay at Hillcrest, it turned out, had not been in vain. I was not going to let Dr. Nelson down; more important, I was not going to let myself down. I remembered all too vividly the moment of panic on the stage when my mind went blank. I sat staring at the two little bags, determined not to open them. The time had finally come when I was able to say no. I pulled myself to my feet and, with a tremendous sense of achievement, dumped the coke into the toilet.

I was sufficiently proud of myself to call Steve and tell him what I had done. We had a long talk, during which I basked in his approval. At the end he said, "Call Ruth again." I decided to follow his advice, but not yet. I was not ready to face another rejection.

Two days later I had a thrilling surprise. My doorbell rang. When I opened the door, there stood Ruth. I pulled her inside and threw my arms around her. She would never know how happy she made me by changing her mind. She would never realize how badly I needed her.

11

A WOMAN'S VOICE came over the telephone. Where had I heard that curious blend of Italian accent overlaid with British? Suddenly I remembered Carla and the Moscow competition. She had called me several times before when she was in New York but had missed me because I was on tour. This time we could see each other. I was delighted.

We met in the lounge of her hotel, the Drake. She turned out to be the kind of elegant Italian woman one ran into in international hotels, handsome, self-assured, with an intense face and sweeping gestures when she spoke. I told her that my friend Steve felt she should have won the first prize instead of me.

She laughed. "I thought so too. It made me not like you when you won."

"I knew that."

"How?"

"You were very cool when we parted."

"You didn't think I'd forgive you, did you?"

"Strange," I said, "how important those things seem at the moment and how insignificant they become years later."

We sat in the bar and brought each other up-to-date. She was married to an industrialist and had two children. "It is not good for an artist," she observed, "to have money."

"It's no fun not to have it."

"True. But something happens to you when you lead a very comfortable life. You no longer work so hard."

She was on her way to play the Sibelius Concerto with the Chicago Symphony. It was obvious, from what she told me, that she had a considerable career in Europe, but she had never caught on in the United States. "Here they want something a little more—how shall I say?—sensational. I simply come out and play the notes. I don't try to put on a show."

"There's no such thing," I objected, "as just playing the notes. You can't avoid putting yourself into it; that's the personal element, what makes one artist different from another, what people come to hear."

Carla considered my view. "I guess it's all a question of how much," she finally said. "One way is to put yourself into the music just enough to say what the composer intended. Another is to take over and make the music express your personality instead of his."

"The great violinists solve the problem in different ways. My ideal," I said, "is Isaac Stern. He has a very strong personality, but he plays it down in favor of the composer. So does Milstein. Heifetz struck the perfect balance; Mischa Elman didn't strike any at all. Kreisler found another way. He just wrapped everything in Viennese charm."

I found it more and more difficult to keep my mind on the discussion. I was reacting instead to my erotic memories of Carla. I remembered her room, the bed that took up most of the space, the icon on the wall, the naked girl in my arms. All these images floated underneath the surface of our conversation, lending it a delightfully romantic quality. There had to be, I decided, an intimate bond between people who had been lovers, no matter how much time had elapsed since they were. Why had she looked me up, I asked myself, if not to recapture something of the passion of our lovemaking? This was a visit inspired by nostalgia; any moment now she would be inviting me up to her room. I found this possibility so attractive that I became aware of a stiffening in my crotch.

This response unleashed a flurry of guilt. Here was I trying hard to reestablish my friendship with Ruth, and at the first opportunity my interest turned elsewhere. What kind of hungry bird was I? This was the kind of behavior that Dr. Nelson labeled immature, the kind I was trying to leave behind me. In any case, it was soon apparent from Carla's conversation that I had let my imagination run away with me. She was very much the wife and mother. She had her feet on the ground, rooted in the practical ways of the music world. To see her as a romantic figure out of my past was utterly unrealistic. She had looked me up to reestablish contact with an old friend and colleague. That I happened to have been briefly her lover might add a touch of drama to the encounter but in no way altered its character. She liked me and was glad to see me; that was about it. My erection died.

I asked her if she had encountered career difficulties as a woman. "The violin," she replied, echoing Amos Schein's view, "is really a man's instrument. Some women made it as violinists. Erica Morini and, before her, Lea Luboshutz. Nowadays Nadja Salerno-Sonnenberg and Anne-Sophie Mutter are having careers. In general, though, I think women do better sticking to the piano. By doing better I mean, of course, in terms of success."

"Is that your only criterion?" I asked, a bit self-righteously.

She gave me that tolerant smile I remembered so well. "What other is there?" she asked innocently.

We parted warmly. I promised to look her up if I ever came to Rome. It was not likely, as I played very little in Italy.

Nostalgia of a different kind was the keynote of my dinner with Sheila and Wally. I thought that a visit with the two people who had been closest to me at the rehab center would help me recapture the special quality of that experience. What I did not realize was that Hillcrest had supplied not only the physical environment but also the common interests that nourished our friendship. Without that environment to fall back on, we really had very little to say to each other. We were like people who have a wonderful time together at a summer resort, only to discover when they meet later in town that they don't have much to talk about. Wally continued to be preoccupied with gay liberation. I considered that an eminently worthy cause, but not one in which I was particularly interested. Sheila had just put out a new line of jeans for women and was in the midst of a promotional campaign aimed at the feminine market. Again a not unworthy cause, but one that failed to engage me. I listened sympathetically as they detailed their plans to impose their pet projects on the world and wondered why the three of us could not recapture the camaraderie that had united us at Hillcrest.

I thought Sheila's goal was on the grandiose side, nothing less than to replace the conventional skirt—especially during the winter months—with jeans. The skirt, she argued, was an obsolete contraption that allowed cold winds to strike a woman in the most vulnerable part of her anatomy. Not only was a pair of jeans warmer, but it allowed the wearer to buttress it with a snug undergarment—leotard or body stocking—that afforded legs and thighs the protection they needed. Her job was to bring the idea to women who had never thought of wearing jeans before, a task her public relations people were equipped to handle. Before her mind's eye stretched a limitless market. The prospect warmed her soul.

Wally was equally optimistic. "Our main task in the gay movement is to fight discrimination, especially when it comes to jobs and housing. There's no use appealing to people's sense of fairness. Much more practical is to make politicians understand that the gay vote can be a decisive factor in any election. Not as big perhaps as the black or Jewish or women's vote, but substantial all the same. Once our political leaders realize this, they'll start catering to the gay community just as they now cater to the other minorities."

We had dinner at an excellent French restaurant; Sheila insisted on picking up the check. Only toward the end of the meal did she mention Patrick O'Hara. "He called me," she told us, "but wouldn't apologize for his behavior. I refused to speak to him."

Wally's comment was short and to the point: "I should've killed him."

They asked if I would be playing in New York; they were eager to come to my next concert. I explained that my schedule was not yet set, but I would keep them informed. We promised each other another reunion before long and parted most amicably, each of us going right back into his own little world.

The following morning a telephone call from Amos Schein summoned me to a dinner that consisted, aside from the host and Valerie, of only Dmitri Stamos and me. Mr. Schein had finally decided upon the disposition of his Stradivarius and wanted us to know about his plan. I was to have the use of the instrument for as long as I wanted it, after which it would go to the music school, my alma mater. In this way Mr. Schein would receive the tax deduction he needed. The school could either sell the Strad and add the money to its endowment fund or keep the instrument to be used by its most talented students. "When Isaac Stern began his career," Mr. Schein declared, "you could pick up a Strad like this for fifty thousand. Ten years from now it'll bring between two and three million. Where else would you find accretion like that?"

Valerie was looking at me in a not especially friendly way. I knew what she was thinking: that my ass kissing had finally borne fruit. As a matter of fact Mr. Schein was simply adding a final benefaction to the long list that had helped my career in every possible way. What his wife thought of his generosity did not concern me in the least.

Mr. Schein had another thought that involved me. He intended, he told us, to endow a chair in violin at the school that I would occupy. "I think it's important for artists to teach. They have something special to pass on to the next generation."

The prospect did not appeal to me. "An artist takes a teaching job," I said, "when he wants to cut down on his playing. Or when he feels his concert career is over. I'm not quite ready for that."

My patron reassured me. "I don't mean to turn you into a drudge. You'll have an assistant who'll take care of your students when you're concertizing. The school won't mind your absences; it's good publicity for them to have a performing artist on their faculty."

I realized that he had set his heart on this plan and decided I was not going to disappoint him. I might even enjoy having a few talented students. Mr. Schein was greatly pleased when I consented.

The rest of the dinner was devoted to Stamos's account of his activities during the war. He had never told the Scheins of his exploits in the Resistance, and I didn't mind hearing the stirring tale once more.

Julia asked me to come for Friday night dinner. Knowing that she had always liked Steve, I brought him along. His presence turned out to be a decided asset; it drew Julia's attention—if only briefly—away from me. She clung to the traditional Friday night menu that her mother had taught her: gefilte fish (the modern touch was that it now came out of a jar), plump matzoh balls floating in chicken soup, followed by the chicken itself, and the bland dessert of stewed prunes and carrots known as tsimmes. She had a new theme: Why didn't I marry Ruth?

"Mom," I said, "marriage is a serious step. Maybe I'm not ready for it."

She waved away my objections. "You're ready, you're ready," she announced. "I always said if you had had a wife and kids to worry about, you might have stayed out of trouble."

"Besides, how d'you know she'd have me? I gave her a lot of trouble in the past."

Julia was hardly prepared to accept the bizarre notion that any woman could possibly turn her son down. "She loved you, right? Which means you could win her back if you played your cards right."

"I'm not a good cardplayer."

"You would be if you put your mind to it."

"I asked her to be my accompanist. She was most reluctant."

"But did she refuse you?"

"Not quite. Once Max fixes my full schedule, I'm going to ask her to share it with me. That'll be the test."

Julia was unflappable. "I can promise you one thing. She'll end by saying yes."

Having settled that, she concentrated on Steve. When and where was he playing, what was his fee, was his manager better than Max or worse, how did his agency compare with mine? Steve carefully explained that all managements had the same goal: to make money. The only way they could do that was to obtain engagements for their artists. But the energy with which they pursued this goal varied from artist to artist, even from season to season. The big question was: did they create an artist's career or simply go along with it. He had never found the answer.

The evening passed pleasantly; I decided to repeat it before long. For better or worse, Julia was the only mother I had. And she had the grace never to remind me how much I owed her.

12

In the next weeks Ruth and I worked steadily on my new program. We met twice a week; at the end of each session I felt a little closer to her and looked forward to the next. Our roles had changed in a very subtle way since the years when we were lovers. Then I had been the dominant member of the team, whose judgments and decisions she accepted without question. Now it was she who was able to call on a core of inner strength, while I relied heavily on her advice and encouragement. A similar change showed itself in her playing. She was more self-assured than I remembered, more assertive. I thoroughly enjoyed our music making.

Max brought me my concert schedule. He had arranged my first recitals to take place not in any of the main music centers but in medium-size cities: the first in Springfield, Massachusetts, then one in Schenectady and another in Trenton. This was all to the good; I would have been terrified to make my comeback in a major hall. The crucial question for me was, Would Ruth be available to play these concerts? Fortunately she was.

Now that I had overcome this obstacle, I faced a more substantial one, my panic. I was paralyzed at the prospect of walking out onstage to confront an audience that knew all about my arrest. As the date of my appearance in Springfield drew closer—it was scheduled for the second week in October—I became increasingly aware that I could not face the public. The problem was not that I was unprepared musically; I was simply not ready psychologically. What if they came to hiss me and jeer? There were so many ways in which they could vent their hostility. The thought unnerved me. At the same time I knew it would be a total defeat for me to postpone the concert or to cancel it. How, under the circumstances, could I concentrate on the music, or even remember it, when my mind conjured up such disasters? I was caught in a trap and saw no way out.

There was nothing for it but to seek help. I traveled up to Hillcrest for a long talk with Dr. Nelson. He tried to convince me that my fear of being punished simply masked my desire to punish myself.

"Why should I want to?" I asked. "Haven't I been punished enough?"

"I might think so and you might," he replied, "but your subconscious obviously doesn't. The problem is, you may try to bolster your courage with a snort of cocaine. Just remember that it will only cloud your brain and harm your playing. My objection is not moral; it's practical."

"I'll remember." I returned to New York to struggle with my demons. Springfield was only a week away, and my panic was unabated. Fortunately the first half of my program consisted of Beethoven's Sonata in E-flat for piano and violin, followed by the lush Richard Strauss Sonata. These being chamber music works, they were performed with the music, which at least removed the danger of a memory lapse.

I also had to fight off a fierce desire to fortify my spirits with a line of coke. Having already said no to this temptation made it easier for me not to give in. It seemed to me that all the fears I had accumulated over the years in connection with playing concerts were now coming back to plague me. I had certainly come a long way from my early fear that my trousers would fall down the instant I came out onstage or that a string of my violin would break. But my imagination seemed to have no difficulty at all in inventing dangers just as threatening.

I tried to lessen my anxiety by discussing it with Ruth, who listened sympathetically, as she always had. When we finally set out for Springfield, I was not in very good shape. I had only one strong asset in this struggle: a fierce determination to come through the ordeal successfully. Since we were going only a fairly short way, instead of flying we traveled by train, which I vastly preferred. As we settled into our chairs, "Seems exactly like old times," I said.

"But it's different."

"How?"

"We're older," she said.

"And wiser?"

"I wonder."

"I remember how excited you used to be starting out on a journey."

"I still am. But less."

"Why?"

"We lose our capacity for excitement. We grow up."

"Maybe I'm trying to give you back what you lost."

"Thanks. I'm not sure I want it back." She turned her soft gray eyes full upon me. "There was a philosopher, I forget his name, who taught that happiness is simply the absence of pain."

"That's a prescription for existing, not for living."

"I learned a lot from it. We grow up hearing that a woman needs a man. A false doctrine if ever there was one. She may even be better off without him."

"What about love?"

Her lips curved in a tolerant smile. "Lots of people would never even fall in love if they hadn't heard about it."

"Apropos of love, is there a man in your life?"

She considered the question. "No. I didn't want anyone else. It seemed to me that the solution to my sorrow—and it was a big sorrow, believe me—could not come from someone else. Because then I'd be putting myself in his power, just as I had put myself in yours. The solution had to come from inside me."

She said this with the utmost composure. I remembered how she had always waited for me to tell her what to think. Now she no longer needed anyone to guide her; she knew her own mind and had faith in what she believed. "You've changed," I said. "You're stronger."

"I had to be." She rested her head on the back of her seat and shut her eyes. The conversation was over.

I threw her a sidelong glance. How strange that I now clung tenaciously to someone I had abandoned so readily in the past.

I tried to recapture the frame of mind in which I had reached that lamentable decision, and couldn't. She now seemed to me to embody all the qualities I treasured. After my experience with Natalia, Ruth seemed so gentle, so human, so real. Could it be that I had needed Natalia in order to make me aware of how much Ruth had to offer? It appeared to me that if I could erase the painful memories I had left her with and overcome her fear of me, I would be happy indeed.

We arrived in Springfield in the early afternoon. Max had booked us into the Marriott Hotel. I had slept badly the night before and was able to take a nap, followed by a shower. Once I was in my tails, my spirits rose. I had arranged for a piano in our rooms; Ruth and I did a final run-through, at the end of which I permitted myself one amphetamine to bolster my mood. We arrived at the hall on time. I had a final flutter of butterflies in my stomach as I came out onstage.

The hall was not full, but there were not too many empty seats. I was greeted with friendly applause. It felt strange to be standing in front of an audience again; after the first few bars my nervousness vanished. The Beethoven Sonata unfolded without mishap. I was greatly aided by the fact that I was playing with the music in front of me. Ruth was totally dependable. The Strauss Sonata, I felt, had all the youthful ardor that the composer had poured into its measures. This was an exuberantly romantic work, and I loved playing it. None of the disasters I had foreseen materialized. On the contrary, I came off well even by my standards.

In the second half of the program I had an opportunity to show off a little. I played four Paganini études, a specialty of mine; the fourth was the famous *La Campanella*, which brought down the house. From there on it was easy sailing. I ended with Saint-Saëns's brilliant Rondo Capriccioso; by this time I had completely won over my audience. My encores were the required crowd pleasers: delightful tidbits by Kreisler and, for the finale, the spectacular *Carmen Variations* of Sarasate. The sustained applause at the end sounded wonderful to me. At last I was back in my natural element, where I belonged.

There was the usual party after the concert. I ate, drank, and enjoyed myself hugely, feeling entirely relaxed for the first time in months. It was after one in the morning when Ruth and I returned to the hotel. I threw myself into the armchair in her room; she called down to order drinks.

"Well, you did it!" she exclaimed. "You should feel much better now."

"I do."

"I hope you remember this for the next time. It's terrible that you put yourself through such torture beforehand. You have to keep telling yourself there's nothing to be afraid of."

"What if the fear and tension are necessary for a good performance?"

"They probably are. The trick is not to let them get out of hand."

I sipped my vodka, savoring the taste. "I was afraid that stuff in the papers about me would change their attitude. It didn't."

"Either they forgot it, or they didn't know about it in the first place."

"I'm a lucky fellow, I guess." I suddenly felt very close to Ruth and wanted her to know about my other mishap—that night on the beach of Long Island Sound. Yet I didn't know how to tell her. "It was not the only awful thing," I finally said, "that happened to me this year."

"I know."

"How?"

"Steve told me."

"I'm glad he did."

"Why did you want to die?"

"It's strange that I did, considering how much I love to be alive."

"Then what got into you?"

"A combination of things. For one, my father's death, for

which I held myself responsible. Plus a crazy feeling that it would be easy to slip away and never have to get up again. Let's say it was a momentary attack of insanity."

"But you're nowhere near insane."

"Which makes it even more strange. Believe me, an experience like that changes the way you look at things."

"How?"

"Your values change. Life suddenly becomes very sweet. I began by wanting to conquer the world. Now I'm content just to be comfortable in it." I leaned back in my chair, feeling very much at home in the world. "Ruth, there's something I've been meaning to ask you."

"What's it now?"

"Will you marry me?"

"What?"

"You heard me."

That thoughtful smile spread slowly from her lips to her eyes. She said nothing.

"I need you," I said. "Badly. Not only as my accompanist but as my wife."

She gave me a searching look. "I don't understand. I was all yours, and all you could think of was to tell me to get lost. Now it turns out you need me. What's the story about the young prince who travels all over the world looking for happiness, and all that time the Bluebird of Happiness is waiting for him in his backyard?"

"So I finally got back to my backyard. What's so strange about that?"

She changed her seat to the armchair opposite, keeping her eyes on me. "Let me explain, Danny. What we're really talking about is courage."

"What do you mean?"

"When we're young, we're able to do a lot of things that don't come so easily later on. Why? Because we don't yet know the risks. We have the courage. The trouble is, as the years go by, we lose it. You lost yours and had to find it again. This concert tonight should convince you that you have it back. I'm happy for you."

She took a sip of her drink, and continued. "When you left me, I lost my courage. I too had to find it again. I had to get over you, I had to conquer the defeat you inflicted on me. As a woman, as a musician, as a human being. Have I regained it? Not quite. That's why my only answer must be 'Sorry, I'm not ready to marry you. Or anyone else, for that matter.' If and when I regain my courage, the answer might be different. It's obvious that you mean a lot to me, or why would I be sitting in a hotel room in Springfield at this moment? But I won't marry you as long as I'm afraid you might live to regret it. This time there must be no question in my mind, no fear in my heart."

"Love always involves taking a chance."

"I know. But I must be sure that you're asking me not only because you need me but because you love me. That'll take time. I need time . . . lots of it. You'll have to be patient."

Again I was aware of the inner composure she had acquired in the years since I had known her. I leaned forward and tried to put my arms around her. She clasped my wrists and drew them firmly away from her. "No, we've had enough of each other for a while. You go to your room, and we'll get some sleep."

"Before I go, do you know what I'd like?"

"What?"

"For us to lie next to each other for a few minutes."

She thought. "That can be arranged. But you must promise not to get fresh."

"What do you consider getting fresh?"

"Like taking your clothes off."

"I promise."

We lay down on one of the beds. I held her hand in mine; we said nothing. Presently I could tell from her regular breathing that she had drifted into sleep. She turned and shifted her position; her head slipped lower on the pillow and came to rest on my shoulder. I remembered the last time it had rested there, on the plane to London. I had been bored and restless then; now the same circumstance filled me with indescribable pleasure. The person I then was appeared to be so different from what I was now; I seemed to have nothing in common with him. Ruth wasn't convinced that I had changed, but she would find out for herself in the coming weeks. Months. Years. I would convince her.

Her sincerity and warmth seemed to me so far above the fake brilliance (and willfulness) that had fascinated me in Natalia. I folded my hands behind my head and surrendered to the feeling of peace that enveloped me. I had done everything possible to ruin my life but had come through nevertheless. My will to fail had been so strong that I had failed even in that. At long last I was free within myself, free from bondage to the drug as well as from the driving ambition that had forced me to seek easy relief. I was able to face an audience again; I understood more about music than I ever had. More important, I understood more about myself. I had escaped the dangers that had threatened me and was none the worse for it. On the contrary, I was much better. I was indeed a lucky fellow.

I raised Ruth's hand to my lips and kissed it, letting my love flow from me to her. Then I turned out the light and lay staring into the dark that enfolded us both in its kindly shadow.